SISTER SANTEE

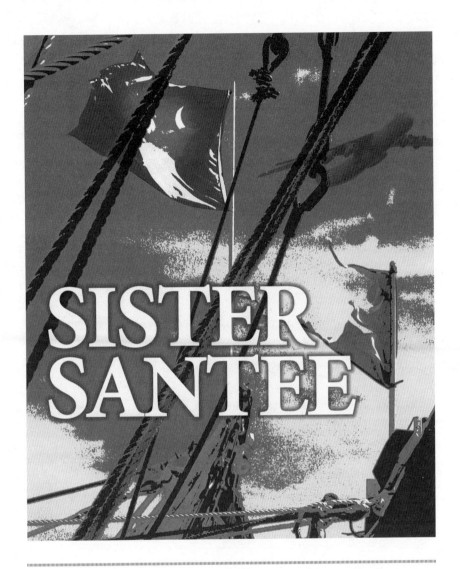

SISTER SANTEE

A SOUTH CAROLINA STORY

by KEN BURGER

EVENING POST
PUBLISHING CO.
Charleston, S.C.

This novel is a work of fiction. Any reference to historical events; to real people, living or dead; or to real locales are intended only to give the fiction a setting in historical reality. Other names, characters, places and incidents either are the product of the author's imagination or are used fictitiously, and their resemblance, if any, to real-life counterparts is entirely coincidental.

Published by
Evening Post Books
Charleston, South Carolina

Copyright © 2011 by Ken Burger
All rights reserved.
First edition

Editors: John M. Burbage and Thomas Cothran
Designer: Gill Guerry

First printing 2011
Printed in the United States of America

A CIP catalog record for this book has been applied for from the Library of Congress.

ISBN: 978-0-9825154-5-7

To Frank Burger,
a better husband, father
and brother than
I will ever be.

ACKNOWLEDGMENTS

I collect names like some people are drawn to coins, stamps and other obsessions. I listen and read and scan the horizon for names that sound like real people. I even dig through the obituaries each day for names. Because you never know where they'll turn up.

Berkeley Aiken, the heroine of this story, is a real person. I met her in the Charlotte airport several years ago. She was a lacrosse player at Presbyterian College. I fell in love with her name and warned her I might use it in a book some day. She smiled. She was young and probably didn't believe me.

This book is splattered with real names of real people who may or may not be anything like the character they became in my imagination. People like Stoney Sanders, Bob Gillespie, Harve Jacobs, Jack McCray and Tom Crawford. Then there are family members who allow me to borrow their names. Bonnie Bezner, Courtney Wilson, Allyson Rhea, Brent, Stacia, Graycen and Grant belong to my wife, children and grandchildren in various forms. They're comfortable names. Names you believe. And I thank them for letting me use them in this book.

There are also many unnamed heroes.

John Burbage of Evening Post Books is the only reason you are reading my words at all. He has the eye of an editor and the ear of a poet. His friendship and confidence are the ingredients that make this journey possible.

My wife, Bonnie, of course, gets a gold medal for missing me when I disappear into that black hole where writers go to write. And, more importantly, for welcoming me back when I crawl out.

Which brings me to Ann McKain and Ruth Coody, our neighbors and friends who enriched my knowledge with a signed copy of "The Santee River" by Henry Savage Jr. of Camden. The book is a well-written saga of the watershed and its many man-made flaws.

Also a tip of the hat to the folks in Jonkoping, Sweden, the birthplace of John Bauer, the artist whose haunting pictures of children and monsters stir souls of all ages and nationalities. It is also the home of my daughter Allyson and her Swedish husband, Tobias, who introduced us to the many wonders of their homeland.

I owe a debt of gratitude to Dan Canterbury, a Delta pilot by day and Air Force Reserve pilot in his spare time. His knowledge of flight in general and C-141 Starlifters in particular kept me within the boundaries of the possible.

And I salute every former and present member of the S.C. Air National Guard at McEntyre Air National Guard Base and Air Force Reservist in the 315th Military Airlift Wing at Charleston Air Force Base whom I had the honor to serve with for 20 years.

A special thanks goes to my friend Frank Glenn, who I portrayed as a drug-running bush pilot. He is a decorated, veteran Vietnam chopper pilot and now a legitimate business guru who is happiest flying someone like me across the rivers and marshes of the Lowcountry in his bright yellow 1947 Piper Cub Classic.

Also, I thank Robin Strickland and Mimi Leroux (another great name) and all the employees at the FedEx Office in Charleston who helped me when I needed technical help, which was often.

As always, I share a small slice of heaven with the residents of Seabrook Island where I escape, walk the beach and discuss story ideas with the dolphins.

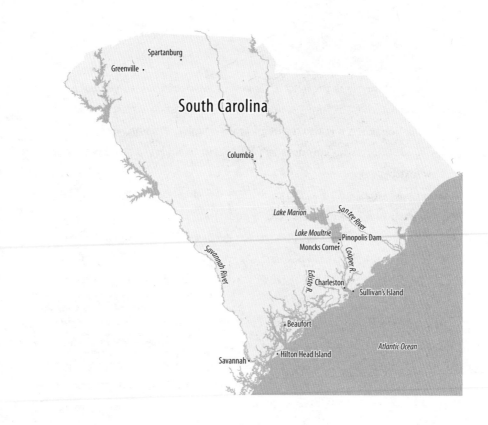

CHAPTER 1

1979

Maceo Mazyck twisted left and right but the straitjacket wouldn't budge. It was wrapped so tight his arms were numb. His camouflage jungle hat and bent aviator sunglasses sat askew on his head. He wore them to hide his imperfection, to disguise him in the pigmented world where he was an outcast, a pink man in a black-and-white universe. He feared light, and hated the flickering fluorescent bulb overhead. Maceo was an albino Negro, a genetic misfit, born under the scorching South Carolina sun, a misprint in a long line of discontent.

While he had no personal memory of slavery, Jim Crow laws, lynching or the Klan, his grandfather Zeke did, and the old man stoked those fears like hot coals in a campfire. On sweltering summer nights he told stories of human cruelty in great detail as his grandsons huddled on his front porch.

Ninety-year-old Ezekiel Manigo Mazyck, hunched and crippled from age and agony, spoke of slavery in whispers, the way his grandfather had done, as if saying the word out loud might bring it thundering back on horsemen riding out of the shadows, throwing torches and swinging rope.

Some children memorize nursery rhymes. Maceo and his playmates remembered tales of torture: An uncle hanged for staring at a white woman; a cousin beaten bloody for no good reason; the brutal rape and murder of an aunt Maceo never met.

Hardly a day of Maceo's life passed without remembering his grandfather spitting in the dirt after nodding and shuffling in deference to white men passing by. An excellent spitter, the old man could summon a wad of mucus from the back of his throat, swirl it around in his mouth and heave it like a oyster minus its shell. He could spray spittle between the gap in his two front teeth, too. If he didn't like people, he'd spritz them in the face, and his lips never moved — fast, like a king snake.

Maceo loved his grandpa Zeke, a blue-black field hand with shiny skin the color of a grackle. Maceo longed to be like the old man: Dark and defiant, but mostly dark.

Old Zeke tried to make his grandson feel comfortable in his own skin, but Maceo's mottled pinkish hue and nappy-blond hair marked him as a mongrel and the runt of the litter, smaller than his older twin brothers, who teased him without mercy. They laughed and said their daddy didn't get a good toehold when he was making Maceo.

Maceo didn't know what that meant exactly. He didn't know much at all. Most days he'd just hide on the boat, out of the scorching sun. He begged God for black skin, although he didn't know all that went along with that peculiar condition. The messages were mixed.

One minute his grandfather stepped aside for white men; the next he swore under his breath he'd slit the crackers' throats and set them on fire. His grandfather hated white people and relished telling stories about them on the porch at night.

One story stood out — the one about Zeke's baby sister, who had been raped and killed. The old man wept when he spoke of Santee, five years younger and the smartest of them all. He'd lower his head, put a finger to his lips, look around and whisper, "Now I'm gone tell y'all 'bout what happened to Sister Santee. I know 'cause I was there. They made me watch."

The boys squirmed when they heard that. They didn't know exactly what rape was, just that it was bad, probably worse than death. But they cheered at the end when old Zeke tracked down the killers and strangled them with his bare hands. Cut 'em up, too. Least that's what he said.

Maceo knew that story by heart. Twenty years later, he broiled in outrage just thinking about what they did to Sister Santee. Then he'd drink. Anger and alcohol were an especially dangerous combination.

The first drink led him down dark paths — to slave ships and rice fields and cemeteries in the woods. The second took him deeper into despair — to a place where he hung by his wrists from chains and bled and twisted and turned in a futile attempt to save Santee as she scratched and screamed and begged for her life.

Maceo's spiral into darkness often landed him in a chair under the glare of the flickering light inside a dingy room on Bull Street where he was covered in his own crap, his veins bulging like bee stings. Everybody in South Carolina knew Bull Street, the 100-year-old asylum for the insane. But only South Carolinians like Maceo Mazyck knew what went on inside that place.

At 5-feet-3-inches and 200 pounds, Maceo was the smallest of the Mazyck brothers. The other two were identical twins, perfect specimens. Maceo was flawed, a by-product, short, stocky, the color of a suckling pig. Sometimes, when brooding, he'd blame his father for his condition. Micah Mazyck was put out of his misery when Maceo was three. He broke down like a mule in a cotton field, went berserk, swung his hoe wildly, and a white man on a horse shot him dead.

Maceo was shelling green beans with his mother in the shade of the back stoop of their cabin when he heard the shot. It came from far away, sharp at first, then soft like an echo rolling through the woods, down the creek and into the yard. His mother jumped up, spilling beans everywhere, and turned toward the noise as she swept up Maceo into her arms, her hands trembling.

That night his father's body was dumped in the dirt beside the lane in front of the cabin. There was a hole between his eyes, which were still open. Maceo watched from the window as his grandfather shuffled up to the corpse, spit in the dirt twice and hobbled off into the darkness.

Twenty years later, Maceo sat in the holding tank on Bull Street twisting and turning, rattling his leg-irons, squinting against the fluorescent flame. Two hundred years of hatred could not be restrained.

CHAPTER 2

G rover Jones Jr. adjusted his red bow tie with his left hand, clicked a retractable ink pen with his right thumb and tried to focus as he worked part time on the night shift inside the state mental hospital on Bull Street.

Junior, as he was known in his family, was 20 years old, a rising senior at South Carolina State College, the only son of a county councilman known to all around Columbia as Grover "Don't Let Nobody Down" Jones.

That had been his father's political mantra for years since he hocked the family car to run radio ads on WWDM, 780-AM, "The Black Spot On Your Dial." Pumping 50,000 watts from a 100-foot tower in Sumter County, WWDM played soul music in South Carolina before people knew it had a name. White people who stumbled across it on the radio often listened in, mostly out of curiosity. If they were riding with a friend, they denounced it as "nigger music" and switched stations immediately. If they were alone, they turned it up.

Grover "Don't Let Nobody Down" Jones used this powerful African-American broadcast channel to get elected to Richland County Council. The seat came open when Councilman Jack McCray, a local civil rights leader, was appointed deputy undersecretary for the assistant director of minority affairs in the U.S. Department of Energy and moved to Washington, D.C.

As a little boy Junior remembered asking what the initials D.C. stood for. His father said, "Da Capital." That always brought laughter from the adults gathered in his parents' living room for penny poker and political policy debates.

Grover Sr. had worked for the U.S. Postal Service since he graduated from Booker T. Washington High School in Columbia. As the first member of his family to graduate and pass the Civil Service exam, he pledged that his son would finish college.

He paid for Junior's education, his wife's monthly trips to the beauty parlor and their three-bedroom ranch in an all-black Columbia neighborhood by working his way up to assistant shift manager. He also moonlighted as a bartender at the all-white Forest Lake Country Club.

Postal pay was not much, but the benefits bolstered Senior's sense of security. He often told his only son about the value of the state retirement system. Senior also dreamed of winning political office. He'd served as vice president of his senior class and secretary-treasurer of the Beta Club at Booker T., and convinced himself that politics was his special calling.

His life changed one Wednesday afternoon when he stepped out of Taylor Street Pharmacy and ran into Amanda Mays, a reporter for WOLO-TV, conducting man-on-the-street interviews about race relations in the Palmetto State. Despite his meek appearance, Senior had a bold baritone voice that became even more commanding when rhetoric was applied. This ability to captivate came through in a sound bite when Amanda asked him for his thoughts.

Senior pondered the question and said, "I am the only son of the only son of the only son of a slave. I have a job. I pay taxes. I have a family. I have more than my father ever dreamed of and less than my son will ever accept. But I am nothing without my brothers. We need to lift everybody up. Don't let nobody down..."

That's where the interview was abruptly cut, even though Senior actually said, "Don't let nobody downgrade you into second-class citizenship."

It didn't matter. The anchorman back at the TV station considered it funny and mocked the phrase, "Don't Let Nobody Down." He said it over and over again on the air in an Amos-and-Andy voice, then added, "Grover 'Don't Let Nobody Down' Jones ... Now that could get you elected to something in this town."

Sure enough, it did.

With the $800 he got for the family's Ford Fairlane, Senior littered his side of town with VOTE FOR GROVER 'DON'T LET NOBODY DOWN' JONES plastic signs; and he ran radio commercials in which he mimicked the TV anchorman's ridicule of the phrase; and Grover Jones got himself elected to fill Jack McCray's vacant seat on County Council.

Unfortunately, his father's success left Junior more confused about when, where and how to be black. While he had the broad shoulders of his father's sharecropper genes, his skin was the color of cappuccino from his mother's homogenized Caribbean legacy.

It was an interesting time in South Carolina: Civil rights was alive, Martin Luther King Jr. was dead, Jim Crow was holding court down at the barbershop and Uncle Tom just bought a house in the suburbs.

None of that mattered much at the moment, in that dingy room with the flickering light on Bull Street, where Junior Jones was trying to act cool in the presence of Maceo Mazyck. Everything about Maceo seemed black — his clothes, his nose, his lips, his hair — but everything was the wrong color, except for the blood trickling out of the prisoner's left ear.

This is how most of Junior's late-night customers arrived: shackled, beaten, bloodied, muddied and mad in both senses of the word. Junior sat at his small metal desk across the room, against the wall, where he had accepted the paperwork from two Berkeley County deputies who had dragged in bound and bloodied Maceo.

"He's all yours," the young cop said as he stamped mud off his boot from an earlier romp through the swamp. "He ain't real big, but beware … the little albino bastard bites. It was all we could do to get him in the trunk of the car."

Maceo's swollen left eye and bleeding ear were evidence of the rifle butt that helped him find his seat next to the spare tire. He was a mess, his jungle hat askew and sunglasses broken, camouflaged pants torn and tattered. From behind the cracked lens of his teardrop shades, Maceo's right eye, pink and bloodshot, stared at Junior.

It wasn't supposed to be like this, Junior thought. When he told his father he wanted a summer job, he wasn't thinking about working in a mental hospital. He remembered his interview. Walking from Rosewood Drive through his middle-class black neighborhood on the south side of Columbia, along the edges of the University of South Carolina campus, past the Capitol building where the Confederate battle flag flew high above the dome, up Bull Street and through the gates of hell.

The Williams Building, designed by the famous South Carolina architect Robert Mills, greeted each visitor to the state mental hospital with the words "South Carolina Lunatic Asylum" chiseled prominently in stone.

Junior assumed that, because his daddy was a councilman, he'd work as a page in the South Carolina House or Senate. But those jobs went to white boys. He landed a position as an admitting clerk on the night shift at the looney bin. At times like this, Grover Jones Sr.'s words about integration echoed in Junior's brain:

"Remember, son, it won't be an overnight thing; our forefathers planted the seeds so we could enjoy the fruits. But don't eat too much too fast or it might make you sick. And be sure to leave some for those who come along behind you."

Junior grew up hearing such tempered testimony. His father spoke of baby steps, one generation at a time. Better and better, higher and higher. On Sunday afternoons, Grover "Don't Let Nobody Down" Jones rode around the city with his son sitting beside him in their wide, second-hand Lincoln. He'd cruise through the worst black neighborhoods, off Hardin Street where he grew up, and point out the druggies, drunks, whores and other no-counts living in the shadows.

"Nigguhs," his father said sternly, making sure his son understood the word. "Like crabs in a bucket, son. Try to get out; they'll pull you back in. They're dangerous, boy, not the white folk. Nigguhs are the real enemy."

All of which convinced Junior Jones he was on the right career path: Getting an education; doing the right thing; knowing the right people. Didn't matter if you were black or white. This is America, by God, and he believed all that. Until he heard about the massacre.

It occurred in Orangeburg in 1968 when state highway troopers surrounded South Carolina State University's campus to put down a protest. A few black State students tried to go bowling in an "all-white" alley across the street. Five hours later, three were dead, 27 lay wounded. They called it "The Orangeburg Massacre."

To Junior Jones and his classmates, it was a teachable moment in history, one he was reminded of every time he entered the Smith-Hammond-Middleton Auditorium, a campus monument to the three students killed when the bullets flew that night.

The fate of those young men was branded on every freshman's psyche at S.C. State. But Senior refused to discuss the massacre, insisting it never be mentioned even at the dinner table. Senior said Gov. Bob McNair was a good Democrat, a good white man. Senior said the whole thing was a tragic misunderstanding, a speed bump on the way forward to the Promised Land.

Little did Junior know that the "way forward" would lead him here, sitting directly across from Maceo Mazyck, an albino who reeked of body odor, puke, excrement, kerosene, pluff mud, wood smoke and ignorance.

Junior carefully picked through Maceo's coat pockets with tweezers for personal items. When Maceo spit through his front teeth, one of the deputies slapped him across the face with a clipboard. It was all part of the admissions process, which included filling out five patient information forms, building a file, making metal dog tags, snapping a mug shot, securing and recording the patient's valuables.

In one of Maceo's front pockets, Junior found a pickled pig's foot, several weeks old, gnawed to the bone. In another were a red Christmas tree light and a one-cent stamp. In his pant pocket he found the first 10 chapters of the Book of Revelation handwritten on notebook paper and cut into strips.

Flipping through Maceo's file, Junior read the diagnosis: "Paranoid-schizo-phrenic," psychiatry's common cold. But it didn't matter. Maceo was a misfit even in a mental hospital. He was aberrant and anomalous and destined to be ignored. Indeed, the night he met Junior Jones was not Maceo's first ride on the Bull. He was a regular. He'd been here three times before, all for 30-day observations during which he was cleaned up, dried out and turned out angrier, more suspicious and meaner than ever.

Then Junior noticed something in the paperwork. Maceo's birthday was the same as his, September 21, although in the space where the birth year should have been registered, someone scrawled, "Unknown." When Junior looked up, Maceo smiled, his gums as pink as his cheeks, his teeth a greenish yellow, jagged, rotted and stained like stumps of an old creek dock. Dark brown slime dripped from his pant leg onto his bare feet.

Junior gagged when the deputies removed the shackles and the straitjacket and left.

CHAPTER 3

Life as an admitting clerk in South Carolina's mental hospital was only slightly better than that of an inmate. Fortunately for Junior Jones, he was just passing through. He thought the way the mentally ill were warehoused in this public dungeon was a crime against humanity.

Once Junior got over the shock of where he worked, he settled into a routine. He arrived at 3 o'clock and left at midnight. In between, he processed a variety of after-hours patients, drove the campus ambulance and smoked pot with the orderlies down in the morgue.

By day, the hospital looked like a college. Ivy-covered architecture graced the entrance; people strolled the grounds and lounged under shade trees. Behind the cloistered scene, however, was a never-ending horror show.

The screams started just after dark, slowly at first. Some had a sensual side to them. But as the night shift withdrew and the drugs wore off, howls of hopelessness bawled from the bowels of the wards.

Junior quickly learned the value of keys. They locked the doors between the wards, sealing one group of chain-smoking psychopaths off from another group of masturbating mutants. He watched his own back. A patient might be firing up a cigarette one minute, setting you ablaze the next.

Junior was always outnumbered, especially at night. That's why nobody was between him and the door when Maceo Mazyck decided to leave. Mistakenly, Junior rose from his chair in a polite attempt to ask the patient to be patient.

"Really, Mr. Mazyck, I do understand," Junior said. "It's late, but we'll be done soon, get you up to bed and you'll be..."

He felt it before he saw it. Actually, he smelled it before that. The pluff mud. The wood smoke. The kerosene. When Maceo's left forearm slammed across Junior's chest, it sent him flailing against the wall with a thud. Maceo, dripping drool, kicked the outer door open with his bare foot and ran into the night. When Junior got his wind back, he unclipped his bow tie, lifted it to his nose and recoiled from the stench. Through the window, under a streetlight, he saw Maceo slinking between parked cars, looking for a way out. Junior tossed his tie across the room, picked up a two-way radio and called security.

Safety Officer George Burr and the boys would pick up Mr. Mazyck before he scaled the wall and, unfortunately, bring him back. "Crazy-ass pink nigger," Junior mumbled as he sniffed his shirt and choked back a dry heave.

CHAPTER 4

George Burr turned the search light toward the chain-link fence on the back-side of the hospital grounds. He'd chased lots of runaways — most of them patients who had earned "yard cards" for good behavior. They were allowed a few hours outside, away from the din of the wards. If one went missing, it was no big deal. They'd usually show up in a dumpster, under a building or in the bushes having sex, and they weren't picky about partners. Few made it over the 10-foot fence topped with razor wire, mainly because they were scared of what was on the other side.

Despite these inconvenient chases, Burr figured he had a good job for a small-town boy who never went to college. Columbia was a happening place for a single man in his 20s. University of South Carolina coeds tended the bars in Five Points and plenty of other eligible women came to town looking for jobs and a good time, not necessarily in that order.

Burr was lanky with long, wavy brown hair he kept tucked under his cap when he was in uniform. He had a garage apartment a few blocks from the hospital where Junior was often invited to weekend parties. Junior liked redneck white girls from small towns like Hemingway, Manning and Saluda. Most of them worked at the Department of Motor Vehicles, County Assessor's Office and Department of Social Services.

The evenings, however, always ended with them going one way and Junior another. While it was a good time to be young and African American, color lines still scratched South Carolina like chalklines on the sidewalks of Orangeburg. Reminders of who was really in charge were obvious.

Chief of Bull Street Security was Tank Barker, a retired Army sergeant who double-dipped his way out of one uniform into another without a day off in between. Compared to what he saw on active duty in the Army, this was cake. He knew the patients were too drugged to do much damage.

But Tank played the game, lecturing his security officers at guard mount each day about the dangers and responsibilities of the job. When he'd turn his back, George Burr would snap from his parade-rest position into his John Travolta, "Saturday Night Fever" pose, and the guys would howl. Tank's turnaround was always a moment too late to catch him. All he ever saw was a silly smile on George Burr's face.

George wasn't smiling the night Junior's call went out over the radio. He steered his Ford Crown Victoria cruiser toward Hope Street and headed for the back fence. That's where they all went, away from the lights.

George shined his spotlight up and down the fence line and saw nothing at first. Then he noticed movement 50 yards to his right. He gunned the car, spun the spotlight and saw a pink foot dragging across the top razor wire, snagging, jerking free and falling toward the other side. Burr slammed on the brakes, jumped out, pulled his pistol and yelled, "Stop, Mister, or I'll shoot!" But he would not pull the trigger. Never had. Never would. Too much paperwork involved.

As Burr keyed his radio microphone to notify city police, he looked up at the wire where Maceo Mazyck went over. There was a small strip of bloodstained camouflage fabric from his pants and a strand of slime dangling from the wire.

Technically, Maceo was a fugitive, but it wasn't as if the cops were actually looking for him. They took the report from hospital security and tossed it on a pile with others they got from security officers of the city's two black colleges, Allen and Benedict.

Later that night, as Maceo rode out of town in the bed of a sharecropper's truck, he saw the Confederate flag flapping in the breeze above the Capitol building in stark contrast to the high-rise office buildings in downtown Columbia.

Maceo spit once, twice, then pulled the heavy red truck tarp over his head as he and the farmer disappeared south into the Lowcountry darkness.

CHAPTER 5

1989

S toney Sanders sat in his office overlooking the Santee Cooper power plant, the last 20 years of his life spent in "governmental affairs," a fancy title for lobbyist. Named for two of South Carolina's Lowcountry rivers — the once-mighty Santee and the uncooperative Cooper — the S.C. Public Service Authority offered hydroelectric power and almost 1,500 jobs in Berkeley County. Santee Cooper's dirty little secret, however, was that clean hydropower totaled only one percent of its output. The rest of the electricity generated by the utility came primarily from carbon-laden coal. So much so, that the state bought Santee Cooper its own coal cars to guarantee a steady flow from Kentucky, West Virginia and Pennsylvania directly into South Carolina.

As Sanders chatted on the phone, he could hear the steady rattle of rail cars creaking and screeching as they dumped loads of black coal into the hoppers that fed the eternal flame. The noise was a small price to pay for progress, he always said, as was the black smoke belching a million tons of pollutants into the blue Carolina sky every day for almost 40 years.

Some said it was not healthy, but few cared because Santee Cooper could do whatever it needed to do in whatever way it wanted to do it. As a quasi-governmental agency, it enjoyed the immunity of its birthright, which allowed it to operate as a state agency one day, a private enterprise the next, depending on which way the political winds blew.

Stoney Sanders thrived in this murky jurisdictional jungle that created its own ecosystem of friends and enemies. His job was to know one from the other. At age 39, Sanders considered himself a lady's man, fit and trim, well compensated, wife dead. His house on Lake Moultrie, the lower of two huge man-made reservoirs, had taken on the aroma of a frat house.

Helen, his late wife, would not have approved of that or the new swimming pool, hot tub and wet bar in the backyard. Nor would she appreciate his new fiberglass pontoon boat docked out back and rigged for "night fishing." Those were Stoney's code words for taking certain politicians out on the lake, laying six lines of cocaine across the mirrored captain's table, rolling up hundred dollar bills and making snow disappear. It was at such a weekend party where Junior Jones leaned against Stoney Sander's backyard bar and sipped white wine. As Junior watched the pontoon boat pull away from the dock, he noted her name on the stern, *The Fine Line*.

Junior snuffled a smile, knowing it referred to the product being consumed and the political path his employer carefully walked. But he was not invited on the excursion. Being a black man invited to a party in Stoney's yard was one thing. Joining Sanders and his cronies on the pontoon boat was above his pay grade in Santee Cooper's Office of Legal Services. He waved to Sanders and the others as they pulled away from the dock. Stoney waved back and smiled.

Although Junior got along with everybody in the utility's administration building in Moncks Corner, he might as well have lived on Mars. As an African American in a company run by Southern whites, he disappeared after work into a figurative black hole. While he did socialize with his fellow employees at work, he never got to really know them, and dating was out of the question.

This not-so-subtle segregation, however, suited Junior because what he did away from work was nobody's business. Junior's father would not understand. It was more important to slowly integrate into the white man's world, Grover "Don't Let Nobody Down" Jones believed. He was a non-combatant and conscientious objector in Dr. King's American dream. Thus, his son toed the line at home. No talk of protest, revolution or use of so-called "safe" drugs, ever.

Senior often repeated the same story about illegal drugs in the black community

— the one about cousin Earl, whose nickname was "Cashew" because his brain wasn't very big. Cashew dealt drugs out of his mother-in-law's house. One-stop shopping, he called it. Pot, powder, rock, crank, uppers, downers, whatever he could get his hands on. He also sold single Pall Mall cigarettes to customers who couldn't afford an entire pack.

One day the Columbia city cops busted him for supplying amphetamines to the wife of a state Supreme Court justice. He did 16 years in Central Correctional Institute, a hundred-year-old prison at the edge of town on the Congaree River. She spent a month at Betty Ford hospital. Junior had no intention of joining Cousin Earl at CCI. He was a lawyer and considered himself above all that.

He wore his hair in a corporate Afro — not too big, not too small, just enough to show his pride without offending his colleagues. He was the only black attorney in Santee Cooper's Office of Legal Services, which had 20 lawyers and 35 paralegals.

When Junior joined Santee Cooper just out of law school, it was considered a prize assignment. He decided not to live in Moncks Corner near the corporate office along the banks of the Tailrace Canal below the Pinopolis Dam. Instead, he accepted an offer to live south of Broad Street in downtown Charleston from his law school chum Ashmead Dawes. Ashmead's parents had a carriage house apartment for rent behind their mansion on Tradd Street.

It was an odd friendship for the times. Junior, a first-generation, college-educated black man chinning himself on the high bar; Ashmead, at the tail end of an inbred dynasty, hanging himself on the family tree.

They met in a first-year study group of the University of South Carolina Law School and soon shared a two-bedroom apartment in the leafy Shandon neighborhood near Five Points in Columbia. At night they'd sit on the second-floor porch, smoking pot, mocking their professors' insistence that law was the glue that kept society from sliding into the abyss.

The law, Junior and Ashmead agreed, kept the rich rich and the poor poor; some people in prison, some out; a few powerful, most powerless; the strong strong and the weak weak. Upon graduation, they tied for 40th-place ranking in their class of 54. Good enough if your family has a law firm on Broad Street or if you're black. So both got jobs they didn't deserve.

Junior enjoyed life, even though his days were spent working on right-of-way easements for power lines. He was paying his dues. His father had planned it all out for him. A few years in the state system, get to know the right people, the lobbyists, the power brokers, the competition. Better to be out of Columbia for a while, get a proper wife, build a grassroots constituency, join the Rotary Club, go to church and carefully lay the groundwork for becoming a good Democratic candidate for governor.

That was the ultimate goal, his father said, for Junior to become the first black governor of South Carolina since Reconstruction. He began calling Junior "Guv'nor" while he was still in law school. It seemed like a silly father-son dream Junior thought as he toiled over blueprints and survey sheets in his Santee Cooper office. Junior loved his father, respected all he had achieved, but his own life would be different.

Junior's nightlife made up for the humdrum of lawyering. Just a few blocks from his Charleston apartment, up East Bay Street in the old Market, Junior found Henry's, a throwback joint where he and Ashmead would slide into a booth with people they'd met at the Garden and Gun Club around the corner.

The Garden and Gun was a glitzy homosexual bar with avant-garde notoriety in staid old Charleston. The club attracted a hip heterosexual crowd that came in late and drunk on Jose Cuervo mixed with prurient curiosity. Junior and Ashmead, as high as cirrus clouds, barhopped until they each found someone to cling to. For Ashmead, his one-night stands included his high school biology teacher in drag. For Junior that night, it was Lena Horne in combat boots.

Quality black companionship was hard to find in Charleston, Junior decided. The good ones left as soon as possible to Northern schools and Northern jobs, far away from the Holy City's slave-owner mentality. Charleston was an old coat brought out of mothballs — a run-down town with an antebellum charm that made it famous. While most Southern cities remodeled after the Civil War, Charleston passed — couldn't afford it. As a result, the city was haughtily tattered, a Confederate-gray symbol of the way things used to be.

Ashley Cooper, a daily columnist for the Charleston Courier, described the port city as "out at the elbow and down at the heel." Cities like Atlanta and Charlotte attracted young people looking for jobs after college. They were the "New South," where banks built skyscrapers; engineering firms flourished and jobs were abundant. Columbia, South Carolina's capital, was poised to be like them but not yet launched.

Junior considered Columbia boring and bureaucratic — "The City of Seven Sundays" — he joked with his white friends. He preferred Charleston. He liked the way blacks and whites, gays and straights, rich and poor quietly accepted each other as passengers in the same leaky lifeboat and in no great hurry to bail.

CHAPTER 6

Maceo Mazyck lived in an old Volkswagen bus bolted to the deck of a bro-ken-down shrimp boat on a brackish bend on the eastern branch halfway up the Cooper River. The locals dubbed the oxbow "Schitt Creek," and it stuck.

In her day, the *Sister Santee* trawled the waters off Charleston with other shrimp boats home-ported from Little River south to Edisto Beach. The *Sister* was wide and sat low when her nets were wet, chugging just beyond the breakers off Sullivan's Island.

The boat was hand-built by Maceo's grandfather Ezekiel, who named it for his baby sister. It looked like all the other shrimp boats — fully rigged with the name painted on the bow and stern — until it could be examined up close. Although built to scale, it was much smaller, and with a lot less net. The Magwoods from Shem Creek had big 60-foot boats with green stripes on the bow. So did the Williams boys out of McClellanville.

When Maceo and other black shrimpers went out, they looked more like the old Mosquito Fleet — small, black-owned fishing skiffs with single sails that used to dot the harbor like mosquitoes hatching on a pond.

The Mazyck brothers scratched out a living aboard the *Sister Santee* until the diesel engine broke down and the nets rotted out. Without money for repairs, they beached the *Sister* on an oyster bed below a bluff where they lived in a row of large rusty cargo containers. When the water was high, the compound looked like any other fish camp. When it was low, it exposed a mud bank littered with discarded machine parts, disc harrows, bicycle wheels and rusty tractor seats.

Maceo chose to live on the boat, inside the old bus, rather than with the others on the bluff. The bus was his grandfather's idea. After the diesel failed, the old man engineered a system where the Volkswagen engine turned a fan belt that turned the shaft and propeller. While it lost some thrust, it pushed the old boat at about six knots. Anywhere else, the sight of an old VW bus bolted to the deck of a wooden shrimp boat would be ridiculous. Not on Schitt Creek.

Maceo's brothers, O'rangejello and Le'monjello, lived on high ground in the metal boxes that once served as shipping containers for the Sea-Land Company. The yard was full of corroded car carcasses and other junk. The compound reeked of dog shit and sewage, neglect and indifference. Maceo liked living on the boat even though it listed three feet to the right every time the tide went out. It was far better than living with his brothers, who were full-time criminals.

If they weren't stealing tires from the highway department bus shed, they were breaking into warehouses and taking fire extinguishers, lawn furniture, diapers, motorcycle parts and whatever else they could sell on the black market. But to make big money, they used the *Sister*.

Just two weeks ago at dusk, when the creek was high and the moon was low in the east, Maceo cranked up the four-cylinder engine, turned the steering wheel of the micro-bus and guided the *Sister Santee* down stream, out through the old rice fields and into the retreating tide. Once in the creek, he and his brothers drifted down river, past miles of untended dikes and ditches, into the harbor, out to the jetties, within sight of land, where they killed the engine, opened cans of Vienna Sausages and sardines and waited.

Maceo especially liked Vienna Sausages. They came in short tin cans, six of them packed tight in their own juices. Homefolks called them "stand-ups" because they were stacked upright in the can. Sardines were "lay-downs," because they were packed flat, swimming in brine and salt. Both came with a built-in key, which fascinated Maceo.

As they finished the second can of stand-ups, a sleek, black cigarette boat appeared just off their bow, its in-board engines bubbling noisily until the captain cut the power and drifted next to the *Sister*. Without conversation among the crews, four footlockers were hoisted over the *Sister's* gunnels and the Mazyck twins stacked them on the deck. The speedboat's engines suddenly roared to life and the sleek black craft quickly disappeared into the night.

Riding the inward tide, the *Sister* sputtered home without running lights as the Mazyck brother's tossed empty sausage and sardine cans over the sides. Next day, a man they knew only as "Rolex" roared down the dirt road to Schitt Creek bluff in a black El Camino. Before the dust could settle, the Mazyck twins had slid the footlockers on to the truck bed. The driver ran down his black-tinted window a few inches and passed them an unmarked envelope. O'rangejello grabbed it, glimpsing the big gold watch on the driver's wrist before he pulled away.

Maceo got none of the cash. He griped about how his brothers left the shrimp boat atop the oyster bed — never the same way twice, which disrupted his sleep when the boat rolled side-to-side with the tide. At high tide his bedroll fit perfectly on the floor of the bus. But at low tide, he slept hard against the sliding doors. He did, however, take comfort in the knowledge that he had masterfully drilled holes in the handles of his pots and pans, allowing them to swing on nails with the shifting tides.

The boat was cold in the winter and hot in the summer, but Maceo didn't care. Anything was better than living with his brothers and Gizelle, a trash-mouth Gullah girl who alternated sleeping with a twin nightly. Gizelle was not much prettier than the pit bulls the Mazycks kept chained under the sprawling oak trees in the driveway.

Maceo had been to dogfights up the road, past Frazier's Store, inside the abandoned red barn. His brothers spent hours taunting those poor animals, poking them with sticks, pissing them off. If a dog weren't mean enough, they'd beat it to death with a brick, or string it live up on a coat hanger from a tree limb.

Maceo didn't have the stomach for any of it. Reminded him of Bull Street. He preferred the company of George Dickel and J.W. Dant.

All his life he'd been lonely this way: Not quite white, hardly black, a pinkish freak in a forgotten sideshow. His brothers were the beautiful beasts — broad shoulders, narrow waists, everything in proportion. Maceo wasn't fully formed — his torso squat, his head too big, his pigmentation the ultimate curse.

At night, as he slept in the bus and rolled with the tide, Maceo often dreamed of being solid black — so black his brothers wouldn't taunt him, so black he could disappear into the night and nobody could find him. He also dreamed of far-off Sweden, where the sun did not shine for six months of the year.

In the glove compartment of the bus he kept a tattered issue of National Geographic magazine he had found in the trash at the "lunatic asylum" on Bull Street years before. The cover story was about Sweden, its dark winters and how the fair-skinned Swedes drank heavily to compensate for the lack of sunshine. He particularly liked the artwork on page 39, a John Bauer print of a small boy leading a large, stooped, hairy creature through the forest at twilight. Snow was falling. The boy showed no fear of the dark, the weather or the brooding ogre.

The lady who drove the Berkeley County bookmobile stopped by the bluff one day and read the National Geographic article to him. She said Bauer, a native of Jonkoping, was a master of painting Swedish scenes that contrasted trolls and children in the deep woods during winter. She read about how Bauer and his wife drowned in a lake when their boat overturned; about how the people of the town honored his memory with a museum filled with his artwork.

Maceo could only imagine there was a place where he could be cold. A paradise where fair-skinned people brushed their stark white hair and shuffled through the snow smiling because the sun had gone away and would not be back for a long, long time. He dreamed of sailing the *Sister* all the way to Sweden, which was somewhere north of Lake Marion, he supposed.

Most nights Maceo fell asleep holding the magazine to his chest, wishing he were somewhere else. But every day he would awaken, his hair still white, his arms still pink, his piebald body still in Schitt Creek, and he would curse and then cry and drink.

One day Maceo — heavily influenced by his friends Dickel and Dant — decided to make a pass at Gizelle, the Gullah slut. His pink penis worked fine, as far as he knew, so when she walked by looking for frogs to gig along the creek bank, Maceo dropped his pants and giggled.

In one swift move, Gizelle turned, raised the three-pronged spear above her head and let it fly toward him. Instinctively, the blood rushed out of Maceo's penis and engorged his brain, which warned him to duck. The gig stuck in the side of the forward cabin of the boat next to where the fire extinguisher was before his brothers sold it.

"Me no touch dat, freakin' pigmy!" Gizelle snarled between yellowed teeth.

The intensity of the threat was lost on Maceo, who blurted out, stuttering, "B-b-but my pee-pee's p-p-pink and your p-p-ussy is too!"

Gizelle was not impressed.

"If I wanted dat, I'd be down on Spruill Avenue," she said and trudged up the embankment. "Ya got nuttin, pigmy," she added.

Enraged, Maceo grabbed a three-foot length of chain he kept onboard, swung it like a lasso and loosed it toward Gizelle. It whizzed by her head and stuck with a thud in the pluff mud.

"B-b-bitch," he screamed as he scampered inside the bus.

While the incident was insignificant, Maceo's stuttering was not. It meant he needed medication. Fights were highlights of Maceo's social life. Mostly he sat in the bus, listening to his transistor radio, watching Schitt Creek rise and fall. Because he had a diagnosis from the state mental hospital, he received a disability check, which his brothers controlled, and food stamps, which he used at Frazier's Store to buy the staples he needed to stay alive.

But his most treasured possessions came from the river, flotsam from boats of people who cooled themselves in the upper lakes in the summertime. Occasionally he found something worth keeping. Like the life preserver he snagged with "U.S. Coast Guard" stamped on the inside. When Maceo fished it out of the water, he found a pistol in a waterproof holster strapped to the side of the float. Probably fell out of a patrol boat or one of those bright orange helicopters that fly up and down the waterways in search of smugglers and drowning victims. The gun, a 38 caliber, had a full clip of 20 rounds.

Maceo fired it a couple of times — once over the heads of his brothers when they threatened to feed him to the dogs; another when somebody other than the county nurse showed up to administer his monthly injection. And maybe a few other times when he was drunk and couldn't remember what he was shooting at. Word got around that he had a gun, so most folks left Maceo alone. They knew he had a pistol; they just didn't know how many bullets he had left.

However, nobody knew about the batch of dynamite the river delivered to him a few years back — six sticks, wrapped tightly in plastic, that bobbed up next to the *Sister* and got hung up in the prop. Maceo feared explosives and didn't touch them for a few days. Eventually, he fished them out of the water and stowed them deep in the bow, just in case. Maceo was always preparing for a time when things would be different — when Armageddon arrived — although he had no idea what that meant.

He shivered in the winter and broiled in the summer. Unlike the bronze sons and daughters of South Carolina who lay about the beaches and rubbed themselves with coconut oil, Maceo wore a hat and shades and long sleeves at all times during daylight. Without this protection, the Southern sun would blister him, even in winter. He always looked bundled up during daylight hours. When the sun didn't torture him, the gnats and mosquitoes did.

Maceo was barely tolerable to others when he got his sleep and his shots. Without them, he was a stuttering, unpredictable pain in the ass. Once a month a lady from the Berkeley County Mental Health Department came out to give him a shot, a concoction of Halperidol and Thorazine, which turned his stuttering into slurring. She said it was like mixing paint: Try a little of this and a little of that until you get it just right.

When it was right, a heavy tarp muffled Maceo's madness, tacked it down tight and kept it from consuming his life. That's why Eleanor Lane was the only social worker Maceo had ever trusted. She talked to him about school and reading and what was going on elsewhere in the world. He smiled when he saw her station wagon coming down the dirt road to the fish camp, kicking up dust through the willow trees. She made him feel human.

When she was late, Maceo worried that she was sick or dead. It had to be one or the other because Miss Eleanor wouldn't just abandon him. If she did not show up on the final workday of the week, tension rose in Maceo's mind, the tarp flapped at the edges and little by little, a big wind ripped it off, and he'd wake up in jail raging like a caged and abused animal.

Fortunately, most of the time, Eleanor showed up like clockwork with a smile on her face and a hypodermic needle in her left coat pocket. She was somewhat pretty, always sweet, Maceo thought. She'd stand on the shore and call his name before tight-roping the long two-by-six plank and coming on board.

Maceo would roll up his sleeve and wait for her to dab his arm with alcohol and give him a shot. Within minutes he felt the chemicals pulsing through his veins, and he relaxed. Sometimes he walked a ways with her back toward her car and they'd stop and sit under a tree and talk for a while. For Maceo, the only days that were better began high above the treetops.

Once a month, if the weather suited and he wasn't manic, Maceo would leave the *Sister* at 3 a.m., hike up the dirt road past Frazier's Store, take a left on the paved road and walk another mile to the Woodboo Fire Tower.

Built by the Civilian Conservation Corps during the Depression, the metal tower was 110 feet through the top of the pine canopy of the Francis Marion National Forest. From up there, a fire spotter could see for miles in any direction. Spotters would climb 100 steps that zigzagged to the top. They'd open a trap door and lift themselves into a small metal cab with large windows.

There was nothing fancy about fire duty. The spotters, both men and women, spent 12 hours alone in that hot little box scanning the forest through big binoculars. Any sign of smoke meant a fire was up and probably running, which meant the rangers had to be alerted. The fire tower had no phone. The spotters pinpointed the origin of the smoke on a Fire-Finders pad, noted the coordinates, climbed down, found a neighbor with a telephone and called it in. Fires often outran the rangers, which meant the air would be filled with smoke for days before it burned itself out.

These days, neither the rangers nor the spotters came around much. Technology rendered the towers obsolete. But not for Maceo. He would arrive at the gunmetal gray tower by 4 a.m., which meant he had another hour to climb the steps. This was not easy for Maceo. His body was crooked and inflexible, his legs were short and his feet hurt if he stood around too long.

But what he lacked in physical ability, he made up for with determination. Step by step, level by level, Maceo would clang his way up the metal steps, never looking down, always focusing on the top. When he arrived, he'd hoist himself into the cab and climb into the chair.

Since Maceo was barely five feet tall, he couldn't see over the railing while seated. So he stood on the spotter's chair, which made him feel like a giant. He'd roll out the dirty windows and admire God's wide green garden. Only the caw of an occasional crow and the hum of the utility's power lines interrupted the silence. Once settled, Maceo awaited the first light of day and would stay until "dayclean," as they say in the Gullah tongue. Dayclean is an acknowledgement that follows the first rays of light. Soon after the sun clears the pink clouds in the eastern sky, the world has a clean start, another chance to get it right.

Maceo liked to swivel on the spotter's chair and scan in all directions. It was his only toy besides the gun. But he stopped twirling once the morning sun inched over the eastern rim, spraying sunshine across the pine tops as far as he could see.

Maceo climbed up there as often as he could. He enjoyed the break of day, before the scalding rays could damage his eyes and skin. He loved the certainty and consistency of each sunrise. First there were the pink reflections off the clouds, followed by a general bluing, followed by a bright stream of light flashing across the horizon.

Some folks never got up early enough to see the sun rise — people like his brothers and their nasty Gullah girl. They slept late every day of their lives. They would be surprised, Maceo thought, at the way the morning sun trickles like a creek just after dead low tide and then floods the landscape. When he was lost in the beauty of a sunrise, Maceo believed there might be a God, although he was probably white and could not be trusted.

Maceo loved the view from atop the tower, where nobody bothered him, called him names or tried to steal his stuff. This was heaven even though the sun itself was hell. As soon as the burst ended, Maceo would clamber down the steel structure before the angle of the sun cut into his flesh. In the shade of willow trees, he made his way home and hid in the *Sister's* shadows.

On good days, after Eleanor's visits and the tarp was on tight, Maceo fished with a cane pole. Sometimes he'd catch a flounder, which he fried with butter in an iron pan. Other times, he settled for crabs, which he caught with a chicken neck tied at the bottom of a drop net. But social life on the creek was limited.

Some afternoons, Maceo stumbled down the dirt road a half-mile to Frazier's Store, a cinderblock building snuggled under the outstretched arms of an ancient oak where locals passed the time. Next to the store was a weathered billboard featuring an old white man and his towheaded grandson holding up a huge striped bass.

"Welcome to Santee Cooper Country — Where the Big Ones Don't Get Away!"

the sign said. The billboard leaned and the paper peeled so that part of the grand-father's head was missing. But the smiles on their faces were ubiquitous from high above the misery of those who lived in the utility's shadow; those who understood the difference between fishing for fun and fishing for food.

Under the big tree, sitting on upturned wooden Coke crates, black men of all ages drank and sang and played harmonicas, smoked, ate fried chicken, told lies and laughed. The place was littered with half-pint liquor bottles, beer cans and chicken bones. The older men rolled their own cigarettes, flipping them around between callused fingers, licking the paper with their bright pink tongues, lighting up with safety matches they'd pop to life on their broken teeth.

Just before sunset, a large man named Mudslide would usually walk twenty yards over to the creek and cast a six-foot-wide hand-made net, then haul in a double handful of wiggling white shrimp.

"Sea roaches," he said as he popped off the heads, squeezed the meat from the shells and de-veined the shrimp with a dirty thumbnail. He'd drop them in a buttery skillet balanced over a can of Sterno. Then he'd sprinkle on some Old Bay seasoning that he pinched from a Prince Albert can.

None of them had jobs. They were "hang-arounds." They'd hang around here, hang around there, hang around mostly under the old live oak in front of Frazier's Store. Shiftless as they were, even they hated to see Maceo headed their way.

"That's one sorry-ass pink nigger come yonder," one would always say.

CHAPTER 7

Despite many differences, Ashmead Dawes and Junior Jones had one thing in common. They were lawyers in love. But not necessarily with each other.

Junior enjoyed living down low on the weekends. Monday through Friday he'd play by the rules — go to work, wear a suit and tie, attend meetings, donate blood, visit shut-ins and do everything else an up-and-coming politician should do. But weekends belonged to him. He seldom went to church and always had a good excuse lined up in case anyone asked. He told the people at the white church he went to the black church, and vice versa. People wanted to believe his story. Like the New York Times said, segregation was dead in the New South.

Perhaps that was true when the Times reporter came snooping around. But Ashmead would not take Junior to the Carolina Yacht Club. He wouldn't take Junior to lunch at Jimmy Dengate's on Rutledge Avenue across from the baseball park either. Jimmy Dengate's was a key club. You had to have a key to get in the front door, and only whites had keys.

But Junior didn't worry much about racism. Few people in his generation marched in the streets, sat-in at lunch counters or cared where they were on the bus. As far as Junior was concerned, Ashmead Dawes was his brother in a new age of opportunity.

The Dawes family arrived in Charleston when it was the third largest city in America, an international seaport that sparked staggering wealth for certain people. The Daweses were not abundantly rich, however. They were generally inept, but each of them looked good. They came from England to the Colonies on a lark, married into respected families, inherited their spouses' land and lived on the fringe of failure from one generation to the next.

Their heritage was longevity, which is important in Charleston. Thus nobody questioned where Ashmead got his money. His great-great-great grandmother, Celeste, married a Middleton. They exchanged rings beside Middleton Plantation's butterfly lakes overlooking the Ashley River, peninsular Charleston's western boundary that snakes past bountiful Lowcountry forests and old rice fields to the Atlantic. But Miss Celeste didn't marry the right Middleton. Otherwise, Ashmead would be rich.

Ashmead, in fact, almost had to go to public high school his senior year because his parents couldn't afford tuition at Porter-Gaud, Charleston's private Episcopal academy. To avoid embarrassment, Ashmead's father sold the family's remaining 500 acres along the upper reaches of the Cooper River, not far from Schitt Creek. In five generations, the Daweses sold off 10,000 acres of inherited plantation land piecemeal to pay bills and avoid work. That last one got Ashmead into the College of Charleston, but unlike his father and grandfather, he had to pay for law school himself.

What Ashmead lacked in intellect he made up for in organizational skills. In college he ran a successful drug business from inside the Nag's Head bar, across the street from the college's vaunted Cistern at the heart of the campus. Black beauties, T-20s, green amps, grass, hash and Quaaludes paid his bills. When he finished the University of South Carolina Law School, he was earning more than this father, who he'd been supporting for a while.

Ashmead hung his shingle below his old man's sign on Broad Street soon after graduation. But Ashmead never practiced law. He sold drugs to politicians, journalists, bankers and judges and other lawyers across the state. Pot was his bread and butter; cocaine was white gold.

Ashmead kept secret the details. All Junior knew was his best friend always had killer dope. It was during a Charleston Symphony concert at Boone Hall Plantation on a pleasant Sunday afternoon when Junior met one of Ashmead's business partners. Junior and Ashmead were sitting cross-legged on blankets on the lawn in the shadow of Ashmead's Bentley and sipping champagne. A heavy-set man walked up and stood beside them. They turned and looked at him, although the setting sun shining directly into Junior's eyes made it hard to see his features.

Ashmead stood, brushed himself off and extended his right hand. Junior saw the man shake Asmead's before slipping something onto his friend's wrist.

"From the boys upstream," the man said, turned and walked away.

"Who was that?" Junior asked.

"Nobody."

"What'd he give you?"

"This," Ashmead said as he held out his wrist.

"A Rolex?" Junior asked.

CHAPTER 8

It was late summer 1989 and people were out in boats enjoying the vast man-made Santee Cooper lakes. The sound of outboard motors drowned out the distant rumble of coal cars that fed the towering Santee Cooper power plant, and a southerly breeze pushed the black smoke up river.

Stocked with striped bass, Lakes Marion and Moultrie, named for two South Carolina Revolutionary War heroes, were a fisherman's paradise — despite all the stumps protruding from the shallows, or maybe because of them.

The digging and dredging and hauling and hacking began during depths of the Depression in the 1930s and continued for years as two great dams were built to hold back the waters of the Congaree and Wateree rivers. Thirty-five plantations, God only knows how many small farms, several little towns, country stores, churches, graveyards and sharecroppers' shanties drowned in the process.

Plantation life, as depicted in "Gone With The Wind," had withered and died. What the boll weevil didn't destroy, a series of bad hurricanes finished off. What had been the placenta of the planter aristocracy had quickly deteriorated into gaunt mansions with crooked chimneys and pane-less windows.

The land was purchased cheap and in large chunks to create a national forest the size of Vermont and two giant lakes that covered one enormous engineering mistake after another. Two hundred thousand acres of prime timberland were leveled at the stump by men with whipsaws and hauled away by mules and the sons of slaves. When they completed 42 miles of earthen dikes and concrete dams, Lakes Moultrie and Marion were born. They held almost 900 trillion gallons of fresh water, a testament to man's belief that nature was his plaything.

But when the Japanese bombed Pearl Harbor, everything changed. As workers were siphoned off to war, huge swaths of old swamp were left littered with dead trees that stuck up out of the water like dinosaur carcasses in a tar pit. Those ghostly stumps provided the best striped-bass habitat in the world, and homegrown fishermen like Stoney Sanders loved it.

Sanders' grandfather was one of 9,000 men who helped clear the land, and his father ran a fish camp on the lower lake near the high ground community of Pinopolis. Stoney was the best water skier on Lake Moultrie, once going barefoot 20-odd miles from Cypress Gardens to Bonneau Beach. That was during the summer between his sophomore and junior years at The Citadel when he worked as a lifeguard and sold fishing licenses and night crawlers for bait at his father's store.

His old man would do just about anything to make a buck. He rented canoes and paddleboats, ran a campground, pumped gas, fixed outboard motors and hand-tied the prettiest fishing lures between Savannah and Wilmington. But business was seasonal, shutting down from Labor Day to Memorial Day. That's when Stoney's father ran his fix-it shop in nearby Elloree. He repaired sewing machines, typewriters and electric fans mostly.

Everybody liked Jerry Sanders, especially his son, who would do just about anything to please his father. Like the day Jerry drove Stoney down to The Citadel campus in Charleston to see the Friday parade. Stoney was 11 at the time, and the sights and sounds of the cadets passing in review and winking at the pretty girls made a profound impression on the boy. Jerry said that if a man were good enough to graduate from The Citadel, he would always have a job because the Corps took care of its own.

At that very moment, the regimental band played "Dixie" and members of the long gray line stiffened with pride.

"Daddy, I want to be a Citadel cadet when I grow up," Stoney said.

Seven years later he signed a ROTC contract with the United States Air Force, committing himself to four years at the military school and six years in the active-duty military. But upon graduation, his test scores weren't good enough to qualify him to fly fighter jets. So he shuttled cargo out of McGuire Air Force in New Jersey. Stoney spent the Vietnam War shuttling dry goods and POVs back and forth across the Atlantic for NATO troops. He never made the "travel team." He never saw the fight and never received any Vietnam War ribbons.

On his desk was a picture of himself on his wedding day wearing dress blues and silver wings affixed to his chest. He married Helen Hart, Miss Lone Star, a buxom blonde who earned a degree in education from the Baptist College near Summerville just days before the wedding. Helen taught third grade in public school when Stoney was stationed in New Jersey.

They seemed to be the perfect couple. After his active-duty stint, Stoney joined the Air Force Reserve and was hired into management training at the sprawling Santee Cooper utility. Helen taught at Moncks Corner Elementary School and molded the minds of nine-year-olds until she died of breast cancer at age 37.

Stoney swore he'd never remarry, but not because he was heartbroken. He had worked his way up in the company to become an executive in the Governmental Affairs Office, where Leona, his secretary, made grown men cry every time she crossed her legs. Stoney's trysts with Leona gave him a keen understanding of oral sex and a wicked cocaine habit. When Leona got high she liked to bite, and every member of the Santee Cooper board knew it.

Stoney was in his office thinking about Leona's legs when Rod Timsdale, chairman of the board, knocked on his door then stuck his head in and said, "Leona must be on break, Stoney. Got a minute?"

"Sure," Stoney replied, straightening some paperwork on his desk.

Timsdale entered along with a man wearing a white linen suit but no tie, brown loafers but no socks, a gold chain around his neck, matching pinky rings and a Rolex watch that hung like a shiny smoked ham from his left wrist.

"You remember John Rhett, don't you?" Timsdale asked.

CHAPTER 9

John Rhett was one of South Carolina's most notorious politicians, which is saying something. The former U.S. Congressman was defrocked a few years earlier after admitting to the FBI that he accepted $50,000 in bribes from some fake Arab sheiks in an undercover sting known as Abscam.

He resigned from Congress and served 13 months of a two-year prison sentence. Still, many South Carolinians admired Rhett because, as he explained to People magazine, he made love to his buxom wife, Tina, on the steps of the U.S. Capitol a few years before. That was the sex scandal of the late 1970s that spotlighted the Horry County con man who never saw a jug of whisky he didn't want to chug, a beautiful woman he didn't want to screw, a joint he didn't want to toke, a line he didn't want to snort or a bribe he didn't want to take.

"I couldn't help it," Rhett told the judge in the Abscam case. "I've got larceny in my veins."

Fresh out of prison, tanned, clear-eyed, reeking of British Sterling and looking for work, ex-Congressman Rhett shook hands with Stoney.

"Good to see you, Bubba. It's been a while. How you doing?" he said.

"Pretty good, John. How 'bout you?"

"Just trying to make a living, son," Rhett said as he sat down. "Being disbarred ain't good when you're in the lawyering business. Thank goodness Rod and the boys on the board have seen clear to send some work my way. I've opened a public relations firm in Myrtle Beach. You know, the usual stuff: Dragons slain, damsels rescued, mountains moved."

The three of them laughed. But Rod Timsdale did not sit down. He was anxious to leave.

"Uh, I thought you and John might need to talk about some of our more pressing issues of the day. I'll be in my office if you need me."

Rhett slipped a flip-top box from his shirt pocket, pulled out a Marlboro, lit up, exhaled and sank back into the big leather chair.

"When did you get out?" Stoney asked.

"Tuesday," Rhett replied, blowing a smoke ring.

"Tough?"

"The travel opportunities were limited, but I did work on my backhand."

Stoney stood, walked to the window and looked out at the utility's tall smokestacks belching black plumes into the summer sky.

"So what now, other than your new PR business?"

"Don't really know yet," Rhett said, pulling off his loafer and scratching his left foot. "I'm starting over with nothing but my charm and good looks."

"Where's Tina?"

"Hollywood. She only calls when she wants more money, more dope or both."

"Tina's a junky?"

"Not really, but her friends are."

"And you help her out?"

"Occasionally," Rhett said, looking Stoney in the eyes for the first time since he walked into the room. "I help people that I like when they're looking."

"Well," Stoney said, glancing toward the door. "I know somebody who's looking."

"Really?" Rhett feigned.

"Yeah, really."

With that, the two men headed out to the parking lot and talked loudly about some great new fishing tackle out in the trunk of Rhett's car. The sun was hot and both men wore sunglasses as they black-slapped and laughed their way out of the administration building. When they got to Rhett's blue Cadillac, he popped the trunk, leaned over and peeled back an Army blanket under which were five Ziploc sandwich bags full of pure white cocaine.

Rhett snatched two, palmed them in his right hand and dropped them into Stoney's left coat pocket.

"How much I owe you?" Stoney whispered.

Rhett shut the trunk, slapped Stoney on the back again and said in a low voice, "Not a thing, pal, because it didn't happen. They put people in jail for that shit."

43

CHAPTER 10

Junior Jones pulled into the driveway at his parents' new house in the Forest Acres section of Columbia. It was a split-level with a sunken den where his father sat watching football and drinking a Heineken. A white plumber lived next door. A carcass of a '71 Camaro, a fiberglass bass boat and a painted concrete lawn jockey were in the neighbor's front yard.

Senior was no longer on County Council. He never lost an election, but he did lose the turf war when the Republicans gerrymandered his district out of existence. He talked about running for the state House of Representatives but never got around to it.

Junior dropped by every few months to check on his folks. His mother still worked at the S&S Cafeteria at Richland Mall where she'd been slicing roast beef for 21 years. When Junior came through the kitchen door, his mother kissed him on the cheek then pointed to the den where his father was watching the Gamecocks play Georgia.

"We'll never get another Democrat elected and we'll never see S.C. State play football on television," he said, shaking his fist at the TV as Junior entered the room. "The news from the front is not good, son."

His father no longer addressed him as "Guv'nor." Senior soured on politics, saying you couldn't get anything done on County Council anymore. Too much partisan infighting and not enough statesmanship, he said. He also noticed that Senior was wearing Hushpuppies — a sure sign of surrender.

"At my last meeting, Councilman Henry Smith, a disabled veteran, took off his artificial leg and banged it on the desk in utter frustration," Senior said. "I wanted to cut off my leg and join him."

All that was left of Senior's political career was a hundred plastic campaign signs stacked up in the tool shed, photographs of him shaking hands with the mayor and a highway commissioner and a plaque thanking him for 20 years service to the people of Richland County.

Junior was about to tell his father about his promotion when he heard the kitchen door open and his mother say, "Oh, Della, do come in. Junior's in the den with Grover. He just drove in from Charleston."

Della Sparks had a thing for Junior since high school. A teller at First National Bank now, she was one of those girls men fall in love with when they walk into her branch, stand in line and hope they will get her when it's their turn to go to the window.

She was a classic African goddess: slightly cross-eyed, shiny black curls framing her full face, pouty lips glistening under candy-apple liner. The most amazing thing about Della, however, was her ass, which could not be seen from the customer side of the teller's window. It was big and round and inviting like a beanbag chair.

"Hey, Della," Junior said, leaning in for a hug, trying to avoid her broad breasts, which served as ballast for her butt. "You still working at the bank?"

With that, Della took his face in her hands and kissed him on the lips, slipping her tongue in and out a few times without Junior's parents noticing.

"I'm fine as communion wine," she said, rubbing her tits against Junior as she turned back toward the kitchen. "Ain't that right, Mrs. Jones? Life sure is good here in the Capital City."

Junior's mother wiped her hands with a dishcloth. "Life is always good when you got the spirit of the Lord in your heart."

Della, whose mother named her after the singer Della Street, broke out into a stanza of "In The Garden."

"I come to the garden alone, while the dew is still on the roses," she sang, reaching out for Junior's hand just as he pretended to lean the other way for a mint in the candy dish. "And the voice I hear, falling on my ear, the Son of God discloses..."

That's when Junior's mother harmonized, "And he walks with me and he talks with me and he tells me I am his own/ And the joy we share as we tarry there, none other has ever known."

They held the last note a few seconds for effect, which reminded Junior of why he no longer attended services at Mount Zion AME Church on Dunbar Street where he was Sunday schooled and baptized in the blood of the cross. He used to envy his white friends who only had to attend church on Easter morning and Christmas Eve and didn't have to stay long. The folks at Mount Zion were just getting warmed up after an hour, or two, or three.

Junior cashed in his communion chips when he went off to college but still put up a good front for his mother, who believed in the power of prayer and a forgiving God. Rather than making a joke about how Jesus could have beaten the rap if he'd had a better lawyer, Junior decided to change the subject.

"I guess this is as good a time as 'any," he said as his father joined the group at halftime. "I have an announcement to make."

"Oh, good," his mother said. "You gonna marry Della?"

Junior laughed uncomfortably the way he always laughed when his parents brought up marriage.

"No, Mom, it's about my job. I've been promoted."

"Great news, Son," Senior said, extending his hand. "What's your new title?"

Junior stepped back, pulled a business card from his shirt pocket and handed it to his father.

The card read:

Grover Cleveland Jones Jr.

Assistant Vice President, Governmental Affairs

Santee Cooper Authority

Junior's father nodded, looked up at his son and smiled. "Congratulations, Guv'nor!"

CHAPTER 11

S oul singer James Brown's purple jump suit was unzipped below his navel and his belly bulged out when he sat down for the interview.

"Don't shoot this," he said, holding his hand up in front of the camera lens. "The Godfather ain't ready yet."

Standing up, he jumped a little off the ground each time he tried to pull the zipper up over his stomach.

Berkeley Aiken started to laugh but managed to maintain her professionalism. As cohost of "Good Morning, Midlands!" for three years, she was the best-known minority face in local journalism. That's because she was the only minority face on local television. And that depended on the definition of minority, and journalism.

The 10 a.m. time slot was filled with promotional interviews for Junior League charity events, Greek Fest, teacher of the year, local cookbook authors and chitchat between Berkeley and her white cohost, Darren Green.

Doubling as a meteorologist, Green was like Playdough. He didn't do anything well on TV but always looked good doing it. Together, they were joined at the hip in the minds of viewers in the Midlands. Some asked when they were going to get married, which was interesting considering he was white — as if racism didn't exist on television. What viewers didn't know was Darren Green was gay, and Berkeley wasn't about to break that story.

Berkeley entered broadcasting through the back door as a reluctant beauty queen, having finished first runner-up for Miss South Carolina in 1982. The State Sentinel did a story on her because she was the first dark-skinned woman to walk the runway in the annual Jaycees-sponsored contest to determine who was the fairest of them all. That landed her an interview at WIS-TV in Columbia. She clinched the job by knowing the answer to the trivia question offered up as a pop quiz for the job seekers. The station's call letters, WIS, she explained, stood for Wonderful Iodine State, a brand the Chamber of Commerce dreamed up during the early 1900s to note an abundance of iodine in the soil.

Even though most of her peers couldn't decide if she was black or white, her dusky almond complexion appealed to the judges. It was the initial step toward landing her dream job as an international television correspondent like Christiane Amanpour on CNN.

A raven-haired journalist, Amanpour was always at the center of the storm, reporting from Lebanon or the West Bank or Paris or wherever big news broke. She was born in Iran and grew up in the palm of the Shah. Her father was a favorite within the puppet regime. When the American-backed government fell to Islamic radicalism, the Amanpour family fled to London. Christiane studied journalism at the University of Rhode Island.

That was encouraging to Berkeley, who attended Columbia College, a small, all-girls school in South Carolina called, affectionately, C-Square. The girl with coffee-colored skin and the unlikely name of Berkeley Aiken often stood in front of her mirror at home, holding her hairbrush like a microphone, practicing sign-offs saying, "This is Berkeley Aiken, reporting from Nairobi," or wherever.

But at WIS-TV, she was still on the way up, interviewing circus clowns and Rotary Club presidents. She came to work every day believing a network executive might be in town for a family funeral, see her work and offer her a job in New York City.

It was an adjunct writing professor who had given her the best advice she ever received in journalism. He said the secret to success was hitting the trifecta — being in the right place, at the right time, with the right stuff. That her skin was caramel and her voice as sweet as coconut cake didn't hurt her chances. Somebody had to be the first minority anchorwoman on national TV and it might as well be her.

"Hair and teeth," James Brown answered without hesitation when she asked about his secret to success. "If a man's got hair and teeth, he's got it all. Course, it helps to have a little funk, too, baby."

Berkeley took his flirtation in stride. During close-ups, he kept touching himself, adjusting his package — so to speak — letting his eyes drift toward her cleavage. A master communicator, The Godfather always knew which camera was live.

"Well, those lucky enough to have tickets to your show Friday night here at the Township Auditorium are certainly in for a treat," Berkeley said. "Now, we're going to take a quick break before Darren brings us up to date on that tropical storm brewing off the coast."

Brown unhooked the microphone from his lapel, handed it to an assistant and leaned in for the kill.

"Mercy, girl, you down right delicious, ain't you? What the hell is you, anyway? Injun, Cuban, Brass Ankle?"

As he moved toward Berkeley, she wished she had worn something more conservative. When he came closer, the 5-foot-5 entertainer's face was eye-level with her tits.

"I'm from Charleston. My father is Jewish, my mother Ethiopian," she said.

Indeed, Berkeley Aiken was many things but white wasn't one of them, and in South Carolina there were only two colors.

"Well, it's nice to meet you, Cleopatra," Brown said, proving he didn't know the difference between Ethiopia and Egypt. "Would you like to see why they call me the hardest working man in show business, baby?"

"I assume it's because of your work ethic," Berkeley said, removing her earpiece and stepping backward.

"It's because of my work ethnic, baby," he said, emphasizing the word "ethnic" while grabbing his crotch. "Tell you what. I'll leave four tickets for you. Bring some of your girlfriends backstage after the show Friday night. We'll party."

CHAPTER 12

B ack on Schitt Creek, Maceo felt a cool breeze kick up from the ocean and wondered if a storm was brewing. When he saw flocks of seabirds headed inland, he knew. Storms off the Atlantic don't give much notice; they suddenly appear at the doorstep, raging. Advance notice comes from nature: A wind shift, a pressure drop, a sense of dread even on a sunny day.

Maceo remembered a previous storm that tore through on a weekend, trashing house trailers, uprooting trees and pitching the *Sister* onto the creek bank. It took a dozen men to wedge the boat back into the water scratched but unharmed. Not much a storm can do to a boat already stripped of its dignity.

Maceo didn't trust hurricanes. They came from different angles and in various sizes, like football players. Some skirted the South Carolina coast en route to Cape Fear, above Calabash. They whipped along the coastline like a halfback on an end sweep looking for a spot to cut up field. Others bore straight in, head down, elbows tucked, like a fullback. The blunt force of landfall slows down the storm, buckles its knees, saps its energy until it collapses somewhere inland, gasping and swinging as it goes down.

Maceo could sense the mood along Schitt Creek was shifting. The old men under the big tree at Frazier's Store had slipped off to higher ground. The grandfather's face in the billboard flapped wildly in the wind. The store was closed, its windows crisscrossed with masking tape. The top branches of palmetto trees were tossing back and forth like the brush of an artist gone mad. The winds rocked the shrimp boat with powerful gusts one minute, dropped to nothing the next. But Maceo's true measure of trouble was the storm brewing inside his head.

As the barometer fell, the pressure tightened the platelets of his skull like wood screws boring into Maceo's brain. Eleanor was due any time now with the medicine.

He wondered if she would make it before the storm. Moaning, Maceo held his head between his pudgy fingers, knowing his brothers were not around to help and he'd have to ride out the storm alone.

Maceo knew it was time to move upriver. By late morning he had been up to the camp, collected several cases of stolen Vienna Sausages, sardines and saltine crackers and loaded them onto the *Sister*. A few bigger boats were already heading inland for safety. He knew the river would soon be filled with shrimp boats and private yachts, lashed to docks, tucked away in shallow creeks like animals digging in when a forest fire roars past.

Down the road he could hear the women of Christ the Great Redeemer Baptist Church singing as they boarded up windows and moved communion cups higher on the shelves.

"Sometimes I'm up, sometimes I'm down,
Sometimes I'm almost to the ground.
You know the storm is passing over,
Hallelu."

As Maceo listened, he moved about the shrimp boat stacking pots and pans and other possible projectiles in the hold of the bow. In the distance he could see clouds gathering darkly, the early outer bands spinning from the eye of a storm, warning Negroes in the field that it was coming.

"Some say Peter, some say Paul.
Ain't but one God for we all.
You know the storm is passing over,
Hallelu."

Slaves in the rice fields knew the signs all too well but had no place to hide. The whites could leave, but the field hands were at the mercy of storms. Many drowned, their bodies found floating in the rice rows, broiling in the hot days that always followed.

One fall a hurricane killed 20 slaves, so the survivors were ordered to build brick shelters for themselves. They constructed igloo-like structures in the rice fields of the Santee Delta. They were designed to deflect the high winds and save the souls who huddled within. So the odd-looking shelters stood, one by one, a mile or so apart. They'd withstand the winds, but those who huddled inside never knew if their shelter would be their tomb as the storm surge flooded ashore.

"The tallest tree in Paradise,
Christians call the Tree of Life,
You know the storm is passing over,
Hallelu."

Maceo hauled three cans of gasoline and a half-gallon of Dickel from his brothers' sheds, stacked them neatly in the back of the VW bus and fired up the engine. The fan belt squeaked as it turned the drive shaft that spun the propeller that sent the fiddler crabs scurrying into their holes in the mud. Maceo poled the old boat off the oyster bank and she bobbed in the water like an ocean liner just christened.

As Maceo pushed forward the throttle, the nasty Gullah girl ran down the bank, splashed into the water knee deep and cried out, "Takes me wi' cha, takes me wi' cha! I is scaid Maceo!"

He turned his head and looked down at her as he slowly pulled back on the throttle. She smiled and waved her skinny arms over her head as she waded out deeper toward him, happy to have gotten his attention.

A mile away, Eleanor's station wagon rumbled down the dirt road, kicking up dust through the willow trees. As she pulled up to the fish camp, she saw that Maceo and his boat were gone. The camp was quiet, except for a steady wind blowing up from the south. Not even the Gullah girl was around.

A gunshot rang out. Just one. Then silence.

Eleanor ran to the water's edge as the shrimp boat turned the bend and cut through the swirl that marked the deep channel. Maceo was at the helm but never looked back as the *Sister* chugged upstream.

"Nineteen," Maceo whispered as he shoved his smoking pistol into the glove compartment and slammed shut the door.

CHAPTER 13

J unior Jones kept his eyes on the road while trying to tune the radio to his favorite FM station in Charleston. He'd been in meetings all day in Columbia on another one of Stoney's little missions.

Meanwhile, a Santee Cooper maintenance crew atop the Pinopolis Dam spotted a steady swirl of water they assumed was escaping through a crack deep below the waterline. Motion sensors strategically located along the barrier had activated, and the crew was dispatched to pinpoint a possible leak. It had happened before. The structure was more than 50 years old and hurriedly completed as World War II broke out. Rumor was contractors pencil-whipped the last three sections of the dam to make a deadline.

Years later, engineers installed the sensors knowing there could be trouble someday. Inspectors decided wood pilings installed at the base of the dam were rotting out. But replacing them posed one headache after another. It was expensive, and preliminary work required excavating layers upon layers of bureaucracy that were in the way.

They were ignoring Armageddon.

A breach in the dam would send a 50-foot–tall wall of water downstream all the way to Charleston, destroying bridges, docks, homes and everything in its path. Geologists estimated the low-lying port city would be inundated with as much as nine feet of water after the initial surge reached the ocean, and would take at least a week before it ran off.

Junior had been reading briefs he delivered that morning to a group of sleepy-eyed rate regulators. The meeting confirmed what he already knew about the state-controlled energy business: Rates never go down.

The relationship between utilities and state officials reminded Junior of how amateur plays were staged in middle school. Everybody learned their lines, delivered them with phony compassion and waited for the applause of interested parties who already knew the outcome.

To give the appearance of oversight, the politicians occasionally added to the drama by railing against the rate increases to get headlines. But reality was quite the contrary. State-owned Santee Cooper and the state-owned Ports Authority were members of the same country club. So too were state universities, colleges and tech schools. All were quasi-governmental entities, created by the state, overseen by state-appointed boards answerable only to a handful of powerful legislators.

Junior learned the secret handshake from two of his office mates. One held his thumb and forefinger together to make a hole while the other stroked it with his middle finger. They had a special quasi-governmental cheer:

Quasimodo, he's our man;
Because zero emissions are a total scam!
Quasimodo, what a sham;
Whether it's a college or a hydro dam!
Quasimodo, you're the best;
Because regulators are such a pest!

During the last Santee Cooper Executive Halloween Party, one of the skits featured drunken lawyers wearing Quasimodo t-shirts mocking the famous hunchback of Notre Dame in Paris. They mocked Junior, too, as the only minority member of the club. "Hey look," one of his colleagues pointed down from the stage at him and said. "Junior came dressed like a nigger!"

Junior took it all in stride. Twice already, he'd been offered better positions with South Carolina Electric and Gas Co. as well as the S.C. the Regulatory Commission in Columbia. Everybody had minority quotas.

So, while thinking about kilowatt differentials, peak summer-usage charts and lucrative job offers, Junior heard talk on the radio of the storm brewing off the coast. As he pushed the company's Chrysler K-car down Interstate-26 toward Moncks Corner, the static on the radio cleared when he hit 96 WAVE. Known for its rock concerts and edgy on-air talent, the WAVE represented a sea change in local broadcasting in the South Carolina Lowcountry. Its irreverent afternoon drive-time team of Atom Taler and the Critic racked up big numbers and made them local celebrities.

"I see on the wire that radar has identified a tropical storm brewing off the coast," Taler said, playing the straight man.

"Yeah," his understated sidekick said. "But they've also picked up a cluster of ICBMs inbound from Havana, so, you know, man, like, don't sweat the thunderstorms."

Junior chuckled as he pulled into a rest area below Orangeburg. He needed to relieve himself ever since his meeting broke up, but the men's room in the Brown Building was out of order. Slowing down at the exit, Junior noticed a line of power-company trucks in the rest area parking lot that looked like a small army in convoy.

Most notably, they were neither his power trucks nor those belonging to SCE&G or Berkeley Electric Cooperative, his utility neighbors. Pulling up next to the trucks, he rolled down his window and read the name on the door — West Virginia Power and Light.

"What's the matter, son, you never seen a real power truck before?" a voice from above asked.

Junior looked up. On the back of the truck was a beer-bellied white man with bulging forearms who was tightening a chain with a ratchet.

Loosening his tie, Junior leaned out over the Santee Cooper logo on his car door and said, "What are you guys doing so far from home?"

The man jumped down off the truck and landed in front of Junior.

"Storm's coming, Einstein. We're here to stage up, go in and fix everything after that hurricane rips your power grid all to shit."

Junior forgot how bad he had to urinate. He walked toward the pay phone outside the men's restroom, picked up the handle and dialed.

"Collect call from Junior Jones," he told the operator. "Thank you, ma'am."

He waited impatiently as the phone rang four times before Leona picked up. "Governmental Affairs, Stoney Sanders' office. May I help you?"

Junior started to blurt something out, but the operator interrupted him by asking if Leona would accept the charges, which she did.

"Leona, this is Junior. What the hell's going on with this storm?"

"Hey, Junior, where are you?"

"Driving back from Columbia. Had meetings all day up there. I'm in the rest area below Orangeburg. West Virginia power trucks are lined up here like it's a Christmas parade or something. What's happening?"

"Oh, you know, Junior, another cover-your-ass drill or something. We do this every time it clouds up. Mr. Timsdale activated the Disaster Preparedness people and everybody's running around looking for reports they never thought they'd have to find."

"Where's Stoney?" Junior asked.

"Oh, he's got Reserve duty — gone on some VIP flight to somewhere or other. He left at noon."

"So, is it serious? What should I do?"

Leona had several answers for that question, some of which included unbuttoning Junior's shirt with her tongue and ripping it off his body with her teeth. But she had yet to cross the color line.

"Oh, hell, Junior, do what I do."

"What's that?"

"Grab a cold case of Coors, a bottle of Everclear, a carton of cigarettes, rolling papers, your stash and meet us at the fishing pier."

"At Folly Beach?" Junior asked.

"Yeah!" she said. "We're having a hurricane party."

CHAPTER 14

Berkeley Aiken did "Good Morning, Midlands!" live at 10 every weekday morning. On weekends, she squeezed in personal appearances in support of her career: Judging picnic tables at the Colonial Cup steeple chase in Camden, handing out Girl Scout merit badges at Dentsville Elementary School, competing in the Gilbert Peach Festival pie-eating contest. It wasn't easy being a television celebrity in South Carolina, but she enjoyed most of it, except having to wrestle with chauvinists like James Brown backstage at Township Auditorium.

But this week would be different. The station manager signed her up for a publicity flight with the Air Force Reserve to Ascension Island in the South Atlantic. It would be a two-day orientation trip with some local politicians and businessmen. She'd look great in a tight-fitting Air Force flight suit standing on the runway and telling the audience about the adventure.

Finally, a real assignment, Berkeley thought. She would meet the crew early the next morning at McEntyre Air National Guard Base near Eastover, between Columbia and Sumter, while weekend anchor Courtney Wilson would fill in for her on the morning show. But first she had to tape a promotion shot for the town of Gadsden's upcoming "Great Congaree Cooter Race." The turtles were boxed up and hauled into the studio where she planned to ad lib a few minutes with the judges. She told them she would not touch a turtle, although one almost snipped off her finger when she wasn't looking. She wasn't paying close attention. Her mind was on her big assignment. She had her scarves already picked out and planned to hit the sack early because she was due on the flight line the next morning at 0730.

"So, what's the deal with this storm?" she asked Darren the weatherman on her way out of the studio. "Is it going to rain or what?"

Darren received his meteorological certification through a correspondence course offered by Mississippi State University. He understood the basic principles: high pressure good/low pressure bad. But that's about it.

"That system's getting stronger, but it's way out there," he said. "It dropped a few millibars last night and picked up speed, headed north/northwest. Doesn't have a name yet but could be a Cat One by tomorrow night. Might hit the coast. Might not. Too early to tell."

Berkeley shrugged and looked at the newsroom assignments posted on the bulletin board. Bob Gillespie, a veteran videographer, was going with her.

CHAPTER 15

George Burr, now 36, through no fault of his own, had been promoted to director of safety at the State Mental Hospital and ran his operation differently than his predecessor, Tank Barker. Since the Reagan administration emptied the nation's mental hospitals, the crazies who were living on the inside were now living on the outside — mostly on the streets.

The sprawling campus he patrolled was a ghost town compared to what it was like when he started working at Bull Street. But that was fine with Capt. Burr. His pay was the same whether he was wrestling a whacko or sipping coffee at his desk. His most pressing problem was paperwork. The state wanted to close the books on all mental patients that came through the system, and there were some glaring omissions — escapees.

During Burr's 18 years on the force, a few patients did make it over the wall, but most were captured or killed within a few days. Only 12 got away, and each was listed on a sheet Capt. Burr had on his desk. He called them "the Dirty Dozen," but not because they were all that smart or that dangerous. They were never found because nobody bothered to look for them.

But the state demanded an accounting of them now. Otherwise, his new operating budget would not be approved. And his new budget included money for the purchase of his new police cruiser. So, holding the list in his teeth, he grabbed his cup of coffee in one hand and a lemon-cream-filled doughnut in the other and kicked open the door to the squad room where Lt. Ralph Cumbee sat sound asleep at his desk.

"Damn it, Ralph, wake your ass up!" Burr yelled.

Cumbee, a 20-year veteran of the force, jerked up his head and grabbed a newspaper like he'd been reading it, and said:

"Present!" before realizing who it was, then added, "Oh, shit, George, I thought you were somebody."

"I am somebody, dammit. I'm the captain, Deputy Dog, the big cheese in this stinking smokehouse. I know it's quiet around here, Ralph, but shit, try to stay awake, OK?"

"Sorry, George. Had a rough night."

"Every night's a rough night for you, Ralph. You need to cut back on the Jack. I'd lock your ass up in the drunk ward if we still had one — let you dry out and find Jesus, or did he get discharged too?"

They laughed at their own predicament.

"I got a job for you, Ralph. It'll get you out of this hellhole for a while. You can spend a couple of days in the Upstate. Go visit your good-for-nothing relatives near Honea Path while finding out what happened to these free birds," Burr said as he handed the list to his lieutenant.

"Do I have to actually find 'em?"

"Hell, no. Just ask around. Hopefully they're dead and you can just check 'em off."

"OK," Ralph said. "When?"

"Well, there are 12 names on this list. I'll split 'em with you. You take the Upstate and I'll take the Lowcountry. I'm headed towards Salters to visit my sister, then work my way down river."

Ralph adjusted his reading glasses and glanced at the paperwork. He remembered some of the names on his list. One was Maceo Mazyck, Schitt Creek Road, Wampee, S.C. Escaped 1979. Whereabouts unknown.

"I remember this one," Ralph said, rubbing his chin. "He's that nasty pink nigger, right? Glad he's yours and not mine."

60

CHAPTER 16

A bright full moon rose, partially blocked by low clouds scudding across the horizon. September in South Carolina is a continuation of summer, with spectacular sunsets and star-splashed nights.

Ashmead and Junior were in good spirits as they walked hand-in-hand, high as kites along the Battery in Charleston, gazing out over the harbor. When they spotted a police car rolling toward them on Murray Boulevard, they loosed their fingertip grip and half-stepped apart. Earlier, at Ashmead's house on Tradd Street, they sipped martinis and snorted cocaine before stepping outside into the storm-stirred air. They had been together on some wild escapades before in the Holy City but had never been so open about their fondness for each other.

"How come you never try to do me?" Junior asked, stepping in front of Ashmead to get his attention. "You do everything to everybody. And I mean everything to everybody. But you don't do me. Why is that?"

Ashmead, bleary-eyed and tired, looked at his friend and said, "Because you're black and we live in Charleston. Because they'd hang us from a live oak in White Point Garden if they knew I was doing a slave. Because, because, because, because. How many reasons do you need?"

Junior stopped suddenly, climbed halfway up the railing overlooking the harbor and spread out his arms as if he wanted to fly home to Africa. A wave slammed against the bulwark and soaked him.

"And because there's nothing worse than wet, kinky hair in bed," Ashmead said, doubling over with laughter. "Now get down from there."

They stumbled across Murray Boulevard singing a stanza of "When the Bullet Hit the Bone" over and over until they climbed the stairs onto the bandstand in the middle of the park where the old oaks formed an umbrella and darkness engulfed them. They joked about their jobs and what fools they were making of society. If only people knew how much they hated the world they lived in. How often they wanted to strip naked and run down Meeting Street, gathering others in their wake, flooding the mayor's office on Broad Street with perverts and dancing jaybird naked on his desktop. They giggled as they described the imaginary romp, and leaned against the posts of the stage.

"We could dance here," Junior said.

"Naked?"

"Why not?"

"Because, because, because, because," Ashmead said as he watched Junior unbutton his shirt.

CHAPTER 17

L t. Col. Stoney Sanders sat at a table in the officer's club dining room with a few fellow Reserve pilots and sipped a Diet Coke. He did not drink liquor the night before a mission. He had 18 years in the system and needed only two more to get a good retirement check and full-bird status. Once a month he got to put on his flight suit and pilot a huge C-141 Starlifter, the Air Force's workhorse cargo plane. It was a rush like no other. Almost.

For several years he'd been in the second seat, training young captains on air-drop simulations over North Field in Orangeburg County. But his new assignment came with a mission. Now he was in the regular rotation to command monthly flights to Ascension Island, a volcanic speck in the Atlantic halfway between South America and Africa.

For the 315th Military Airlift Wing, an all-Reserve outfit, it was a twice-monthly mail run from Charleston to Antigua in the Caribbean, and then out over the Atlantic to the tiny equatorial island that served as an antenna farm for NASA, the CIA and God only knows who else. Cargo usually consisted of food, beer, liquor, mail and golf balls for the one-hole golf course played by the 35 spooks assigned to the volcanic isle.

This trip, however, would include 20 civilians — mayors, businessmen and media types. The Public Affairs Office called such runs "familiarization flights," designed to generate support back home among employers of Guard and Reserve troops. But Stoney did not care what people thought any more. Since Helen's death, he'd fallen in with an interesting crowd, mostly Delta airline jockeys who flew with him on the weekends. Sometimes they went to McGuire in New Jersey or Dover in Delaware, laying over in Atlantic City, where Stoney fell in love with roulette.

He gambled only a little at first, just enough to satisfy the jag of his cocaine rush.

But one thing led to another, which led to more cocaine, which led to huge debts, all of which brought him to this particular trip. The plan was simple: Stoney would pick up a duffel bag of cocaine while refueling in Antigua, smuggle it home and sell it. He'd save $10,000 of the proceeds to pay back his new best friend, John Rhett.

Stoney looked at his watch, a standard-issue Timex with a Velcro strap that he planned to replace soon with a new Rolex. He pushed back from the table at the club and said, "Show time is oh-dark-thirty, boys. Gotta get some shuteye."

CHAPTER 18

T he big plane barely gained altitude from Charleston Air Force Base when Stoney dropped the flaps and put it on final approach for the 29er runway at McEntyre. The small Air National Guard base outside Columbia was only a 20-minute hop from Charleston. After landing and loading the passengers, Stoney and his crew would lift off and head south for Antigua, a five-hour flight for a short layover before the long haul to Ascension.

As Stoney forced the big cargo plane downward, he lined up with the runway and pushed hard on the yoke, leaving 10,000 feet. Five generations of pilots who flew these big birds hated to land them. The cockpit joke was that General Knowledge said you had to fly them into the ground to get them down.

But pound for pound, this was Stoney's airplane of choice. He loved the way it looked on the runway, its long wings hanging like muscular arms, its engines staggered underneath, its camouflaged paint suggesting the reality of war.

Nothing in the military, however, escapes ridicule. When the brass decided to switch the C-141s from the original white-top, gray-bottom scheme to the green-and-gray camo colors, the crews renamed their craft "Starlizards" instead of Star-lifters.

Stoney, almost 40 years old, was now one of the old guys in the unit.

But everybody in blue knew about McEntyre, a good-old-boys club for statehouse politicians who ran the South Carolina Air National Guard.

The commanding general, in fact, was the lieutenant governor, and members of his command staff were cronies who liked having F-16s fueled and waiting whenever they wanted to go flying on weekends. Mostly they dumped dummy bombs on dummy targets at Poinsette Firing Range, a designated military drop zone on the edge of Manchester State Forest east of Columbia. But they were fighter jocks and wanted everybody to know it.

The 169th Tactical Fighter Group was known by its "Swamp Fox" call sign, and Stoney instantly recognized the nose art when two fighters dropped in on his wings as he was making his final approach.

"Pretty boys," Stoney muttered into his headset. "I hate fighter jocks, don't you, Buck?"

Maj. John Buckston, his co-pilot, was a UPS pilot out of Charlotte who spent a tour flying Air Force One when he was on active duty.

"Yeah, they can't fly real airplanes, so they gave them toys," Buck said. "Wan'na rock their world?"

Stoney goosed the Starlifter and waggled its wings. The plane was so massive that the burst of prop wash pummeled their cocky escorts enough to give them a scare right where all the dignitaries who had gathered on the ground to watch the landing could see it.

Col. Jack Hamby, commander of the 169th and pilot of the F-16 Fighting Falcon on Stoney's right wing, felt the turbulence and adjusted quickly as his bird bumped hard and settled down quickly.

"Damn trash haulers," he said to his wingman, Capt. Jim Jakes. "Criss-cross their nose and hit 'em with the afterburners."

With that, the pilots of the two fighter planes zoomed ahead of the descending cargo plane, flew a crossing pattern, pulled back on their sticks and hit the power. Flames flew out their tails like dragon's breath as they climbed into the clouds.

Standing in a roped-off area beside the runway, Berkeley Aiken turned to the man in uniform next to her and asked, "Wow! Was that for us?"

The public affairs tech sergeant sighed and said, "Little boys and their expensive toys, Ma'am."

CHAPTER 19

M aceo poured brown liquor into a paper cup as he steered the old boat through one after another of the serpentine turns of the upper Cooper River. Plowing upstream against the current was slow going, but Maceo was in no hurry. He sat in the driver's seat and watched the people along the riverbank pack up lawn chairs and coolers and crab traps and head inland. Most of them were wearing Clemson hats and shirts.

College football permeates the culture of South Carolina, even though most of the folks in these swamps never went to college. Maceo did not understand college football, but he did know one thing: He hated Clemson. Clemson fans — always dressed in orange and purple attire — lived all along the Santee, Wando and Cooper rivers, and they had tormented him his entire life. Bleached-blond boys often brought their buddies in their daddies' 20-foot Grady Whites to gawk at the Pink Nigger who lived up Schitt Creek.

When they roared past the *Sister Santee*, the drivers of the boats would often electronically raise one of the two outboard engines just out of the water, rev the motor and spray water. It was their way of shooting Maceo the bird.

In recent years Maceo had even become part of a scavenger hunt in a fraternity's initiation rites. Kappa Sigma wannabes from Clemson had to piss off Parris

Mountain in Greenville, steal something from an SCE&G city bus in Columbia, ride the rollercoaster at Myrtle Beach, take a picture of the albino of Schitt Creek and spray paint their name on the graffiti-covered skiff beached alongside Folly Road in Charleston — all in one day.

That's why Maceo hated Clemson. Just the sight of a tiger paw made him itchy. But not that day. Maceo was in charge. He wore his hat pulled down low on his head like a riverboat man, like the one in the stories the library lady read about Tom Sawyer and Huck Finn. Maceo couldn't read, but he listened well.

When he was younger, the woman from the Berkeley County Library drove the bookmobile down to the fish camp on Sunday afternoons and read to the children. She always stopped in a shady spot and spread out a blanket, far away from the drunken lay-abouts outside Frazier's Store. Children gathered around and sat cross-legged and listened to her read from the books she toted in a crocus sack.

Maceo was too old and too ugly to join the kids, so he'd sneak through the shrubs and find a spot where he could hear what she said. His favorite character was Jim, the muscular runaway slave who floated down the river with Huck Finn. He liked that Jim was gentle and kind, and that Huck was surprised to learn about it. Huck never considered colored people as being real human beings until he met Jim.

Maceo was thinking about this when the shallow keel of the *Sister* dragged the sandy bottom. Jerking the wheel to the port, Maceo leaned left and steered the boat off a bar. While the Cooper River was not as big or famous as the mighty Mississippi, it was a force to be reckoned with. One of South Carolina's many black rivers, the Cooper was stained a cola color by layers of decayed leaves from overhanging trees as it wound down from one side to the next on a slide to the sea.

After Maceo scraped a few barnacles off the bottom of the boat, he managed to steer the *Sister* back into deep water where he planned to drop anchor and straight-hook brown liquor from his jug. He scurried to the bow, grabbed an umbrella and popped it open to protect him from streaks of sunlight that broke through between the swirling clouds. He chose a faded yellow one with traces of Tweety Bird on each side.

Eleanor always brought him umbrellas that people left at the Social Services office: A Batman umbrella with a hole in it, a Western Auto umbrella with a bent handle, a Roy Rogers umbrella that was missing a panel and others scattered about the boat.

Holding his Tweety Bird bumper shoot high over his head, he kicked a crankcase anchor from a '58 Oldsmobile over the side and watched the rope slip out until the block hit bottom and the line pulled tight.

"Mark Twain," Maceo hollered, looking around to see if anyone onshore was watching. But the river was empty, except for some cormorants sitting on dock posts with their wings spread wide and drying. Under the late morning sun, Maceo fell asleep at the wheel of the VW van as the anchor line held the shrimp boat snug into the current. But sleep was no escape. He dreamed he was in the water neck deep and holding onto branches of willow oaks that leaned low into the river.

Maceo's mind struggled in fear behind his closed eyelids, his breathing quick and deep, interrupted by chokes caused by mouthfuls of river water that tasted like death. Straining to remain afloat, he struggled to keep his head above water. He could see Sister Santee fighting for her life just beyond his reach. He stretched his hand out to her as he tiptoed on the bottom. He touched her fingers but could not get a grip. He watched hopelessly as her hand slowly disappeared into a whirlpool of tannin-stained river water.

Then he woke up, tired and angry and alone again. So he lifted his half-gallon jug of Dickel and drank until an edge of the tarp pulled loose and flapped twice in the wind. He stood, steadying himself as best he could, and unfolded a towel he had designed as a banner he made using paint he stole from his brothers. The towel was blue. Maceo had carefully striped it with bright yellow pigment to make it look like the flag of Sweden he had seen in National Geographic. Someday he would sail the *Sister* into Stockholm harbor and be welcomed by people who loved him.

Clipping the flag to the rigging, he slowly hauled it skyward. The makeshift signet fluttered once, and then snapped in a gust of wind atop the rusty mast.

CHAPTER 20

In her day, Santee Mazyck was the prettiest girl on the river — that's what everybody who knew her said. She could also set trotlines, skin the catch and cook a perfect catfish stew before the sun was high enough to make shade on the riverbank. Her older brother Ezekiel taught her how to do all that.

She lived way up the creek among aunts and uncles and cousins in shanty houses with doors and window frames painted blue to keep out evil spirits. They huddled on heirs' property that nobody else wanted at the time. She was exceptionally smart, Ezekiel said. She could have finished high school and gotten a good job. No Mazyck from that neck of the woods had ever graduated from high school before.

But Santee loved to sing. She was a member of the Christ the Great Redeemer Baptist Church choir. Members of the congregation said the Lord had sprinkled angel dust on her vocal chords soon after she was born. By 16 she was the lead singer in a quartet that won first place in the Hell Hole Swamp Festival's "Gospel Music Extravaganza" competition.

Soon afterward, because her family needed the money, Sister quit school and went to work for a white couple that owned the big house on an old plantation not far away. She took care of their two-year-old daughter and managed to save for a train ticket to New York City. She planned to go up there someday and see Miss Ella Fitzgerald sing in person. Santee heard Ella sing on a record that the white lady played on her phonograph.

"Oh, lullaby of birdland,
that's what I always hear,
when you sigh,
Never in my worldland,

could there be ways to reveal,
in a phrase how I feel."

Santee memorized the words, although she had no idea what they meant. She often tried to match the sound of Ella's voice as she sang along with the record, and the white lady liked the way Santee sang. The white lady even asked her to sing that song to the members of her sewing circle one evening when they gathered on the back porch.

"Have you ever heard two turtle doves,
bill and coo, when they love.
That's the kind of magic music we make with our lips,
When we kiss."

The ladies gathered every Wednesday night and sewed while the men played poker down at the boathouse and got drunk. When one of the men came up to the house for more whisky, he heard Santee's voice and walked up to the porch to see who it belonged to, then stumbled back to tell his buddies.

"That's some mighty fine black snatch up there on the porch singing to the ladies," he told them. "Who she belong to?

"That's Zeke Mazyck's baby sister," one of the men said. "You know him. He's the one who sassed you that day about laying your crab traps along the river. You told him you'd shoot his black ass if he did it again."

"And there's a weepy old willow,
He really knows how to cry.
That's how I'd cry in my pillow,
If you should tell me farewell and goodbye."

A little after dark, Ezekiel walked out of the shadows on the path along the river en route to the big house. It was time for Sister to come home. As Ezekiel cut between the boathouse and the house, one of the drunks saw him and shouted:

"Well, well, look who's coming, boys! Shine a light on that black sum-bitch.

Looks like that nigger Zeke we just been talkin' 'bout. Yeah, that's him. We been talkin' 'bout you, boy. You comin' to fetch that pretty little sister of yours?"

Ezekiel ignored them as he climbed the hill to the house, where he stopped at the porch and told Santee it was time to go home. Ezekiel held Santee's hand and they headed back down the path. He glanced over at the boathouse and nobody was there.

"Come on, Sister, hurry along now. It's getting late," he said.

"Yea, boy, it's too late," a deep voice erupted from the shadows as five men surrounded Ezekiel and Santee.

The last time Ezekiel saw his sister alive he was neck deep in the water and she was being dragged down the path, her pretty dress torn and her mouth full of blood. That was just before one of the men broke Ezekiel's arm in two places and shoved him off the bank into the river. Santee screamed in the darkness, cried out for her mother, begged them to stop, and then there was silence.

Late the next day, a fisherman saw Sister's hand sticking up from the water, three bends down from the big house where she and Ella sang so sweetly for the sewing circle the night before.

"Lullaby of birdland whisper low,
kiss me sweet, and we'll go.
Flying high in birdland,
High in the sky up above,
All because we're in love."

CHAPTER 21

Herman Bishop III, son of a state legislator from Bamberg County, finished Clemson University in 1978 with a degree in accounting and a minor in inferiority, a complex combination.

After three years of selling condos on Hilton Head Island, the former high school football lineman joined forces with a client named Bob "The Boss" Bellingham, who was bringing boatloads of marijuana into the Lowcountry and didn't know how to launder his accumulating cash.

Weighing in at 235 pounds, Bishop had been a pretty good pulling guard at Robert E. Lee Academy near Ehrhardt, but was nowhere near good enough to play college ball. He assumed he'd lose weight at Clemson. He did not.

When he took a job at the Hilton Head Development Co., he was up to 350 pounds, which weighed heavily on his social life. But his bosses loved his ability to crunch numbers in a back room away from the customers. Not long afterward, much to his father's dismay, Bishop quit his day job, bought three Cadillacs and moved into an oceanfront mansion behind the security gates of Sea Pines Plantation.

When his old man asked where he got the money, all Bishop said was, "Good investments, Dad."

Herman Bishop met Bob the Boss at a Waffle House one Sunday morning as each fed their fetish for cheap food served up by desperate women. Both dated Waffle House waitresses because most didn't care what a man looked like as long as he didn't beat them up.

Bob came down from Ohio to sell boats and found the drug business in South Carolina much more profitable. Eventually, with the help of some locals, Bellingham and Bishop were smuggling in South American marijuana by the ton.

Bob cashed in and returned to Columbus. That's when Bishop turned a four-boat operation into the largest drug-smuggling cartel that had ever operated along the east coast. Which is why he parked next to Memorial Stadium for Clemson's home games after arriving at the county airport in his own private plane and escorted by a large, hairy bodyguard known as Larry.

"I don't care if he cheated, he won the national championship and that's what it's all about," Bishop often said about Clemson's football coach Danny Ford. Bishop sent several of Coach Ford's players envelopes stuffed with $5,000 in cash after the Tigers beat Nebraska in the 1981 Orange Bowl. "I was there. I rented an entire hotel on South Beach and we were cooking for a bunch of hungry country boys from Po-ass, South Carolina."

"Cooking" was Bishop's favorite word. When things were cooking, he was making money. And the way he spent it, he always needed more. Jewelry, cars, women, drugs, helicopters — his appetites were insatiable.

In five years, Bishop's enterprise imported more than 175 tons of marijuana through the quiet creeks of the South Carolina Lowcountry. That's about 16 shrimp-boat-loads a week, every week. He also commanded a small air force of renegade pilots who transformed the state's rural airstrips into bustling late-night drug-drop zones.

Bishop and his man Larry flew into Clemson the night before, held a business meeting on a houseboat in the middle of Lake Hartwell, then staged an elaborate tailgate party before the noon kickoff against the University of Virginia.

The only thing Bishop didn't like about Clemson was its namby-pamby schedule in the Atlantic Coast Conference. Playing Duke, Virginia and Wake Forest irritated him. Clemson belonged in the Southeastern Conference, Bishop thought, along with Georgia, Tennessee, Alabama and Auburn.

A year earlier, he tried to make that happen, wining and dining the SEC Commissioner on a private yacht off Sea Island, Georgia, where he made the pitch to expand the league by bringing in Clemson and Georgia Tech. He had Roy Cramer convinced it would work, giving the SEC a 12-member conference that could be divided into east and west divisions, thus creating a championship game that would make millions.

But the deal fell through when Bobby Robinson, Clemson's goody-goody Christian athletic director, balked. He even threatened to blab to the NCAA about booster tampering. Bishop withheld his IPTAY donation until the last minute, claiming he was going to offer the same deal to the University of South Carolina if Clemson didn't come around. But his unabashed hatred for the Gamecocks significantly weakened his argument. So he continued to concentrate on smuggling drugs.

"We're good for the local economy," Bishop said loud enough for everyone at the party to hear. "We're a home-grown industry that creates jobs and puts groceries on the table. We employ more people and have a bigger payroll than the Navy Shipyard in Charleston."

Nobody would argue with Bishop, who suddenly raised his left arm, looked at his flashy watch and declared it was time to leave.

"Ain't you going to stick around for the game, Rolex?" somebody asked.

"Can't," he said. "Got something cooking over at the Esso Club."

CHAPTER 22

S toney greeted the passengers at the doorway to his aircraft and noticed Berkeley Aiken's breasts bouncing up the stairway. She did look great in a flight suit.

"Welcome to the *Spirit of Charleston*, Ma'am. My name is Colonel Sanders and we hope you have an interesting and informative flight. We'll do whatever we can to make you comfortable. If there's anything you need, just ask me or one of the crew."

Berkeley accepted his hand, giggled and said, "But, Colonel Sanders, won't you be busy frying the chicken?"

Sanders smiled. It reminded him how much he didn't like civilians. He loved the military and everything about it, especially the straightforward way it catalogued people; the way everything he needed to know about a person was on the uniform for all to see. Reading uniforms was elementary: The nametag, the stripes, the bars, the service ribbons. Lots of ribbons stacked on a chest plate explained where the wearer had served and when. They designated how well the wearer could shoot a rifle and his general attitude about service to the country. Couldn't see all that right off the bat in the real world.

Behind Berkeley on the climb into the cargo bay were the rest of the traveling circus: Berkeley's unshaven photographer, Bob Gillespie; a town councilman from Swansea; the mayor of Gadsden; a Methodist minister from Camden; a banker from Sumter; the travel writer for the Charlotte Observer; a radio talk-show host from Columbia; a priest from Irmo; an ad sales rep from the Orangeburg Times and Democrat newspaper; and a car dealer from Cayce. But Col. Sanders didn't know exactly who they were. None wore uniforms.

The group was escorted by Technical Sergeant Tom Crawford of the 315th Public Affairs Office. In civilian life, Crawford worked in public relations for Southern

Bell. He had served in Vietnam, according to his ribbons.

The crew — including the co-pilot, a navigator and three loadmasters — helped everyone get comfortable in airline seats installed along the walls of the airplane's cavernous cargo section, which looked like the inside of a huge a shotgun shell. Beyond the special passenger seats were 12 pallets of tightly packed provisions headed for Ascension Island.

"May I have your attention, please," Stoney said, holding up his hand as the passengers got situated. "My name is Lt. Col. Stoney Sanders, your aircraft commander on this flight. In real life, I work for a little power company down the road called Santee Cooper. You might have heard of it."

The group chuckled appropriately.

"On behalf of the United States Air Force and the 315th Military Airlift Wing at Charleston Air Force Base, I'd like to welcome you to this orientation flight designed to give community leaders a better understanding of the Air Force Reserve and what your employees and neighbors who work with us do when they report for duty once a month."

The group mumbled among themselves, joking about various weekend warriors they knew. As the civilians looked around, checking their seat belts, Billy Glover, the car dealer from Cayce, raised his hand.

"Uh, Lieutenant Colonel, sir, could you tell us about the storm that's headed this way and whether or not it's going to be a problem."

Stoney turned to his navigator, Capt. Cliff Hendrix, a high-school chemistry teacher.

"The system is approximately 500 miles east of the Lesser Antilles," Hendrix read from a printout he was holding. "It has reached tropical storm strength and has been given the name Hugo, according the National Weather Service. Hurricane hunters from the 53rd Weather Reconnaissance Squadron, manned by Air Force Reservists, are en route from Keesler Air Force Base in Biloxi, Mississippi, to enter the storm and assess strength and direction. At this time, the storm is expected to take a northern turn and possibly skirt the eastern seaboard of the United States. We will, of course, keep you informed in this matter and never put you or this mission in jeopardy. Thank you."

The civilians gave Capt. Hendrix a round of applause and settled back into their seats for takeoff.

"I just hope we get back on time," said Glover, the Chevy dealer. "I've got an important meeting with my sales managers."

Berkeley Aiken, strapped into the seat next to him near the small porthole window behind the right wing, nodded as the engines began to spin and whine. The aircraft taxied out to the runway. The loadmasters checked the passengers before strapping themselves into the web seats along the bulkhead.

The thrust pushed the passengers back in their seats. They held on tight to the armrests as the plane lifted quickly off the runway and seemed to float horizontally into the sky.

"Oh my," the priest from Irmo said as Col. Sanders banked the big bird to a heading of south, southeast.

CHAPTER 23

John Rhett walked into the Esso Club on the edge of the Clemson campus, ordered a ginger ale at the bar and took a seat in a back booth. The Esso Club was an old gas station converted into a student bar over the years. The tables were scarred with names carved in over the ages and the floor was always sticky from vomit and stale beer.

Rhett — dressed in a beige Haspel summer suit — breathed in the odors of indulgence and let them roam through his brain cells before letting them out slowly. There was a time when his life revolved around booze. As hard as Rhett tried to be a Southern gentleman, his redneck, trailer-park, cock-fighting bloodline kept getting him in more trouble than he could talk his way out of.

If it wasn't booze, it was drugs. And if it wasn't drugs, it was sex. His appetite for immorality was unparalleled in South Carolina politics, which took some doing in a state famous for electing liars and egomaniacs.

But it was power, the ultimate high, that finally brought Rhett down. And he knew it would happen again. The day he stepped off the plane at National Airport, got into a limousine and crossed the Potomac, he knew he was hooked. He saw the Washington Monument to his left, the Capitol building shining in the distance and the White House down the street. The scent of power was in the air that lovely winter's day; he tasted it in the snowflakes that fell upon his lips. Nectar of the gods.

Washington was his Eden, and his beautiful young bride, Tina, was Eve. They ate all the fruits, flaunted themselves in the halls of Congress, made love on the Capitol steps and made headlines, too. John Rhett was shameless in the city that has no shame. He fell eventually — but not before going to hell and back before admitting his weaknesses. He was a narcissistic drunkard, a powerless man at the axis of world power. But he didn't realize he was an alcoholic until he heard the cell door slam behind him.

It's easy to quit drinking in prison. Rhett swore off the juice and took on Jesus as his personal savior. But trouble always found him. During his visits to the prison chapel for confession, he met a priest who asked a favor. Would Rhett smuggle a few packets of happy dust for inmates who needed "a religious experience?" The packets would be tucked inside tiny little Bibles that John passed out to the born-agains on Sunday mornings. And he could keep some for himself.

It was a good gig, something that Rhett needed to satisfy his larcenous soul and adventurous spirit. Until he got caught. His two-year sentence for the Abscam shenanigans multiplied by 10 for possession of cocaine with intent to distribute, near a church — unless he agreed to help authorities in the war on drugs.

So a deal was cut in the prison library with born-again federal drug agent Sid Rice, who was not amused by Rhett's attitude or his plight, but willing to play the game. Therefore, when Herman "Rolex" Bishop walked into the Esso Club that sunny day in Clemson, he had no idea he was about to shake hands with the devil.

CHAPTER 24

R olex always wore sunglasses, even in a dingy bar, and always entered the Esso Club through the back door. He waved off the bartender's attention because he already had a scotch and water with a twist in hand. He joined Rhett at the back booth and asked the former congressman to change seats. Rolex always sat with his back to the wall.

Herman Bishop III was obese but he was not a big man on campus when he attended Clemson. He frequented the Esso Club as a student, pretending to be cool, watching frat boys guzzle beer and nuzzle coeds. He tried to be like them but failed. They didn't give bids to fat boys. They took ugly boys and stupid boys, but not fat ones. Bad for the Sigma Nu image. Not cool enough for Kappa Alpha Order. Even the Sig Eps blackballed all 300 pounds of Herman Bishop III.

He resented the cliques and the pretty girls who only dated pretty boys whose daddies had lots of money. Despite being a member of the S.C. House of Representatives, his father, Herman Bishop Jr., was an outsider, of the merchant class, from Bamberg.

Herman thought graduating from Clemson would get him in to the closed society of South Carolina gentlemen. He took a job in Hilton Head to impress a girl from Cameron whose father was a cotton farmer in Calhoun County. He figured Sea Island real estate would quickly make him rich. He soon found himself on the fast track of international drug smuggling, which made him richer.

"My man," Rolex said as he stuck out his pudgy hand, hung heavy with jewelry that jangled as they shook. "What's the word?"

Rhett clinked glasses with Rolex and quickly drained his.

"Business is good," Rhett said. "I've got a guy who can bring in 20 kilos a month, like clockwork. Good stuff."

"Where from?"

"Down south. Really good stuff. No problem."

"Air or sea?" Rolex asked.

"Air," Rhett answered.

"The feds are all over that now. DEA's tracking flights. Shot one down last month."

"No problemo, amigo."

"Why not?"

Rhett stirred his drink with an orange swizzle stick.

"They don't shoot down Air Force jets."

CHAPTER 25

T he electrical wiring was ripped out of the *Sister Santee* long before Maceo moved in. But he had a dependable transistor radio he kept on the dash of the old bus. He didn't listen to the news because he didn't understand it. But he enjoyed music and could pick up WBBB, a beach, boogie and blues station out of Orangeburg. He liked the old songs best. Brother James Brown and Wicked Wilson Pickett. When the horns kicked in, Maceo closed his eyes and pretended he was one of the Famous Flames, dancing and playing a saxophone.

The music was interrupted occasionally by reports that the storm was strengthening. As the crow flies, it was only 30 miles from Schitt Creek up the Cooper River to refuge near the Pinopolis Dam. But Maceo was no crow and the river meandered like a snake. He noticed windows and doors of shacks along the way were boarded; that johnboats and lawn furniture had been moved to higher ground.

People in Santee Cooper Country respected water. At least once a year the river rose into their yards, threatening everything they owned, which wasn't much. The 80-mile-wide flood plain was littered with poor white trash, folks who lived in broken-down shanties and rusty trailers between the National Forest and paper-mill tree plantations where a billion pines separated them from the rest of the world.

It was a good place to hide; where truck drivers parked big rigs under trees next to mobile homes that hadn't moved in 25 years. Fishing, hunting, guiding, growing marijuana, shooting each other and sitting in jail took up most of the inhabitants' spare time.

Created during the Great Depression, the Francis Marion National Forest was a 225,000-acre expanse of sand and clay that was cleared and planted and farmed with loblolly pines. In the middle of it were 2,000 acres of hardwood wetlands called Hell Hole Swamp. Certain powerful South Carolina politicians who hailed from the area called themselves the Hell Hole Swamp Gang. They included former U.S. Congressman Mendel Rivers, former Governor Bob McNair, state Senator Rembert Dennis and Columbia Mayor Lester Bates.

One year, at a political stump meeting in Galivant's Ferry, the flowing-white-haired Rivers was delivering a speech and referred to his hardscrabble upbringing in Hell Hole Swamp. That's when a farmer dressed in overalls shouted out from the back of the crowd, "All swamps are hell holes, Mendel!"

And he was right. The mushy center of the forest was a no-man's land where alligators topped the food chain and towering cypress trees blocked out both the sun and people. It was quiet out there, except for the wind rustling the pine needles, the rattle of coal cars and the rumbling hum of electricity in the power lines.

Maceo sometimes thought he could hear himself think out there in Santee Cooper Country. He could hear his brain clicking through the choices he had to make,scraping and scratching throughout the process. Today, though, he simply turned off his brain and got himself into a sort of trance as he drove *Sister Santee* upriver.

The *Sister* was almost to the U.S. Highway 17-A overpass when he saw a police car stop in the middle of the bridge. Shifting the *Sister's* engine into neutral, Maceo slowed to a stop and stared at the white Ford cruiser with a decal on the door.

On the bridge, Officer George Burr got out of the car and looked over the side for crappy beds along the river's edge. An avid angler, Burr planned to catch some pan fish while down in this neck of the woods.

His morning visit with Sue Ellen, his older sister, went as usual. The roof of her doublewide outside the village of Salters in Williamsburg County was leaking and she didn't have enough money to fix it. She also didn't have enough money to feed her two kids since her husband, Edgar, lost his right arm at the sawmill two years ago. George gave her two hundred dollars and thanked God he was not married. If he caught some fish, he'd give them to her. Wouldn't have to clean them that way.

Looking over the side of the bridge, he thought he saw a nice sandy bed where fish might gather under a cypress tree fifty yards downstream. Then he noticed the shrimp boat, drifting in the distance. He tried to read the letters on the bow. Shrimp boats had been a fascination of his since he was a boy and dreamed of running away from home. Wasn't until he worked as a striker on one the summer of his junior year in high school that he cured himself of the notion. Hot, boring, backbreaking days trolling the sandy shallows off Seabrook and Kiawah islands taught him what a shrimper's life was really like.

While he watched rich people sun bathing on the beach, he sorted out jellyfish and horseshoe crabs and other slimy by-catch on the deck, shoveling it all back into the water where seagulls circled and swooped and squabbled and screamed a constant cacophony as the slop splattered into the sea.

The boat he worked on was the *Mary Penny,* out of Cherry Point on Bohicket Creek. It was named for the owner's daughter. George liked to record the shrimp-boat names painted carefully on the bow and at the stern. He found them interesting, even if the people in them were not. Unable to make out the letters on this particular boat, George lifted his binoculars and focused.

"Now that's odd," he mumbled to himself as he zeroed in on the old VW bus, then scanned toward the aft and spotted loosely rigged nets hanging from the trawl. Squinting, George tried to make out the faded green letters, twisting the lenses for sharper focus. Gradually, the boat turned sideways and George saw the words *Sister Santee* stenciled on the bow.

"What a nice name," he said to himself.

As George lowered the glasses, he heard a logging truck rumbling his way.

"Crap!" George screamed.

The truck driver pulled on his air horn, but never hit the brakes. No way he could stop in time. George climbed onto the railing and jumped just as the Kenworth, loaded with logs, clipped the back right fender of the patrol car and flipped it like a pancake over the other side.

Both cruiser and cop hit the water 20 feet apart at the same time.

Maceo gunned the VW engine and headed to the rescue. By the time he reached

George Burr, the car had filled with water and only its trunk and rear wheels were visible. Swept along by the current, Burr grabbed a line Maceo threw his way and clambered up the side of the old boat, having shed his boots. As he crawled over the gunnels and onto the deck, he looked up and saw the muzzle of a .38 caliber revolver aimed right between his eyes.

"W-w-welcome to the S-s-sister, M-m-m-mister," Maceo said with a crooked smile, the pistol cocked and ready in one hand and the faded Tweety Bird umbrella in the other. Maceo loosed a rope from a hook next to him and the net on the deck snapped up Burr, throwing his bare heels above his head, trapping him like a giant catfish, swinging back and forth four feet off the deck.

As Burr twisted and bobbed, Maceo's grin broadened. He hated white people, and now he had snagged one of his very own.

CHAPTER 26

Junior Jones sat on a high stool at Henry's bar on North Market Street in Charleston. It was 10 a.m. and above the bar images of the Atlantic storm flickered across the TV screen.

Junior sipped a Bloody Mary, drowning his father's dream of him becoming South Carolina's first African-American governor since Reconstruction. It was over. It ended the night before when he kissed Ashmead Dawes on the lips on the bandstand in the middle of White Point Garden. Their moment of passion was disrupted by the glare of a large flashlight held by a cop and the question, "What the hell you boys doing up there?"

Junior didn't want to be the governor anyway. He could do better, he thought, as he focused on the television screen.

"I don't want to unduly alarm anyone," Channel 5 weatherman Charlie Hall said, "but Hugo is a monster hurricane and it's headed our way. It could make landfall anywhere between Savannah and Cape Hatteras in two days. State officials have issued a voluntary evacuation request for residents of all South Carolina beaches. So, if you want to leave, do so now."

Junior leaned over the bar, grabbed the remote control and switched off the set.

"Hey, I was watching that!" a man sitting in a booth hollered. "We got a hurricane headed our way."

Junior swung round on the stool, looked at the man who was wearing khaki pants and a pink Polo golf shirt, and asked, "I'm going dancing. Care to join me?"

Junior didn't wait for an answer. He slammed a ten-dollar bill on the bar and left, got into his company car and headed to Folly Beach. Leona and her friends would surely be at the pier by now. Overhead, a huge C-141 cargo plane left long white condensation trails seaward over the Charleston peninsula.

CHAPTER 27

Berkeley Aiken and cameraman Bob Gillespie were the first two civilians invited to visit the flight deck as the Starlifter approached the coastline and headed south-southeast. The cockpit didn't provide as good a view as Gillespie had hoped. The pilot and co-pilot were wedged into their seats and the cameraman's lens was not wide enough.

The pilots flipped buttons and turned dials on the main control panel. The navigator was crammed in behind the co-pilot and faced another wall full of switches and gauges. He had a fold-down desktop on which he had unfolded a map.

"Welcome to the flight deck," Major Hendrix, the navigator, said, swiveling his chair as the visitors squeezed in for a better look. "We've got headsets for you."

Colonel Sanders, all puffed up in his new leather U.S. Air Force flight jacket, motioned for Berkeley and Bob to pick up the headsets. Berkeley spread the earphones with her perfectly manicured hands and slipped them over her ears, careful not to tousle her hair any more than she wanted it tousled. She used her best TV voice to test the microphone.

Bob, still flustered about not having the right camera lens, put his headset on backward. Stoney signaled to him to turn it around, which he did with a silly grin.

"OK now, can everybody hear me?" Stoney asked.

"Where's the volume control?" Berkeley responded. "I can't hear myself."

"It's the little switch on the bottom left of the console, young lady. Got it?"

"10-4," Bob said.

"10-4," Berkeley chimed in.

Bob swung his video camera to his shoulder and began filming again. He managed to get Berkeley and the two pilots in the viewer as light streamed in through the windows and illuminated the control panels.

"Good," Stoney said. "I'm turning the airplane over to my copilot, Major Buckston here, and he'll take us up to 32,000 feet. Look over to your left and you'll see the Morris Island Lighthouse, and just beyond is Fort Sumter, where the War of Northern Aggression began more than a century ago."

Berkeley nodded as she looked at the two landmarks as well as the two long, parallel, man made rock jetties that marked the entrance to Charleston Harbor. She remembered the breezy summer day when her father took her sailing — how she let out the jib of their 18-foot Y-Flyer, and how their boat whisked past scores of competitors in a Sunfish regatta off James Island across from the Charleston Battery.

"Few people get to see the South Carolina coastline from this perspective," she reported as Bob held his camera steady on her profile then panned toward the window and to the harbor. "But for members of the Air Force Reserve, this spectacular view is part of their regular commute. Today we are the guests of the 315th Military Airlift Wing of Charleston en route to Antigua for a brief layover and then on to Ascension Island, a volcanic peak in the middle of the vast South Atlantic. We're glad you could join us on 'Good Morning, Midlands!' So sit back and enjoy the ride."

Bob gave her a thumbs up and shifted in his seat to get another side-angle shot of Berkeley in the cockpit with the crew.

"Ever been up in an Air Force plane?" she looked into the camera and asked. "Well, I'm TV-10's Berkeley Aiken and invite you to stay tuned to 'Good Morning, Midlands!' It will be the ride of your life."

Another thumbs up from Bob, and Berkeley relaxed her smile. She enjoyed filming teasers for her show. Everything she knew about television she learned from watching it.

She was the daughter of a Charleston Courier editorial writer and grew up in a fine home in downtown Charleston, where she attended Ashley Hall School for Girls and dated boys from Porter Gaud. From there, she went to all-girl Columbia College, having been turned down by the University of North Carolina at Chapel Hill. So she settled for being editor of the Columbia College student newspaper. During the summer she took writing courses nearby at the University of South Carolina. She also excelled in judo, which inspired a series of articles in the USC newspaper.

Suddenly, with a jerk, Berkeley swatted at something crawling up her leg. She reached down and grabbed Stoney Sanders' hand, twisted his wrist and locked it against her knee.

"Whoa, little lady, you're fast," he winced. "I need the flight log there behind you between the seats. Hand it to me, please?"

"Sorry, Colonel. You scared me. Never been this high before."

"Really?" Stoney smirked as he straightened his headset and raked his fingers through the patch of thinning hair on the back of his head. "No problem, Missy. Let me remind you that it's cramped up here on the flight deck. So be very careful what you touch."

Bob, who heard all this through his headset, interrupted: "So, Colonel, where are the parachutes in case we have to bail for some reason? You never know…"

"No parachutes on this plane," Stoney barked as the plane pulled up and away over the Gulf Stream. "But there is a lifeboat, and I'm in charge of that too."

CHAPTER 28

George Burr hung upside down and spun slowly in the netting of the *Sister Santee*. Each time he turned round he was looking down the barrel of a .38 caliber widow-maker in the grungy hands of a state-certified maniac. He had found Maceo Mazyck.

"Mr. Mazyck," George gasped. "I've been looking for you, man. I've got good news. The government owes you money. They sent me here to give it to you."

At each turn of the net, George searched Maceo's vacant eyes for a hint of what might come next. All he saw was madness. Maceo wrapped his pink lips around the top of the brown liquor bottle he held in his left hand, threw his head back and sucked down a half-pint's worth of whisky. At the same time he placed his right thumb on the hammer of the pistol he held in is other hand and cocked it. George smelled the stench of Maceo at each turn — a nasty combination of sweat, gear grease, urine, feces and rotgut whisky. "F-f-f-fuck you," Maceo sputtered. "I know you. H-h-hospital m-m-man."

He has a good memory, George thought as he spun round again, then said:

"Yep, that's me, good ol' Dancing George, your friend and confidant. You remember the games we played in Columbia? Hide and seek outback by the big fence? We had fun didn't we, Maceo?"

Maceo hadn't been hauled into the State Hospital since Reagan emptied the wards and the cops quit chasing him through the swamps. Now, they simply waited for Maceo to sober up a little, get hungry and exit the jungle. Then they beat the crap out of him and left him there.

"H-how m-m-much?" Maceo asked, looking quickly over his shoulder as the boat puttered closer to the bridge.

"Oh, um, the money," George answered. "Lots of money, Mr. Mazyck. Let me out of this net and I'll tell you about it. I'm a little dizzy right now."

"How m-much m-m-money?"

"Oh, maybe a million or so, Mr. Mazyck, enough to buy a new boat, take a vacation, build a house..."

Maceo pondered that for a moment. He'd never taken a vacation.

"W-w-where?"

"Where? Oh, yeah, uh, the vacation. Well, um, how about Mexico? Ever been to Mexico, Maceo? Lots of tequila and pretty senoritas there for sure. You'd have a blast down there."

All Maceo knew about Mexico was it was even hotter than South Carolina. "S-s-Sweden. I w-want to g-go to Sweden."

"Sure. No problem. You can go to Sweden. That would be nice."

Maceo lowered the barrel of the gun slightly and George wrenched his hand through the slimy webbing of the net in a futile attempt to disarm his captor.

Maceo stepped back and raised the pistol to George's head.

"I'm g-g-gonna k-k-kill you."

"But Sweden's a neutral country," George said, swallowing hard.

CHAPTER 29

Two miles upriver, Father Rudisill finished filling the feeders in the huge hen house at Mepkin Abbey. The retreat was part of a 3,000-acre rice plantation once owned by magazine publisher Henry Luce of New York. His widow, Claire, who had converted to Roman Catholicism, left Mepkin Abbey to a group of Trappist monks from Kentucky. They built a chapel overlooking the Cooper River. The monks added a dormitory near the chapel and scattered a few guest accommodations for use by guilt-ridden souls seeking weekend escapes from reality.

As Father Rudisill, the abbot, emptied the last bag of scratch into a feed trough, a heavyset monk attired in a black and white hooded habit and sandals rolled through the front gate on a rusty bicycle. Father Rudisill walked over to the man, who handed the abbot an envelope.

"Thank you, Brother John," he said as he slipped the envelope into his pocket.

Brother John wobbled into a nearby garden and knelt clumsily before a statue of the Virgin Mary. Just beyond the garden stood the chapel, from which could be heard a roomful of monks and a handful of congregants groaning incomprehensible chants and muffled prayers.

Brother John shuffled to his dormitory room, which overlooked the river. Father Rudisill did not know Brother John's given name, which was not unusual, but he did know it was an alias. Brother John's actual name topped a list of drug smugglers that the FBI in cooperation with the State Law Enforcement Division had posted on a huge flip chart in the "War Room" at SLED headquarters in Columbia. This posed a serious problem for Herman Bishop III/ aka Rolex/ aka Brother John.

Brother John walked to the window of his room, lifted his left arm and pulled back the heavy sleeve of his habit with his right hand so he could check the time. As the second hand of his diamond-studded wristwatch swept past high noon, Brother John issued a deep sigh. The problem will be solved in exactly two hours, he reassured himself, before managing a nervous chuckle.

CHAPTER 30

B rent Lee, his wife, Stacia, and their children, Graycen and Grant, were anchored in the family's 18-foot Carolina Skiff just off Seabrook Island near the mouth of Privateer Creek. Graycen, 9, saw three large fins slice through water.

"Sharks!" she yelled.

Gently, three bottle-nosed dolphins rolled off the bow and blew out a mixture of air and seawater from holes behind their heads.

Graycen's 5-year-old brother shoved his sister back into her seat, saying, "They ain't sharks. Those are dolphins, you know, like Flipper."

As the boat rocked in the surf, Graycen fell and bumped her mother's oversized purse, which barked. Suddenly, from deep within the canvas bag, out popped the head of a miniature schnauzer. The dog squinted, as if to ask what all the ruckus was about.

"Down, Cocky," Brent said with a laugh. "Down, boy, nobody called for a guard dog."

Cocky slipped back into the coolness of the purse.

"They're just playing, guys," Brent said as he pointed to the dolphins. "But I'm not. Grant, you listen to me. Be nice to your sister."

Normally, Brent wouldn't take the boat out on a day when local forecasters were hyperventilating on storm warnings. But Special Agent Lee had been working hard in Columbia as head of a combined state and federal anti-drug-smuggling task force and had not seen his kids in more than a month. He promised them a boat ride, and here they were, bobbing on the waves just offshore.

Stacia was glad Brent was back in town. She didn't like his being away for so long. It reminded her of his Army days when he disappeared to Panama for weeks trying to stop the flow of illegal drugs into the United States.

Stacia met Brent when he was stationed at Fort Bragg, near her hometown of Pinehurst, N.C. Her father was general manager of a company than owned and operated several exclusive golf courses in the Tar Heel State. She was a waitress at the venerable Pine Crest Inn when she first saw her future husband.

Special Forces Lt. Brent Lee walked into the bar one Friday afternoon with three of his fellow officers, all Airborne Rangers who loved to play golf. She knew they were soldiers by their closely cropped haircuts.

Brent was sorting out the bets when Stacia smiled and asked him what he'd like to drink. He looked straight into her ocean-blue eyes and whispered, "A double, please ma'am, of what you got."

It wasn't the first time Stacia was propositioned by a weekend golfer. But the Guilford College senior wasn't interested in swaggering soldiers. She had visited Fort Bragg and seen the married housing, which certainly was not anything worth bragging about, she joked. However, exactly one year after first laying eyes on Brent Lee, Stacia exchanged rings and vows with him at the altar of the Fort Bragg chapel. Forty paratroopers formed the traditional arch as the newlyweds left the church, climbed into his Porsche convertible and headed to the Outer Banks.

Two years later, when Brent left the Army to attend law school at the University of South Carolina, Stacia took a job at the Big and Tall Shop in Columbia's Richland Mall. She stood only five feet on her tiptoes and could barely see over the clothing racks.

Brent got his law degree and a job in the U.S. Attorney's office in Columbia where he specialized in federal drug cases — shuffling papers mostly. He liked jumping out of airplanes better. When he was told he was going to be transferred to headquarters in Washington, Brent and Stacia agreed he should look for another job, maybe in his hometown of Charleston. Sid Rice, one of his law school classmates, had called saying he needed a young, local prosecutor to help with a huge federal drug-smuggling sting.

Now, after 14 months of undercover investigations, Brent and his team were ready to slam the door on Herman "Rolex" Bishop III. But the smuggling kingpin received a tip that his arrest warrant had been issued, promptly "got religion," and disappeared.

CHAPTER 31

In the distance Brent heard the whine of a cigarette boat in Bohicket Creek and saw a huge rooster tail winding through the marsh. Soon he saw the speedboat as the operator maneuvered the final curves of the deep-water creek between Seabrook Island and Rockville. Boat jockeys were common in the waters around the village where the last big regatta of the season draws thousands of drunks who pretend to watch the races.

So Brent paid little attention when the sleek craft, took a hard left and sped toward them. Probably going down the Edisto, past Deveaux Bank and out into deep water, Brent thought.

Stacia was searching through their plastic cooler for some juice for the children when Grant screamed, "Look, mommy, that boat is going to hit us!"

"Don't be silly, darling," she said raising her head to see what was causing all the commotion.

Brent, who was checking the depth finder to determine if the dolphins had gone under the boat, also looked up and saw the long, black craft speeding their way. He began waving his hands over his head and squinting to see if the driver had spotted them. But the sun reflected brightly off the windshield of the errant craft.

He continued to wave his arms frantically, then yelled, "Hold on tight, he might hit us!"

Fumbling with the ignition key, Brent managed to get the Johnson outboard motor cranked and shoved the throttle forward with his right elbow. He snagged Graycen in his left arm as the engine roared to life. Stacia and Grant hit the deck hard near the stern. The black cigarette boat missed them by only a few feet as it cut close behind them and banked sharply toward open water.

"Damn you!" Brent yelled and shook his fist as the black boat turned back toward the creek. Graycen cried. Blood ran down Grant's leg where he cut it on the metal cooler handle. Stacia, having hit her head on the deck, lay stunned at the stern.

Brent grabbed his field glasses from the center console and searched for a name on the back of the black boat. It had none.

CHAPTER 32

It seemed like the perfect hideout, but now Brother John wasn't so sure. As a boy, he visited Mepkin Abbey with his mother. Emmy Lou Rooney was a devout Roman Catholic, a Charleston native and a graduate of Bishop England High School. She often said it was ironic that she married a man named Bishop.

But Emmy Lou's married life in the farming community of Bamberg was far removed from her childhood in metropolitan Charleston. There was no Roman Catholic church in Bamberg and, as far as she could tell, no Catholics. Emmy Lou's husband, Herman Jr., was a Baptist who seldom went to church. His passion was politics, which he toted self-righteously like a cross while serving in the S.C. House of Representatives for 20 years.

So each fall, Emmy Lou and their only son, Herman III, retreated to Mepkin Abbey where a sanctimonious sense of belonging engulfed her like the long habits hid the monks from reality. At Mepkin, Emmy Lou and little Herman slept in single beds in a stark room furnished only with a chair and desk. They listened all night to barred owls hoo-hoo-hooing and to crickets scratching and bullfrogs croaking and God only knows what else that contributed to the so-called sounds of silence surrounding them.

Herman could not recall a single autumn when he did not accompany his mother on the sojourn. She loaded him and a couple of changes of clothes into the family car, placed her rosary beads in her son's hands and taught him by rote how to Hail Mary and all the rest of the celestial cast as she drove the back roads of Bamberg, Dorchester and Berkeley counties en route to the abbey.

"Jesus loves you, son. Never forget that," she'd say.

Herman hated Mepkin Abbey at first because children were considered a nuisance there. But Emmy Lou begged her way in with her boy, vowing he would be no trouble, adding she needed him there with her to find peace of mind. Mostly, Herman played hide-and-seek alone among the statues of saints in the gardens, which is precisely what he was doing in the guise of Brother John. He appreciated Mepkin Abbey now, especially since the monks didn't say anything to anybody and lost souls were always welcome, for a small fee.

The only manmade sounds on the sprawling grounds of the abbey were guttural. They came from the chapel at least twice a day in between the shuffle of sandaled feet back and forth from the giant hen house and mushroom farm. The chickens, of course, were another matter. They cackled and clucked and squawked and fussed and laid golden-brown eggs, which were hand selected and slipped into soft pockets before being carefully placed in cardboard cartons that bore Mepkin Abbey labels. The eggs sold exceptionally well in local grocery stores to folks who appreciated good value while helping with the Lord's work.

Brother John soon left his room, hobbled down the bluff to the river and rested his hulk on a bench from which he watched storm clouds gathering. There was a rustle of leaves in the wind and he sensed a presence behind him. He turned quickly and got a glimpse of someone in a dark frock staring from behind a trellis covered with cassia pods. He quickly looked left then right for others before spotting a man in a fishing boat near an old rice field dike adjacent to the river. A glimmer of glass, reflecting the sun, flashed from the boat. Brother John quickly stood and scurried farther down the trail to the riverbank. The fisherman fired up his boat's engine and sped off upriver.

Herman Bishop III loved boats, and now he had lots of them ranging in size from a 12-foot aluminum johnboat to his 150-foot oceangoing yacht, complete with captain and crew. He relished the lifestyle the drug trade afforded him and wanted the world to know he had big boats, big houses and big-breasted women who flashed them on his command. But things were changing. It was more expensive to buy off small-town cops, and state authorities were no longer clueless and careless about guarding the South Carolina coastline from dope runners.

Time was running out for Herman Bishop III, and he knew it. He already sold two of his mansions and recently fired his bodyguard, Larry, because he couldn't account for where he was the weekend before. A trained accountant, Herman had an excellent sense about things not adding up. Not even the cloistered grounds of

Mepkin Abbey felt safe.

As Brother John scampered up the shady lane toward the front gate, he had to pause and wait for a group of visitors from Traveler's Rest to pass en route to the conference center. He planned to take the abbey's ancient bicycle and escape into the countryside. Monks did this often and the locals were accustomed to seeing the hooded brothers pedal past like faceless angels. But as Brother John waited for the group to pass, he noticed a police car waiting at the gate.

CHAPTER 33

B erkeley Aiken awoke as the wheels of the jet touched down in Antigua. She had fallen asleep after taping an interview with Tom Crawford, a loadmaster, about how much cargo the big plane could transport. Now she looked out the side porthole at palm trees outlined against the orange Caribbean sky.

"Welcome to Antigua," Sgt. Crawford announced as the plane turned on the narrow runway and taxied down a bumpy apron ramp. "We'll deplane here while we take on fuel. We'll have an early supper in the officer's mess, where you can freshen up before our departure for Ascension later tonight."

Berkeley heard the words but couldn't put them in order. The cobwebs of a sound sleep still clouded her brain. Pulling out her compact, she glanced into the tiny mirror and blinked a few times. She looked good and she knew it. Looks were just about everything in her world.

Berkeley refreshed her lipstick, powdered her cheeks and brushed her eyelashes a few times to achieve the "maximum minimum," a term she learned the first day on the job. The rule for television personalities was that, while you can't always look great, maintaining a maximum minimum is a must at all times.

Christiane Amanpour never looked perfect while she was dodging bullets in Kosovo or interviewing a jihadist in a cave. Christiane's thick black hair was always slightly mussed. Her skin was smooth and brown and she seldom wore makeup. But she always maintained her maximum minimum. Christiane's secret was the way she wore her scarves, sometimes wrapped around her shoulders, other times draped over her head. And she had piercing dark eyes and spoke with a distinct British accent. Berkeley had studied Christiane carefully on TV.

As the front-end crew sat in the cockpit shutting down the engines and going through the usual checklists, Berkeley and the others climbed into a blue Air Force bus that awaited them. Sitting next to the open window, Berkeley let the balmy Caribbean breeze brush her hair as the bus left the runway onto a road filled with potholes and strewn with trash.

Antigua, she realized,was a poor country. Not quite Ethiopia, but close. She had visited her mother's native land when she was in middle school, a trip that left a lasting impression. She learned how different the world was beyond the protective walls of her youth.

While her mother had come from a family of privilege, there was no escaping the stench of Ethiopian starvation and filth that filled Berkeley's nostrils as they drove past the refugee camps where the unwashed lived. She remembered her father saying they were like the concentration camps of World War II. But it was primarily through her mother that Berkeley learned the history of Ethiopia, a land so ancient it was mentioned twice in the "Iliad" and three times in the "Odyssey."

Her school nickname, in fact, was "Lucy," given to her by classmates at Ashley Hall when they studied the African nations and read about the world's oldest human fossil found in the Awash Valley. At first, Berkeley didn't like being compared to an Ethiopian fossil, but grew to identify with her dignity and accepted the nickname with pride.

But Antigua's squalor repulsed her. She turned her eyes away from the garbage and trash swirling in the wake of the blue shuttle bus as it made its way toward the beach. Reaching into her purse, she pulled out a black and brown scarf, draped it over her shoulders then pulled it across her face and pretended she was the crown princess of cable TV.

CHAPTER 34

Josh Jenkins joined the Berkeley County Sheriff's Office soon after he completed a six-year hitch in the Navy. Jenkins, a deep-sea diver, had been stationed in Naples, Fla. and Norfolk, Va. before finishing his tours of duty and returning to his South Carolina home in Round O — a village named for an Indian chief who had a purple circle tattooed on his chest.

But Jenkins enjoyed his time in the military, especially the order it provided in his life. His African-American father was an alcoholic who left home when he was seven. His white mother raised him on the family farm in Colleton County with his grandparents where he avoided the worst of South Carolina's scorn for his mulatto skin. He traded in his Navy whites for the gray and tan uniform of the Berkeley County Sheriff's Department soon after his girlfriend, Dora Ann Simms, got pregnant with their daughter, Stephanie, now two years old.

Jenkins worked for a year as a patrolman before joining the department's search-and-rescue squad. It put him in some of the Lowcountry's darkest rivers, lakes and ponds groping for the bodies of drowning victims. He liked his job, except every now and then when he'd come face to face with a submerged corpse, its eyes open and mouth agape. He'd been spooked more than once by such bloated specters.

Josh Jenkins was a kind-hearted man. The members of the Berkeley County Sheriff's Department had raised $5,000 for the monks of Mepkin Abbey and he was happy to be chosen to present the check to Father Rudisill.

Every year the sheriff's deputies participated in a special alligator hunt in Hell Hole Swamp. Each officer paid $50 for the privilege of shooting a gator, dragging it back to the station and measuring it tip to tail. The biggest gator won a $100 gift certificate to Bubba's Outdoor Emporium in Moncks Corner. The federal government's endangered species act did not apply to the Berkeley County Sheriff's

Department, especially since alligators eat hunting dogs.

"How big was the gator this year?" the Father Rudisill asked as he put the check into the pocket of his habit.

"Fourteen feet, eight inches," Josh said, leaning back against his cruiser. "Seems like they get bigger every year."

"Well," the Abbott said, "we prefer that God's creations not be sacrificed like this, but we appreciate what you gentlemen do."

"Actually, a hundred of them suckers gave their lives this year," Josh said.

Through a large camellia bush, Herman aka "Rolex" aka "Brother John" Bishop III watched the cop talking to the monk and figured he was the subject. One of Bishop's runners was picked up two weeks earlier and held for two days before going back to work on Hilton Head Island. When Bishop found the wire under the man's shirt, he ripped it off and threatened to cut his heart out.

Bishop had not killed anybody but came very close that day. Now he was frustrated. Everything was unraveling. What he didn't know was the feds already had all the evidence needed to indict him under the government's new Drug Kingpin Statute.

If and when they nailed him, Rolex would spend the rest of his life in prison with no chance for parole.

That thought turned Herman's spine to ice.

CHAPTER 35

Stoney Sanders lifted himself out of the pilot's seat of the C-141, shuffled down the crew stairs, dropped into the cargo bay and headed to the rear of the aircraft where the big back doors were wide open.

The passengers had already left for drinks and supper at the officers' club. Stoney told his co-pilot and loadmasters to hop on the crew bus and he'd be along later after checking with maintenance about a rear-hatch warning light that was flickering. As the crew pulled away, a man emerged from a tool shed at the edge of the runway carrying a duffel bag and a rifle.

U.S. warplanes never sit unguarded while on foreign soil, although sometimes the guards themselves are not Air Force issue. Several men with M-16 rifles stood around the aircraft as the man approached the rear of the plane, exchanged a few words, then strolled up the back ramp to where Stoney was standing.

"My friend sends a special gift to *Senor* Stoney," the man said smiling through a scraggly mustache and beard. A marijuana joint jutted from behind his right ear. He dropped the duffel bag at Stoney's feet next to a pallet of Budweiser beer and smiled. "You are *Senor* Stoney, *si?*"

Stoney looked down at the green bag, stuffed and pulled tight, then directly into the man's dark eyes and said, "You sure as shit better hope so, *Poncho.*"

The man fingered his weapon nervously for a moment and returned the stare. "This is no game we're playing, *comprende?*"

"No, no, I mean, yes, yes, uh, *si, si,* I got it. We're cool, man," Stoney stammered. "I'm Lieutenant Colonel Stoney Sanders and welcome aboard my aircraft."

Stoney led the man into the cavernous cargo compartment between the pallets of strapped-down payload. When they reached the platform leading up to the cockpit, Stoney lifted a ladder from the bottom and swung it up. There, behind the steps, was a narrow panel that he popped open with his hand. He stuffed the duffel bag inside the compartment, closed the panel, handed the man an envelope and dropped the crew steps back down into place.

"Remarkable aircraft," Stoney said.

The man looked him in the eye and blinked once.

"Local herb?" Stoney asked, pointing to the fat joint behind the man's right ear.

The man smiled.

"From Colombia. *Es muy bueno, Senor* Stoney. Want some?"

"*Si! Si! Amigo.*"

The man grabbed the joint from behind his ear, twirled it between his fingers and handed it to Stoney, who slid it inside a small zippered sleeve pocket of his flight suit.

"Nice doing business with you, Poncho," Stoney said with a smile.

The man looked at Stoney, blinked once, threw his M-16 across his shoulder, turned, walked to the back of the plane, down the ramp and disappeared into the Caribbean darkness.

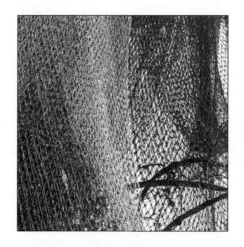

CHAPTER 36

George Burr knew he was in serious danger as he dangled in the shrimp net. He saw the trunk of his Crown Victoria sticking out of the water under the bridge. As soon as he hit the water he removed his pistol belt and boots so he would not drown. Now he was hanging in a trawl trying to reason with a lunatic pointing a loaded .38 between his eyes.

"Where we going, Maceo?"

Maceo turned his head quickly, looked up river and said, "I'm g-going to hell and you're g-going with me."

No telling what Maceo Mazyck would do and George knew it. He'd seen his share of madmen who missed their meds. The tarp comes off completely and the demons emerge full force. But in two decades of chasing crazies, he'd never fired his weapon or had one fired at him.

He enjoyed playing the role of a real cop, riding around in his police cruiser. It made him feel good when the neighborhood children called him Officer George. He liked wearing his uniform, too. It fit his trim body perfectly, and women often flirted with him. They were impressed by his good looks and his small-town charm.

George's own childhood had been a nightmare. His father drove pulpwood trucks, drank a lot and disappeared for long periods of time. He never knew his mother. George and his sister moved out as soon as they were old enough. So George had been around whackos all his life. Some were certified. Some were not.

"OK, Maceo," he said, as he continued to slowly spin in the net. "How about turning this boat around and let's get on down to Cypress Landing. It's not far. We can ride out the storm there, just the two of us. What 'cha think?"

Maceo pulled the trigger and shot George in the right foot, taking off a toe, splattering blood everywhere and putting a hole through the boat.

"Holy Shit, you shot me, you crazy bastard! I'm bleeding. I'm dying! Damn, Maceo, get my ass out of this net and take me to the hospital!"

The crack of the pistol's report reverberated through the silence of the ageless forest. George Burr stared at his bloody foot. His white sock was sopping red. He tried to say something, but passed out from shock before words got to his lips.

"Eighteen," Maceo muttered.

CHAPTER 37

Berkeley Aiken's childhood had not been exactly normal. Neither was her father. Bernard Achem had been a CIA operative since the 1960s when he started and quelled a political coup in southern Africa. His daughter, Berqua Achem, was born in Rhodesia after the Ethiopian uprising in 1961. It was in Rhodesia, now called Zimbabwe, where Bernard met her mother, Makeda, whose family had been assassinated.

A quiet man, Bernard Ishmael Achem began his career as an analyst for the Mossad, the Israeli Political Action and Liaison Department. Eventually, he moved to the Collections Department, which did the dirty work. He'd narrowly escaped the Nazi ovens in Poland, but his parents did not. Bernie Achem, in fact, barely remembered his mother and father, who handed him off to relatives just before they were taken.

Smuggled to America, he was raised in New Jersey by aunts and uncles, educated at Yale and joined the Israeli Army. He was decorated for valor in the Six Day War before returning to the United States, where he earned a law degree at Georgetown University and settled down to raise his family in Charleston, the home of his college roommate, Pierre Darby.

The Darbys, owners of the Charleston Courier newspaper, came from a long line of French Huguenots who settled the Santee River Basin and got rich growing indigo and rice. Bored with plantation life, some moved into Charleston proper and invested in the newspaper, eventually sending their sons off to New England colleges where they intermingled with America's elite. Over time, they became involved with the CIA and piddled in political juntas and other democratic efforts around the world.

Pierre's grandfather and namesake helped Woodrow Wilson fight a clandestine war in Europe when the country's official stance was neutrality. The Darbys also built and maintained a para-military training site on the family's 8,000-acre spread near Billings, Montana, for use by the CIA.

Bernie Aiken, as he was known to the locals, assumed the role of an editorial writer for his friend's newspaper. Occasionally, he wrote op-ed pieces dealing with esoteric issues in the Middle East and along the NATO watchtowers. People waved when he walked down King Street wearing his trademark seersucker suits during hot Charleston summers. But whenever his special talents were needed elsewhere in the world, he told his family he was attending an editorial conference and disappeared for weeks.

Through it all, Bernie raised Berkeley to be a Southern lady, changing her name to help her fit in. Her parents even put aside their Jewish and Muslim heritages and sent their daughter to Bethel United Methodist Church, a few blocks from their Tradd Street home. They seldom attended, but it was a good spiritual environment for Berkeley because Methodists don't keep score.

Everything about her childhood was aimed toward her becoming the wife of someone important, someone with a stable, normal life. But there was a problem. Instead of watching "The Martha Stewart Show," on television, Berkeley got hooked on CNN.

CHAPTER 38

Ashmead let the hot water from the shower pulse on his head, as he stood naked, knowing the answer was not good. His doctor at the Medical University said the results of his blood work were troubling, but not to worry. He would re-run them and get back to him.

But Ashmead knew. His weight was down considerably. His hair had thinned. His energy was drained. Like most of his friends, he treated AIDS as a black problem, primarily among heroin and crack addicts. Needles were never his thing. So he thought he was safe, sort of.

He had been with men whose names he did not know, didn't want to know; men from New York, passing through, looking for fun with a Southern accent. Ashmead was usually available, sitting in the back booth at Henry's — a so-called Charleston blueblood who took on all comers. He had condoms but they never left his dresser drawer. Passion wears no clothes, knows no fear.

But he should have known. Sin never goes unpunished. Perhaps another age, more enlightened, like the Romans, would have allowed light to shine in this dark place. But in his world, his reality, it's a flashlight in the eyes, a stick across the buttocks and a warning to never come back again, ever.

Sometimes Ashmead had talked Junior Jones into participating in three-ways, usually when he was exceptionally trashed. He loved Junior, his blackness, his funny sayings and cavalier attitude about sex. Ashmead hoped to God he wouldn't kill his best friend loving him as he did. He hoped those nights of lust were not a death sentence.

The red blotches on his back and legs were certainly not heat rash, as he tried to convince his mother. And he had not slept in months, which in his mind was worse than death itself. Best to sleep through it all than try and stare it down at 3 a.m. AIDS has no schedule, no conscience, no heart.

As the hot shower water ran down his face, Ashmead cried, not for his own lost soul, but for those he stained along the way. He meant no harm. Honest to God. He was just having fun, which is what he was raised to do.

His crowd always arrived drunk and dissolute. How drunk, how screwed up, how maniacal, how debased, how utterly disgusting can a well-born, well-groomed, well-educated worthless bastard be? There were no rules, really, just a lot of money available to pay for the consequences. Worthwhile charities learned long ago to take their money and wash it well before spreading it around among the less fortunate.

But for Ashmead, it was time to pay for his indulgences. Of all possible fates, his would be priceless, one that could not be bribed or postponed, like cancer, which at least would be an honorable death.

Ashmead's knees weakened, and he fell sobbing onto the shower floor.

CHAPTER 39

Maceo lifted his head up from the steering wheel of the VW bus and was face to face with a great blue heron. The majestic blue and gray bird stood as still as a painting on the bow of the boat trying to determine if Maceo was alive or dead.

It was a tough call. Maceo was drunk, under-medicated and wide awake. A triple threat. When he pulled the pistol up and aimed it at the giant bird, the heron lifted off the bow with a loud squawk, spread its five-foot wingspan and flew elegantly to a perch on the riverbank.

Maceo fired wildly.

"S-s-Seventeen," he said, swaying.

At the aft, George Burr moaned, his right foot wrapped tight with duct tape, as was his mouth. Though storm clouds gathered, the afternoon sun cut a hot streak across the deck. George wriggled into a sliver of shade cast by the rigging. He had decided he was going to die. He just didn't know when. At least he had stopped shaking. Burr learned something that day about himself that almost 20 years in law enforcement had not taught him — he was a coward. The bullet only grazed his toe, causing it to gush blood. Not enough to kill him, although he did go into shock.

It was the first time he had been on the other end of a gun barrel. He had not realized until then the dehumanizing effect it had on people, sane or insane. In the brief moment before the shot was fired, George's body convulsed, completely uncontrollable, totally unnerving. So complete was his fear that he lost control of his bowels.

As he lay on the deck, squirming, he could smell himself, the sweat that covered his body, the blood on his foot, the feces in his pants. He wept. He did not want to die this way.

Maceo staggered toward the stern and looked down at Burr and grinned as orange rays of sunlight slanted across the tops of trees. The first fingers of night clutched the boat from all sides, like willows leaning from the shore.

Later, Maceo steered the Sister close to the west bank to avoid gusting winds. He popped open a can of Viennas and tossed one back toward to George. The meat hit the deck and rolled in the sand and slime. Maceo cut the engine, walked over to George, picked up the sausage, wiped it on his pant leg, ripped the tape from his prisoner's mouth, shoved the meat inside and slapped the tape shut again.

"F-f-feeding t-time at the z-zoo," he said as he looked Burr in the eyes. "J-just like at the h-h-hospital. B-back on the wards, b-b-boss. H-how you like it?"

George felt the sand and grit in his mouth as he swallowed it whole. He gagged several times trying to force the grit through his gullet. But bile bubbled up from his small intestine and gushed through his nose.

"N-n-now you know," Maceo sneered as he turned away. "P-p-pretty sh-sh-shitty, huh?"

CHAPTER 40

At the Folly Beach Pier, a drunk Citadel cadet leaned over the edge of the rail and heaved as a buddy held his belt to keep him from falling into the breakers. College kids started early — around noon — celebrating the first big hurricane of the season. Most had never experienced one.

Below in the roiling Atlantic, four surfers were riding high and "shooting the pier" — a risky maneuver that included dodging the barnacled pilings that held the huge bar and dance hall in place over the ocean's edge. Upstairs, leaning out over a rail, a group of sorority girls from the College of Charleston giggled and pointed at the suntanned surfer boys.

"I'll have one of those to go," gushed Leona, who was sitting at the bar with a group of Santee Cooper secretaries. "I need a big stiff one." The bartender handed out 12-ounce red plastic cups of a potent fruity concoction called a Hurricane, the special of the day.

"I hear cops are going to shut us down before dark. Storm's getting worse and they're worried about lawsuits," he said.

"I propose a toast to some real class action," Leona quipped as she held high her cup. Cheers and laughter spread all the way around the horseshoe bar as a series of exceptionally big waves slammed against the pier sending sea spray over the top rail.

Junior was the only black person on the pier. The janitor had the good sense to not show up for work that day. But Junior was used to being the only black face in a sea of white smiles. He carried a fake Santee Cooper business card that said, "Grover Jones Jr., Token Negro," which never failed to get a few laughs.

He was the only African-American lawyer on the company's payroll. He was one of only three blacks who worked in the entire administration complex, the others being a middle-aged filing clerk and an elderly cleaning lady, who ironed businessmen's shirts on the side.

By late afternoon, the dance floor was full and loud. Junior sat quietly on a stool watching the action as the dark hand of night lowered the shade in the eastern sky.

CHAPTER 41

Stoney Sanders slipped into the side door of the Quonset hut just as Staff Sergeant Perry Barnes delivered his punch line to the mesmerized civilians.

"... And thanks for flying with the U.S. Air Force, Madam!" he said with a flourish.

Everybody at the table convulsed in laughter.

"Oh, atten-hut," Barnes barked, noting Sanders' entry. "Our fearless leader has arrived."

A lieutenant colonel outranks a staff sergeant by a factor of ten and could scold said sergeant fiercely for implied insubordination. But Sanders had been in the Reserves for too long to give a damn.

"As you were, Sergeant," Stoney said with a wave of his hand. "Your fearless leader apologizes for not buying the first round. May I get the next one?"

The World War II vintage metal building they were in served as an officer's mess and non-com roadhouse. The Air Force facility in Antigua would never pass inspection in Washington, and Sgt. Barnes liked it that way. It's part of the beauty of travel, he explained to Berkeley.

A preacher's kid, Perry Barnes grew up in Ridgeville, one of the sawmill villages that ringed the great forests of Santee Cooper Country. He was a shy child, "Indian shy," people used to say. He'd heard his mother was pure Cherokee and his father was a no-count drunk. He never knew either of them.

Perry was adopted in his first year of life by a Pentecostal preacher whose goal in life was to save Perry's savage soul from the Devil. He believed everything he read in the Bible and defended his faith with a razor strap. Consequently, Perry lived in fear as a child. He endured those beatings until he joined the Marines. The recruiter never asked about his scars. Perry celebrated his 17th birthday in boot camp on Parris Island, where he decided somebody would have to kill him to hurt him more than he had suffered at home.

Now he was on the island of Antigua serving as a sergeant in the U.S. Air Force and entertaining civilians. It had been an interesting ride.

"Are you telling war stories again, Sergeant?" Sanders asked. "Perry's a real war hero, y'all. He's got ribbons that four-star generals don't have. Hell, he's got ribbons generals have never seen before!"

The civilians turned their attention back and forth from Sanders to Perry like fans at a tennis match. The ball was in Perry's court, but he wasn't going to play.

"We all serve when called upon, Colonel," Perry said as he fiddled with his fork, trying to avoid the stares. "We all wear the same uniform."

Stoney wasn't satisfied.

"Word in the squadron is you tend to disappear for weeks, sometimes months at a time, Sergeant. Are we so short on loadmasters that they ship you off on special assignments? Somebody said you visited the Kremlin more than the ambassador. Didn't you start out as a Marine, Sergeant? Your personnel folder must be a mess."

Perry searched for a response that would deflect the Colonel's curiosity about his career, but decided to use his favorite line about transferring from the Marine Corps into the Air Force: "This is the only service that sends its officers into battle instead of the enlisted swine."

Stoney Sanders laughed along with the others, then stepped back and offered everyone a snappy salute.

"Well put, Sergeant. Now, last call for the flight crew. Show time is 2100 hours. Destination Ascension Island."

The civilians raised their beer bottles in a toast to a safe journey.

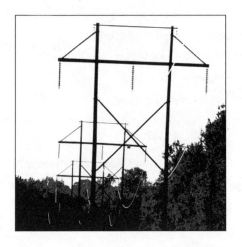

CHAPTER 42

S keeter Simms dialed Junior's beeper number for the fourth time and typed
the same message: "Call office immediately."

Skeeter had been a Santee Cooper lineman for 25 years before a live wire fried
his right arm one night during a thunderstorm. He woke up flat on his back at the
base of a power pole and all he could see was stars, even though the storm clouds
never broke. He could have retired on disability but declined after being offered a
job as an inspector on the Pinopolis Dam.

He liked his new job but missed his "pole cat" buddies, who could walk up a
power pole toting 40 pounds of gear in no time flat. They were like brothers. When
the weather got nasty and the lines went down, they were out there fixing them no
matter what. His favorite tune was "Wichita Lineman."

It was gone in a flash. There was no such thing as a one-armed pole cat and he
didn't listen to music much anymore. But his wife, Odethia, was happy that Skeeter
had recovered and still had a job. Being a dam inspector was safer, too, she liked
to remind her husband. Unless, of course, the dam broke.

* * *

The light on Junior Jones' beeper illuminated the glove compartment of his
company car parked outside the Folly Beach Pier. Junior was otherwise engaged.

Intoxicated, actually, on liquor and Leona's luscious legs. She was dancing with Santee Cooper's new vice president of risk management, a handsome Midwesterner who wore a three-piece suit to the pier party. Leona was unbuttoning the big guy's vest and Junior decided to get a closer look.

"You two having a private party or would you like to add a little local color?" Junior asked over the sounds of Southern beach music. The three of them laughed and huddled and swayed to the beat of a tune titled "I Who Have Nothing" by a local band called the Melody Makers. By the time it got to the second chorus, Leona had her hand halfway down the front of Junior's pants.

* * *

Skeeter didn't know who to call next. As Santee Cooper's interim director of disaster preparedness, he knew that in the case of an emergency he was supposed to first notify Quentin Robinson, the chief engineer, and then Stoney Sanders, the head of public affairs. But Quentin wasn't home, Stoney was out of the country and Junior Jones, who was covering for Sanders, didn't answer his beeper.

Unfazed, Skeeter propped his feet up on his desk, ate his sandwich and stared out along the spine of the dam, a 138-foot tall concrete-and-dirt structure that stretched a mile along the east side of Lake Moultrie. The Santee Cooper complex included a five-turbine power plant and a 70-foot-tall lock that lifted boats up and down between the Tailrace Canal and the lower lake.

The dam held back 400 trillion gallons of water in the 94-square-mile Lake Moultrie reservoir, which doubled as a hydro-electric power source and inland fishing and boating Mecca. Few people gave a second thought about the worst-case scenario.

The first person to notice the warning light on the dam's aging monitoring system was Wendell Metzger, who drank coffee from a Thermos and seldom said anything to anybody. But when Wendell spoke, people listened.

"Got a blinker."

"Where?" Skeeter asked, putting down his sandwich.

"Quad four."

"Has it happened before?" Skeeter asked.

"Only once, 10 years ago. False alarm."

"What caused it?"

"Bad wiring."

"Think that's what this is?"

"Maybe."

"Call down to Maintenance. Get somebody up here to check it out," Skeeter said.

"OK."

"By the way, Wendell, what exactly does that flashing light mean?"

"Breach," Wendell muttered.

Skeeter had been to a seminar in Columbia a few months earlier where a skinny bureaucrat wearing wire-rim glasses laid out the possibilities of dam break and what might happen. The man said a 50-foot-tall wall of water would roll like a tsunami down the Cooper River, knocking down bridges and buildings and drowning everything in its path until it reached the Atlantic. Charleston, the man said, would be under at least nine feet of water within two hours.

Skeeter tossed the remainder of his sandwich in a trashcan and walked out of his office atop the dam and over to the rail, gazed down the line again and wondered if that nerdy bureaucrat knew what he was talking about.

CHAPTER 43

M aceo dropped the makeshift anchor at the last bend in the Cooper River before the Pinopolis Dam. The line screamed out until the weight hit bottom. The rope soon became taut and the boat settled against the current at midstream. The sun was setting behind the pines as a pair of ospreys swept past on the swirling wind.

Maceo envied the graceful hawk-like birds that mated for life. He admired their ability to hover over fish before diving feet first and snagging them in their powerful talons. He often sat in the shade of one of his umbrellas and watched a large cast of South Carolina's wetland birds — ospreys, herons, gulls, pelicans, ibises, cormorants — as they passed overhead in formation in assigned flight paths. He wondered why the birds never collided.

He wished people would go about their daily lives without crossing paths too; that he could walk past the men who gathered in front of Frazier's Store and not be harassed by them. He wished that he could hover like an osprey so he could see Eleanor's station wagon coming.

She came once a month to give Maceo his injection, but this time she was late. It took her longer than usual that morning to put on her makeup. Ronnie, her boyfriend, had backhanded her the night before and left a nasty bruise below her right eye. Ronnie was drunk, again, and she tried to reason with him. She got her psychology degree from Coastal Carolina University and was trying to use it.

As she stood alone on the banks of Schitt Creek and looked for Maceo's boat, Eleanor felt the pain of her bruised face and the hopelessness of her life. Everything, it seemed at that moment, disappeared with the tide. Maceo, his brothers and even the Gullah girl were gone. The store was closed. No one sat under the old oak tree and the grandfather's face on the tattered billboard was flapping wildly in the wind.

Out in the water she saw what looked like a body floating facedown. But when she looked again, it was gone. It began to rain, so she walked slowly to her car, got in, adjusted the rearview mirror, checked her makeup and cried.

CHAPTER 44

Brent Lee kissed his wife and watched his family back out of the driveway in their silver, second-hand mini-van. They were headed for higher ground.

Cocky, the family dog, smashed his nose against the side window as Brent waved goodbye. He could have gone with them but didn't want to miss the show. Federal agents were closing the net on Herman "Rolex" Bishop. As the van rounded the corner, a black Honda fell in close behind, but Brent never saw it. Thinking that his family was safely on the road to his mother-in-law's house in North Carolina, he went inside his house and placed a call to Sid Rice.

"How close are we?" he asked his boss.

"Close," Rice responded.

"You want me downtown?"

"No, stay where you are, and keep your radio handy. I might need you later tonight, so be ready."

Brent walked into the kitchen and opened the refrigerator. Stacia left some pot roast and grilled chicken for him. A box of Krispy Kreme doughnuts was on the kitchen counter along with a note : "You can eat them all. I love you. S"

Brent loved Krispy Kremes and joked that the first time he tasted one, he knew he wanted to go into law enforcement. He broke the seal on the cellophane box, lifted the cover, fingered a soft, warm doughnut and took a bite. The combination of sugar and fried dough satisfied something deep within his soul. The crack cocaine of the South, he thought.

He finished the first one in three bites and downed another one without thinking. He was reaching for the third when he heard the neighbor's dog bark out back. Licking his fingers, he walked slowly to the sliding glass door and scanned the yard for movement. The neighbor's mutt was trying to dig under the fence. Then he saw a boot sticking out from behind his riding lawn mower. A military boot.

Stepping back, Brent reached for his gun, slammed in a clip and scooped up his radio.

"Base, this is Gamecock One," he whispered as he pressed the transmit button. "Do you read me, Sid?"

"This is Base," Sid replied. "What's up, Bo?"

"An unidentified in my backyard," Brent said, stooping down behind the kitchen counter.

"Want me to call the cops?" Sid asked.

"Naw. Not yet."

"Roger, Standing by."

Brent crawled into the living room, slipped out the front door and back along the fence with his gun raised and ready to fire. He thought about the mysterious speedboat in the Edisto River and decided it was no accident. Reaching down, he picked up a rock and tossed it toward the aluminum tool shed. As it clanged off the metal roof, a kid with a power-pump water soaker stepped out from behind the building.

"No fair throwing rocks," the boy said.

Brent aimed his pistol directly at the child's forehead.

"Drop it!" Brent shouted.

The kid dropped his plastic water gun.

"Who the hell are you?"

"I'm Tommy Keller. I live behind you. My friends and I are playing Army."

Brent lowered his weapon, slipped it in his front pocket and walked toward Tommy, who was soon surrounded by four other boys, each armed and laughing and squirting each other.

"Where'd you get those boots, son?" Brent asked.

"They're my dad's. He was in 'Nam. Said I could have them when I got big enough."

Brent shook his head, managed a smile and walked back into his house. The phone was ringing.

CHAPTER 45

Herman "Rolex" Bishop sat in a Jeep at the end of a grass runway of what used to be Sampit Plantation near Hell Hole Swamp. Nobody came to Hell Hole unless they were cruising timber, lost or running from the law.

Owned by the Winthrop family of Boston, Sampit was a 23,000-acre long-leaf pine plantation. Crooners Bing Crosby and Phil Harrison used to fly in for long weekends shooting quail and poking prostitutes at the Wampee Lodge. Normally, Rolex would not be seen at one of his drop sites. But this time was different.

He heard the hum of his custom-made Douglas DC-3. The old tail dragger was World War II vintage and still dependable. Government officials never thought the aircraft would still be flying today in the war on drugs — especially for the other side. With a range of almost a thousand miles, and capable of short-field landings and take-offs on unconventional airstrips, it was the drug dealer's transport plane of choice.

As Rolex watched the landing lights get brighter, he glanced at a black suitcase on the back seat of the Jeep. Inside was enough pharmaceutical-grade cocaine to keep him in senoritas and tequila sunrises for the rest of his life. And, this time tomorrow, if all went well, three 18-wheelers, fake fuel tanks crammed with cash, would clear Customs and meet him in his new home of Veracruz.

Rolex considered trying to move his entire operation to Mexico, but decided against it. He'd made 50 fortunes already. Why risk it for more? As the airplane circled in preparation for landing, Rolex grabbed the suitcase, walked to the end of the grassy runway and ignited a railroad flare.

CHAPTER 46

B rent had never seen a custom-made aircraft like the old DC-3 that sat idling at Hawthorne Air Services adjacent to Charleston International Airport. When Sid called and said to meet him, he had no idea they were going for a flight — especially in a plane like this, in weather like this.

Perfectly restored, it once belonged to a mafia don in French Lick, Indiana, a hot springs resort frequented by Chicago mobsters. The plane had leather seats and ivory inlaid paneling. As the team of drug agents lifted off into the blustery Carolina night, Brent looked down on Interstate-26, a wide concrete ribbon that stretched from Charleston to Columbia to Asheville, N.C. Traffic was bumper to bumper as residents fled the approaching storm. Somewhere on that road, he thought, Stacia, Graycen and Grant were in the mini-van halfway to grandma's house.

As clouds obscured his view, the old plane climbed without strain.

"Intel says this could be it," Rice said to the agents on board, carefully handing each one a black-and-white photo of Herman "Rolex" Bishop III. "This man is wanted under our new kingpin statute. If we do this right, he'll walk right into our arms and we'll put this fat sum-bitch away for good."

Brent's heart was banging like the bells of St. Michael's on the inside of his chest.

"The Air Force was going to give us AWACS support but scrubbed it due to weather," Rice continued. "We're on our own, men. But nobody's expecting us. Least of all Mr. Bishop."

CHAPTER 47

George Burr's right foot throbbed and he worried about infection. But Maceo Mazyck was in no hurry to get him medical attention.

Two larger boats passed by Maceo's shrimp boat within an hour. He stared at them blankly and twitched. George knew madness when he saw it. He'd spent 20 years working on Bull Street and had seen it all. Schizophrenia was bad. Paranoia made it worse; a storm swirled in Maceo's brain.

Maceo shook his head in a futile attempt to gain his balance. He heard something in the wind — a whimpering. He looked toward the shore and saw someone in the water among the willows that hung out over the river. It was a woman, clinging to a limb and facing up as water rushed over the length of her body. She slowly lost her grip, her arm outstretched, her slender fingers reaching, reaching, and then she was gone.

Santee Mazyck's rape and murder had haunted Maceo for as long as he could remember. His grandfather made sure of that. The old man told the story over and over again, each time adding a little more detail: Sister's song, Sister's screams, Sister's rape, Sister's pleas for her life, Sister's murder and the deathly silence that followed.

Maceo tried to erase these things from his clouded mind. But he could not do it. And each episode ended the same way, with Santee's face disappearing into the deep and her outstretched hand and fingers reaching out, always.

As Maceo stared into his madness, George scrutinized the pistol that his captor held in his hand. How many bullets are left? Can I wrench it from his grip? Will he shoot me in the back of my head, or will it happen face to face? George had no clue, and his strength was fading.

Maceo twitched once, twice, grabbed the gun with both hands and spun around as if someone had walked up behind him. It was only the wind. But with each gust, each jangle of the rigging, each creak of the old wooden boat, he turned and aimed but did not fire. He stalked from bow to stern and from stern to bow for what seemed like hours to George. Maceo mumbled continuously, pounded his head violently with the palm of his left hand as if he were trying to knock some sense into himself. He bellowed incomprehensible curses toward the heavens when he slipped in George's feces and vomit. He reached over, took a swipe of the slime in his left hand and rubbed it through his own hair. The stench attracted gulls that circled and squawked and dove close to the stern. One clawed at Maceo's head and the madman turned and fired wildly into the air as the flock of birds dispersed momentarily.

"S-s-s-sixteen," Maceo said.

George tried to count the spent rounds: One in his foot, one at the blue heron, another at the gull. Can't be the first time he's fired the gun. How many bullets does the clip hold? Twelve? Twenty?

Maceo, now grasping an opened black umbrella in one hand and the gun in the other, sat on the deck and stared at George. The madman slowly turned the barrel of the pistol towards George and said, "W-w-with one p-p-pull of this trig-g-ger I can bl-o-o-ow you to hell w-where you and all the rest of them c-c-cops at B-b-Bull Street belong."

George tried to clear his throat so he could speak. Sure, he thought, some of his colleagues had taken the stick to a patient or two. But those patients were crazy and didn't listen and the stick got their attention.

Maceo remembered what it was like breathing with cracked ribs. The guards on the night shift were the worst, especially when they'd been drinking. They kicked and beat him with sticks and tormented him and laughed, always slamming the door on their way out. The nurses were guilty, too. It was the nurses that always let the guards in, then looked the other way.

Maceo aimed the gun at Burr's left foot and fired.

"F-f-fifteen."

CHAPTER 48

The drone of the night flight east across the Atlantic put all the passengers to sleep except Berkeley Aiken, wedged in her seat between the car dealer and local mayor, both snoring like old men in a barbershop.

She thumbed through a magazine but could not concentrate. So she tried meditation, closing her eyes and clearing her mind, a transcendental technique she developed not long after becoming a motherless child. Her mother's name, Markeda, was her mantra and the source of her strength. As much as she loved her father and sought to emulate him, it was her mother's wherewithal that impressed her most.

Markeda Aiken was a princess, her father often said, and indeed she looked the part — dark eyes set perfectly in a face that could be Cleopatra's, the mysterious queen of the ancients, the perfect combination of femininity, beauty, authority and beneficence. There was no company her mother did not improve.

Berkeley was only 13 when Markeda died. She needed her mother more than ever at that time when her body's transformation from childhood to womanhood began. Her father did the best he could to help Berkeley adjust, but he couldn't be with her constantly. He was often away on assignment.

It was also a time when boys began looking at her differently, as if she no longer was a playmate but more like a plaything. She remembered kissing one for the first time and liking it immensely, but she was not sure what to do next and had no one she could talk to about it. She struggled to remain her father's little girl and to excel as a student, shine as a debutante and succeed as a sorority girl.

It was a difficult balancing act. While she never thought she was as pretty as her mother or as smart as her father, Berkeley Aiken possessed a natural beauty, a vibrant, engaging curiosity and a comfortable demeanor that served her well. She pondered all this while sitting there between those sonorous, snorting, wheezing old men.

She remembered the loadmaster said earlier that the original C-141 was extended 22 feet to allow for in-air refueling; that engineers figured out how to do it without affecting the plane's integrity. She had been curious about this sort of thing ever since she was in high school at Ashley Hall. She took Professor Penn Hagood's military history course, an unlikely class for a private girls' school, but quite popular.

So she got up from her seat and headed aft to search for signs of the extended section of the lumbering craft. As Berkeley slowly slid her palms along the walls of the plane feeling for welding marks, she saw Sgt. Perry Barnes crouched behind one of the tarp-draped pallets staring at something on the floor. His face was strangely illuminated. His skin tanned brown like leather. His features were handsome, like a fox, she thought, and his hair was dark and glistened like an otter out of water. He turned toward her and his eyes met hers. His were as rich and as brown as her mother's, Berkeley thought, as rich and as brown as her own.

She had talked with Perry Barnes earlier in the day and she liked what she saw then as well as now. His aura was magisterial — but not of this world — like that of an old soul, a story untold. As she moved close to him, he held up his right hand, cautioning her to approach with care. He pointed to the floor of the cargo bay. That's where Berkeley saw a strange glow and cut her eyes back toward Perry, who cupped his hand to her ear and whispered, "St. Elmo's Fire."

She looked back down at the fist-sized ball of blue luminescence hovering between two large pallets. Like ancient sailors who first noted the phenomenal glow, Berkeley and Perry stood spellbound in the darkness, transfixed on the gaseous, glowing sphere that appeared from nowhere as the plane streaked through the night at 35,000 feet.

"It's an atmospheric electrical field," Perry said. "Nobody seems to know how or why it shows up like this."

The glowing orb slipped between them and up the far wall before vanishing.

"Pretty cool, huh?" Perry said.

"Yeah," Berkeley said with a warm smile. "Got any more magic tricks?"

CHAPTER 49

S toney Sanders sat in the cockpit and punched new coordinates into the flight computer that would guide the Starlifter through the night to Ascension's Wide Awake Airfield. A rising sun usually greets Charleston-based C-141s as pilots negotiate the short and narrow runway. Better be wide-awake when doing so, the story goes.

"Two hours, six minutes to destination," Stoney said to co-pilot John Buckston. "How about you take the ship so I can take a stroll."

Major Buckston straightened his headset and glanced across the instrument panel. "Co-pilot has the aircraft, Sir."

Sanders hoisted himself out of his seat, climbed down the crew ladder and entered a small latrine at the front of the cargo bay. As he stood there, he felt the gentle sway of the airplane speeding through the darkness, the big jet engines constantly churning, ever faithful. He thought about how little he was in the big picture; a puppet on a string, a delivery boy who hauled things — machines, ammo, canned beans, beer, bar soap, whatever it took to make the world a safer place; a lackey of some star-laden general sitting in a control room in a secret mountain somewhere.

Stoney wondered if anyone actually was in charge since so many flights are disrupted by last-minute changes in scheduling — the biggest inconvenience for being in the system. That's how the pilots and crew describe their bit parts — "being in the system." Once airborne, they're in the system, always subject to somebody else's whim. Stoney lost count of the times he sat on the tarmac at Rhine Mien Air Base in Germany, ready for a straight shot home, and the radio cracked and new orders were issued: Divert to Homestead, Fla., to pick up passengers; drop in on Thouley in Greenland to get pallets and deliver to McGuire Air Base, N.J.

The crew never complained openly about being jacked around, but always groaned. Nobody in Central Command cared that they were Reservists; that they had jobs back home and were expected to report to them as usual on Monday mornings.

As Sanders left the latrine he saw Berkeley and Perry huddled back near the cargo bay. They were smiling and laughing and way too cozy, the colonel decided. Berkeley rose first and inched forward through the pallets toward her seat. Stoney met her half way.

"Everything okay?" he asked.

"Yes sir. I was just talking with your 'load' back there," she giggled. "Sergeant Barnes said to call him a load rather than a loadmaster. Very interesting group of people, Colonel."

"Yes ma'am," Sanders snapped back. "Enlisted men are the riff-raff of the Air Force, ma'am. Unlike officers, these particular ones possess common sense and therefore bear considerable watching. They are not to be trusted. That's why we make them salute, so we can see their hands at all times."

Berkeley played along with Sanders' ego. "And to think I sat there and let that awful little man talk to me about personal things like jet lag and the meaning of life when I could have been in the cockpit with a gentleman such as yourself learning about landing gear assembly and glide ratios."

Sanders smirked. "Can I get you something to eat, something to drink? We'll be there in a few hours. Don't want to land on an extinct volcano on an empty stomach."

"I'm fine, thank you," Berkeley said, "although I would like to interview the pilot, if you've got a minute?"

"Sure thing," he said, unconsciously tightening the belly straps on his flight suit. "Where?"

"Over next to the crew ladder. Not as noisy."

Berkeley reached into her travel bag and pulled out a tape recorder the size of a cigar box. "No need to wake up Bob for this one. I'll use this recorder for voice-overs."

"Good," Stoney said, smoothing his hair again with his hand. "I don't have a good side, anyway."

"That's what I've heard," Berkeley said without smiling.

CHAPTER 50

While Stoney Sanders bragged about piloting his C-141 workhorse, a WC-130 lifted off from Keesler Air Force in Biloxi, Mississippi on a special mission. At the controls of the big turbo-prop was Major Bonnie Bezner, an Air Force Reserve pilot with 1,200 hours flying time into and out of hurricanes.

She was a member of the 53rd Weather Reconnaissance Squadron, the only unit in the United States Air Force that did such work. It was a special assignment for Bezner, commander of an all-female crew. The co-pilot was Lieutenant Allyson Rhea and the five crew-women were enlisted technicians. Newspaper photographers and TV cameras recorded their departure, "The first time an all-girl crew has manned this type mission, pardon the pun," a local reporter said.

"His name is Hugo," Bonnie said into her helmet microphone as the plane climbed to a cruising altitude of 16,000 feet over the Gulf of Mexico, "which is French and masculine. Glad they finally decided to give these storms men's names. We girls were getting a bad reputation of destroying things for no particular reason. Truth is, we always have a reason," which brought a smile to everyone on the flight. For the next eleven hours they would pierce Hugo's armor and monitor the temperature and other aspects of the storm.

What started as a heat-stoked wave off the west coast of Africa five days earlier had been stirred by the Earth's rotation and twisted into a powerful tropical storm with winds at 50 miles per hour. That's when the National Weather Service assigned it a computer-generated name.

"The screen watchers say Hugo has potential to be monster," Bonnie added. "Steering currents are aligned for an East Coast hit. He could turn out, though. Never know."

Bonnie, an Air Force Academy graduate, always wanted to be an F-16 jet jockey, but finding flight school an unfriendly place for women, she settled for bulky cargo planes that flew into places that were even more obscure than the Moon. Planes like the WC-130 Hercules; places like the core of killer hurricanes.

Just the thought of penetrating the eye-wall of a Category 4 hurricane with winds averaging 150 miles an hour made her thighs tingle. Of course, she couldn't say that out loud. The Air Force was a man's world and always would be. Men could joke about rough-and-tumble "hard-dick landings" and the like. Not so for the ladies.

Bonnie knew she had to be careful applying her skills in the cockpit and being one of the boys at the bar back at the base. But she always kept her colleagues at arm's length. Besides, she had a steady boyfriend — Alex, her Maine coon cat, who weighed 20 pounds and ate almost that much daily.

Alex was home and waiting for her safe return, Bonnie thought as she readied herself to rendezvous with a killer.

CHAPTER 51

A steady wind blew in off the harbor clattering the high palmetto fronds as Ashmead Dawes sat listening on a park bench in White Point Garden. He watched the moon rise in breaks behind black clouds and people scurrying into the wind along the High Battery. They were getting a feel for the approaching storm before deciding whether to hunker down or flee.

"Hugo" is an odd name for a hurricane, Ashmead thought. "Ashmead" is an odd name too, he reminded himself. He would turn 40 tomorrow, September 21, 1989. Turning 40 is a checkpoint along life's highway, a time to measure his successes and failures.

While 40 is young for a banker, it's old for a baseball player. Both are in the prime of their lives, but one profits from experience while the other only remembers it. Same goes for bureaucrats and ballerinas. But Ashmead was none of them. He was a well-educated dope pusher refined by the pleasantries of an aristocratic Southern upbringing, learned in the ways of the law, but worthless except to his clients, many of them dead, dying or waiting to do so while wasting away in jail.

Now the joint federal and state drug task force was closing in on Ashmead, many of his friends and lovers were infected with AIDS, and he was miserable. There was a time when business and pleasure were a perfect mix for him. One begot the other, the difference being he charged for one and did the other for free.

Ashmead searched through the clouds for a glimpse of the North Star while he considered his pedigree. He thought about his Charleston ancestors — the women and children who sat nervously in the parlors of their mansions as Yankee shells rained down on the city during the Civil War while their husbands and fathers and sons in tattered gray uniforms were worn down, undernourished and spread thin from Louisiana to Richmond in a hopeless effort to turn back the invaders.

Ashmead, like most of his friends, grew up fascinated with the firing on Fort Sumter in Charleston Harbor at the start of the war, the devastating defeat of the Confederates, the spitefulness of the Yankee conquerors, the insatiable greed of the carpetbaggers and scalawags, the fear of retribution by the freed masses of former slaves and the insult his people endured for 14 years of so-called Reconstruction. He also wondered about the secret lives of some of his Confederate heroes. Surely homosexuals were in the ranks of those glorious men in gray. He certainly would have served had he been around back then.

As a modern Rebel, however, he no longer held his childhood grudge against Northerners. Many were his neighbors now. They lived downtown, shopped at the Harris Teeter on East Bay, belonged to the Carolina Yacht Club, sent their daughters to Ashley Hall and their sons to Porter Gaud. Their children were his customers, and some of them his lovers.

As a police car slowly passed by on Murray Boulevard, Ashmead uncrossed his skinny legs left over right, then re-crossed them right over left, and stared at the cop who was staring at him. Such self-righteous, hypocritical bastards, Ashmead thought. They just love to bust queers having a little fun among the spiked cannons and granite monuments in White Point Garden.

Some police officers were gay, too, but like professional athletes, they couldn't be open about it. They'd be banned from the playing fields and locker rooms of life. Ashmead tried to draw some spit for the cop who was eyeing him. But Ashmead's mouth was hopelessly dry. His entire body felt that way. He could not swallow without pain. He cried without tears.

So he just sat there on the battery bench, searching for stars and slowly dying, wondering who would be the first to find him and what his people would think. Would it be a tourist out for a morning run? Or perhaps a homeless person searching for a place to sleep would stumble upon his body. Maybe Hurricane Hugo's storm surge would wash him out to sea and no one would ever know what happened to him.

Ashmead didn't care. He did not care about anything anymore. So he stuck his right hand into his pants pocket, pulled out his father's old .38 special and turned its barrel snuggly to his chest. He glanced back at the bandstand where he and Junior held each other on another night in his hometown, another night, when the air was saturated with the aroma of oleander and salty sea spray. Then he pulled the trigger.

CHAPTER 52

It was dusk on the Cooper River when Maceo Mazyck wrapped more duct tape to stop the bleeding on George Burr's other wounded foot. But the Bull Street cop passed out anyway. Maceo's more immediate problem was the gaping hole in the bottom of the boat created when the bullet ripped off his captive's toe en route to the bottom of the river.

Looking down into the shrimp boat's hold, Maceo watched the water streaming in, listing the vessel toward her port side. He flipped the switch for the bilge pump, which was too slow to keep up with the steady flow. So he went to the bow and winched up the engine block from the river bottom to head upstream. The movement of the boat might slow the leak. Perhaps he would run aground on a sandbar and keep her from sinking.

His mind was a jumble of thoughts where people like Eleanor and Sister Santee became blurred in the murkiness. His stomach was a sour mash of Vienna Sausages, sardines and George Dickel Tennessee whisky. So he held the bottle to his lips, turned back his head and sucked down another slug. Suddenly, he saw something moving along the riverbank. As he focused on the darkening forest, he heard whistles and calls of what sounded like men, and then saw them moving through the mist. They wore buckskins and carried flintlocks.

Maceo had heard stories about a Revolutionary War general called the "Swamp Fox" and his brigade of men, both black and white, who time and again terrorized the British before disappearing into the Lowcountry swallows of sweet gums, laurel oaks and cypress trees. Maceo saw a silhouette of the famous general astride his faithful steed. The smoke from the men's smudge pots lingered low while the gray moss swayed subtly in the gloom of the swamp.

Maceo blinked, and it all went away. Darkness enveloped the *Sister Santee* and the moon winked from behind the rolling clouds while Maceo piloted the boat up the silvery ribbon of river that snaked its way through the forests toward the massive Santee Cooper dam. Maceo flipped on a small transistor radio mounted in the dashboard of the VW bus and slowly turned the tuning knob. He settled on a station out of Nashville playing Andy Williams' version of "Moon River."

The madman smiled.

CHAPTER 53

Stacia Lee clutched her children close to her as she struggled to figure out where they were and where they were going. She had taken Graycen and Grant with her into the ladies room at the rest area on Interstate Highway 26 just south of Columbia. As they returned to the car, two men grabbed her from behind, cupped her mouth and nose with a chloroform-soaked rag and dragged her and the children into a delivery van.

Now all three were bound together in the bedroom of a log cabin and Graycen was crying.

"Shut that kid up or I'll shut her up for you," a voice from the next room boomed.

Stacia leaned her head forward, feeling the drug's lingering effects, and put her forehead close to Graycen's face.

"Please be quiet, baby," she whispered. "Mommy's here. Everything's going to be all right."

But she knew everything was not all right. Surely it had something to do with her husband's new job and that black boat which almost rammed them on the river the day before.

Grant, the youngest, awoke, and started to cry.

"OK, children," Stacia said in her best kindergarten teacher's voice. "We're playing a little game called cops and robbers."

"Mommy, are we the cops or the robbers?" Grant asked.

"We're the prisoners," she said. "But soon the cops, including Daddy, will rescue us from the robbers."

"Who are the robbers?" Graycen queried.

"They're the bad guys," Stacia said, scrunching up her face to give her words more meaning.

"But don't worry because Daddy's on his way to save us just in time."

"Just in time before what?" Grant asked.

"Not sure about that," Stacia whispered, "but he'll be here, just like on television."

CHAPTER 54

B rent Lee felt his stomach flip as the DC-3 hit an air pocket on its descent toward the grass airfield at Sampit Plantation. By instinct, he fingered the safety on the rifle lying across his lap. Looking around in the darkness of the passenger cabin, he saw the silhouettes of five other agents, all armed and braced for landing. Up front, sitting next to the pilot, was Sid Rice, his face illuminated by the green glow of the instrument panel. Behind him was another man, whose face he could not see in the shadows.

On the ground, a single railroad flare burned brightly, giving the pilot a target for landing. The 2,000-foot runway was rarely used and pockmarked with holes dug by gopher turtles. Deer, temporarily blinded by the landing lights, darted across the strip. Frank Glenn, a former chopper pilot in Vietnam, could fly anything and proved it time and again to his government handlers. After they caught him two years ago bringing hashish into Owens Field in Columbia, he agreed to provide personal piloting services to avoid jail time.

"I see somebody standing at the end of the runway," Glenn said. "Don't know if others are in the woods."

Sid Rice kept his eyes on the runway, hoping Rolex hadn't been tipped off. Anytime you're negotiating with drug dealers, there's likelihood of a double-cross.

He also knew that no matter how much planning went into an operation such as this, at least 10 percent of the people involved would not get the message. That margin of error could be deadly.

Rice and his agents had been on Herman Bishop's trail for 12 months, slowly closing in, hoping he'd try to make a run for it. With the help of informants, they knew exactly when, where and how he intended to get away.

Rice planned to have him walk right into their trap, nice and easy. No shooting.

Nobody gets hurt. All they had to do was land the plane, taxi up to Bishop and welcome him aboard.

"You ready, Congressman?" Rice said to the man sitting in the dark behind him.

"Ready," John Rhett said.

CHAPTER 55

Rolex waited restlessly. A lightning bolt illuminated the sky and he felt a tightening in his gut, a sure sign that something was amiss. He could see the plane coming in and knew something wasn't right.

He'd had the same feeling before when things got dicey down at the docks. He instinctively knew when the cops were too close or somebody was about to screw him. While he made millions running drugs, he'd lost almost that much again to people who ripped him off. Some of them got their brains bashed when he caught up with them. Most just slithered away, not worth the effort.

Herman Bishop's first and most important rule was not to go to jail. He'd let a lot of things slide because of this. He also vowed never to kill a cop. He knew what happened to cop killers. He also knew he wouldn't last a week in prison. He was too plump, too desirable. Besides, too many of his ex-associates were in there waiting to get even with him.

While his original plan was to stay in Charleston until Christmas and take advantage of the holiday sales, he knew someone was setting him up. He couldn't figure out who it was or where it was, but he knew it. Now he wanted out. If he could just get away with one last load, he'd never show his face in South Carolina again. He'd have enough money to live happily in Mexico or Guatemala or maybe even Buenos Aires for the rest of his life.

As the wheels of the DC-3 touched down on the grass field, the plane's landing lights reflected off Rolex's glasses. Standing alongside the runway, between two tall pine trees, Rolex bent slightly, picked up the suitcase and stepped out into the open.

Frank Glenn turned the tail-dragger around and taxied toward his passenger. Dry grass flew in every direction as he gunned the starboard engine. The aircraft rolled steadily across the field.

Rolex studied the aircraft he had owned for five years and used on numerous drug drops. With its aluminum fuselage, the DC-3 was light — perfect for short-field landings and take-offs. When empty it bounced on its rubber wheels when crossing bumpy terrain. Herman had joked with his pilots about it, said it was like a carnival ride at the State Fair. They preferred to fly the plane with a heavy load because it handled so much better on the ground and in the air.

Rolex eyed the cockpit window, looking for Bud Willis, his regular pilot, who was actually sitting in the Charleston County Jail. Dawn would break any minute now. But squinting through the fading glare of the landing lights, Rolex saw a pilot in aviator sunglasses wearing a cowboy hat, just like Willis always wore. But something was wrong. The plane should be bouncing. It should be empty.

Rolex took one step backward, fingering the suitcase. As the DC-3 rolled to a stop, the side door fell open and the stairs unfolded to the ground. He pretended to wave to the pilot, shoved his hand into his coat pocket and pulled out a handgun with a silencer.

The first shot went through the plane's door and hit John Rhett in the left shoulder. The second shattered the windshield and the third flattened the airplane's left tire. As Rhett fell back, several federal agents scrambled over him and exited the aircraft. Unable to see through the windshield, Sid Rice jumped out of the co-pilot's seat and opened the escape hatch on the roof of the cockpit. He popped up, lowered his M-16 to where Rolex had been standing and fired three bursts. But Rolex had already disappeared into the forest.

Brent Lee's feet hit the ground as the pilot shut down the engines. An eerie quiet surrounded him. Then, off in the distance, he heard the winding of a Jeep's gears fading into the night. Brent found the remains of the suitcase in the woods, cocaine splattered on the ground and half way up a pine tree. Herman Bishop apparently was running away from the airstrip when a round from one of Sid Rice's three M-16 bursts hit the suitcase and the hollow-point cartridge exploded on impact.

"That's a million bucks worth of coke," Brent said when Rice arrived with a bigger searchlight. "Have you got a crime-scene crew on the way?"

Brent kicked the undergrowth with his right foot, getting cocaine powder all over his boots. He also noticed a book of matches that was burned around the edges, and picked it up.

"Son of a bitch," Rice said. "Wonder what spooked him?"

Brent didn't know what made the fat boy run, but noticed Jeep tracks and motioned for his men to mark them for the lab technicians.

"Don't take it personally, boss," Brent said. "We'll flush this piece of shit. He ain't that smart. After all, he went to Clemson."

The levity loosened the tight corners of Rice's grimace. He looked up at his friend, attempted a smile and said, "You're right, pal."

Another agent walked up, whispered something in Rice's ear, then ran back to the plane. Rice's smile quickly faded. He looked Brent straight in the eyes and said, "They got Stacia and the kids."

Brent stuffed the burned matchbook in his pocket, his knees buckled and he dropped to the forest floor.

CHAPTER 56

Junior woke up with Leona stretched naked across the bottom of the bed and a Citadel cadet snoring loudly on the floor against the wall, a blue plastic pot bong between his legs. At first, Junior didn't know where he was. He could hear waves crashing in the distance and the closer sounds of passing cars. The room was dark and dingy and reeked of sex, cigarette smoke and stale alcohol.

As Junior reached for his watch on the nightstand, he knocked an empty glass onto the floor next to the cadet. The noise startled him.

"What?" the boy croaked and opened his eyes, which darted around the room.

"Good morning!" Junior chimed, leaning over and looking the blonde-headed young man in the face. "I'm your drill sergeant, boy. Your black drill sergeant, boy. Now get your ass up off the deck and give me 20. Now!"

Instinctively, the cadet assumed the push-up position and began pumping his body up and down and counting, "One, drill sergeant, two, drill sergeant ..."

Junior rolled back laughing on the bed. It took three more push-ups before the cadet realized where he was, or rather, wasn't.

"What happened?" he asked as he dropped his chest to the grimy carpet.

"The party went into overtime, boy," Junior said. "You had a great time."

The cadet sat up, rubbed his eyes and asked, "What day is it?"

"Could be Wednesday," Junior replied. "But it feels like Monday, don't it?"

The cadet scrambled to his feet and gathered up his uniform as he headed for the door.

"Who's she?" he asked, looking back at Leona.

"My wife, and I'll kill you if I find out you got anything off her last night. And then I'm going over to that dinky little military school of yours and tell everybody that you got drunk and sucked my black dick."

The boy jerked on his pants, grabbed his shoes, threw his uniform blouse over his shoulder and ran out the door.

The gray morning light slanting into the room hit Junior right in the face. He shaded his eyes with his hand, moving it slightly to see the sign just outside the door: "The Holloway Inn, Folly Beach."

As the sun's rays stabbed at his brain, Junior rolled over and Leona moaned. She squirmed and giggled and slithered up his legs, feeling her way past his boxer shorts, dragging her bountiful breasts across his loin and stomach and dangling them in his face. Junior felt like hell, but loved waking up with white women and boys. But doing so in Ashmead's house on Tradd Street was one thing; doing so in a fleabag motel on Folly Beach could get him killed.

CHAPTER 57

Maceo raised a Minnie Mouse umbrella and strolled onto the deck as the sun rose through gray skies. Earlier, in the darkness, he beached the boat on a sandbar on an inside bank of one of the Cooper River's many bends. So he was surprised when he awoke and the boat was afloat and tugging at the anchor line.

He looked up, then down the river and saw it had risen several feet above the sandbar and spilled over its banks. Normally, such a sudden rise meant Santee Cooper had released millions of gallons of lake water into the river. That was standard procedure after heavy rains. But it was supposed to be done gradually, from various release points along the dam.

As Maceo walked to the stern, he noticed George was unconscious but shivering — like a drugged patient in a back ward on Bull Street, Maceo thought with a laugh. Then he heard a whirring sound, something metallic and out of place. He looked upstream and saw a bridge, then spotted someone swimming. Moving to the starboard side, Maceo squatted and squinted for a better look. The swimmer hooked a cable to the bumper of a car, half-submerged and snagged on a fallen cypress trunk at the river's edge.

The swimmer waved his arms over his head, signaling a tow-truck driver who had parked his rig at a landing next to the bridge. When the driver engaged the truck's winch, the car creaked and groaned and arose from the river spilling coke-colored water from its windows like a fountain. It was a Ford Crown Victoria. There was no body inside.

The swimmer moved quickly to the driver's side of the hulk and looked inside. In an instant, he turned and issued a thumb's down sign, and the urgency of the moment sagged along with the winch cable.

In a few minutes, another Crown Victoria stopped on the bridge, blue lights flashing, and the officer inside leaned out the window and yelled to the tow-truck driver.

"You catch something, Peanut?" the cop asked.

"Looks like a state vehicle, Bo."

"What's that insignia on the side door say, can you read it?"

"You know I can't read."

"Well, hell," the cop said as he stepped out of his cruiser with binoculars in hand and looked downriver. "Let's see, it says S.C. State Department of Mental Health."

"Really?"

"Yeah, wonder what they're doing way down here? Thought those boys just ate doughnuts and howled at the moon over on Bull Street."

"Looks like this one howled his ass right over the side of the bridge, don't it?"

"Any other markings, Peanut?"

"Got some fresh scrapes up there on the bridge railings and a couple of chunks missing from one of the posts."

"I don't see no skid marks up here. Did you, Peanut?"

"Nope."

"No body?"

"Nope."

"Well, don't waste time looking. This storm's shut everything down. Yank that thing in and get the hell out'a here."

Maceo looked back at George Burr, now awake with a strand of toilet tissue in his hands, feebly waving it like a flag to get the cop's attention.

With one quick step, Maceo planted his left foot on the deck and kicked George in the face with his right foot. As he watched his catch spinning round in the shrimp net, he muttered, "White people. Dam m-m-mother-f-f-fucking white p-p-people."

CHAPTER 58

At 2,000 feet the *Spirit of Charleston* broke through the cloud cover and Ascension Island came into view. Lieutenant Colonel Stoney Sanders was at the controls of the Air Force's huge C-141 Starlifter, pushing slowly forward on the yoke, listening to his co-pilot call out altitudes.

"Fifteen hundred and steady, you're right on it, colonel," he said. "Everything's clear. It's your plane to land, Sir."

Television newswoman Berkeley Aiken was strapped into the navigator's seat just behind the co-pilot. Navigator Cliff Hendrix had relinquished his spot so she could get a better view of the approach.

"It's so brown," she said, looking out at Ascension, "and so blue and so green."

Berkeley was fascinated with the island, a mile-wide swath of brown volcanic rock in the middle of the big, blue Atlantic. It looked like a large piece of jagged coal from the bottom of a gas grill that had been dropped into a babbling brook. At the center of the island was a giant, green pimple pushing through a condensation cloud.

"It's the ugliest and prettiest island I've ever seen," she said, adjusting her headset so the microphone was in front of her mouth."

To her left, cameraman Bob Gillespie shot video over the pilot's shoulder.

"She's something different," Sanders said, adding, "Five hundred feet, flaps and landing gear are down, runway in sight. Roger, prepare for landing."

The cargo plane's big wheels screeched on contact with the asphalt runway. Everyone aboard fell forward into their seatbelts as Sanders engaged the reverse thrusters and applied the brakes.

Finding Ascension Island in the vast blueness of the South Atlantic was one thing, stopping the big plane on the short runway was the highlight of his trip. Sanders swung the bird around and taxied back to a couple of rundown buildings.

"Tradition has it that the flight commander buys the first round at the Volcano Club," he announced over the intercom as the passengers gathered their gear in the cargo bay. "After that, there's a one-hole golf course to play, plenty of good fishing and a volcano to climb. Please note that ground time on Ascension Island is limited, so enjoy our unique home away from home. Crewmembers, you know the drill, so get some rest. Show time for departure is 1100 hours Zulu, a 16-hour turnaround."

With that the engines whined down and the mammoth rear door opened, allowing the equatorial heat to rush into the airplane. As Berkeley climbed down the steps onto what looked like the surface of the moon, she took Perry Barnes' outstretched hand and steadied herself. From the roof of the Volcano Lounge, four technicians clapped and hollered and cheered when they saw her. There were no pretty girls on Ascension Island.

Berkeley blushed, feeling like a dumb blonde on a Bob Hope Tour. Perry turned to her and said, "If you'd like to climb Green Mountain, I'll be happy to be your guide."

"Sounds great!" she said.

"And I can't wait to show you the giant goldfish," he said.

"Giant goldfish?"

"Yeah, the mountain is an extinct volcano, and at the top is the blowout. Over the years, it filled with rainwater, at least 20 feet deep."

"So where did the goldfish come from?" she asked.

"Air crews," Perry said. "We've been flying in here for years. Over time, crewmembers brought along some carp and stocked the pond. Every crew designates somebody to climb up there and feed them. I volunteered us. You can bring your cameraman if you want."

"Sure," Berkeley said, looking around and then back toward the big plane. That's when she noticed something strange. As Stoney Sanders stepped down from the ladder onto the tarmac, two men met him and began what looked like an intense conversation. Then, one of the men slapped handcuffs on the pilot as they walked briskly to the headquarters shack.

"What's going on with Colonel Sanders?" she asked Perry, who had been looking the other way. "They handcuffed him."

"Who knows," Perry said, hoisting his duffel bag to his shoulder. "He and the station manager, Sam Tompkins, have been playing practical jokes on each other for years. One time Sam shut down all the lights, radar and radio signals just as Stoney was about to land. Almost lost the bird, the crew and a damned good station manager.

"Another time, Stoney buzzed the Volcano Club on his final approach, an absolute no-no in the Air Force. But, hey, they figure this far from home, it's their Air Force."

CHAPTER 59

I nside the Ascension Island station manager's building, a grim Sam Tompkins told his friend Stoney Sanders he didn't know what this was all about. He said he'd gotten direct orders to detain the colonel as soon as he landed.

Tompkins was a stocky soul, 60 years old and ready to retire from government service. He'd worked security in the Pentagon for years after his stint in the Marine Corps. He landed the Ascension job as a last-stop before he punched his ticket on the government gravy train.

"Probably some screw-up with your clearance paperwork, Colonel," he said as he folded the pilot's flight jacket over the cuffs so others wouldn't see them. "Please don't take it personally, Stoney. I'm just following orders."

Sam was dressed in khaki shorts, a Hawaiian shirt and sandals. His job was more serious than his appearance. Ascension Island was a square-mile chunk of exposed volcanic rock strategically located between South America and Africa. It served as a clandestine refueling station for U.S. bombers en route to Italy during World War II. Now, it was the perfect place for American high-power antennas that tracked what everybody else in the world was up to.

The antenna farm was operated by the CIA and served as host to both the British and German intelligence services. It also served as a downrange tracking station for NASA, which gave it a degree of legitimacy.

"I'm sure this is some kind of mistake," Stoney said to Sam, his island fishing buddy. "They've probably lost my shot record or have me mixed up with a Russian spy or something. You don't have to watch me like a prisoner, Sam. I mean, really, where's anybody going to run to around here?"

Sam refilled his coffee cup and poured one for Stoney.

"This has got to be a circle jerk," Sam said. "I've sent for a clarification. Should hear back from Langley soon. You sure this isn't one of your practical jokes, Stoney?"

"Wish it was, pal, and thanks for the vote of confidence. I'd hate to think that you, of all people, thought I was a bad guy."

They continued to sit there waiting in the early morning light, sipping coffee, staring at the radio receiver.

"Let's go fishing, Sam," Stoney said.

"Soon as we get this thing cleared up. The boat's rigged and ready and the wahoo are running," Sam replied.

CHAPTER 60

After he got back on his feet, Brent Lee couldn't get out of the woods fast enough. But the tire of the aircraft had been shot out, and it would be grounded for hours. So he took off running after Rolex and the Jeep in desperation to save his family. Surely Rolex knew where they were.

Sid Rice yelled for Brent to wait for backup, but knew his friend would not stop. When they were in college, Brent's nickname was Bulldog because of his tenacity playing intramural rugby. Sid had seen the hyper side of his friend before and knew that when the Bulldog was loose, nothing would stop him.

After running more than a mile up the dirt road, Brent exited on S.C. Highway 41 and saw the Jeep's skid marks on the pavement. Rolex was headed north. Brent continued to give chase through the flat pinelands toward Bonneau, the nearest community several miles up the highway. A long-distance runner in high school, Brent was still in good shape. He had already shed his jacket and tie as he dashed through the early-morning mist, his shoulder holster and gun flapping against his body and his rubber-soled hiking boots slapping the pavement at a steady pace.

It would only be a matter of time before a car would pass and he'd flag it down, he thought. He hoofed it past several dead possums and the carcass of a young doe, all victims of passing vehicles. Crows squawked in the tree tops and buzzards started to circle in the gray morning sky. It was like running through the Valley of Death, Brent decided.

After more than three miles, a car appeared on the road ahead and was coming his way. Gasping for breath, Brent stopped, bent over with his hands on his knees and waited for the driver to get close enough to see him. But the car turned off on a dirt road and disappeared into the forest. Taking a deep breath, Brent set off again. His heart felt like it was exploding, but he kept running.

Meanwhile, Stacia held Grant and Graycen close to her bosom, muffling their cries, wondering where she was and worried about what the men who drugged her planned to do to her children. She never saw her captors' faces. They wore Halloween masks: Donald Duck, Daffy Duck, Popeye the Sailor Man. Young Grant recognized Popeye, raised his own right forearm, pointed to his muscle and said, "Spinach!"

The man in the mask slammed the door and left them alone in the dark. The noise caused Cocky the dog to squirm inside Stacia's big handbag. She slipped her hand down into the bag and slipped the pet some treats she had saved for him.

Drenched in sweat, Brent leaned against a road sign that said "Bonneau 8 miles." He had given up hope of catching Rolex when he heard the rumble of another vehicle approaching from his rear. Turning to flag down the driver, he heard the engine gearing down as it got closer, and then he realized it was a Jeep.

He reached for his shoulder holster but his gun was not there. He'd lost it during his mad dash. So he dove into a ditch alongside the road. As the Jeep rolled up and stopped, Brent readied himself to pounce.

"Hey, Buddy, looks like you need a ride," the driver hollered.

"Uh, who are you?" Brent asked.

"Ted Turner. Who the hell are you?"

Brent immediately recognized the man's distinct high-pitched accent and his carefully trimmed mustache. It was Captain Outrageous himself, winner of the America's Cup and owner of Brent's beloved Atlanta Braves.

"What are you doing here?" Brent asked.

"Looking for land," Turner said, standing up in the topless Jeep and sweeping his hand around in a semi-circle. "Best time to buy land is right after a disaster, and we got one on the way. Need a ride?"

"I need a miracle," Brent said.

"Well, hell, that's what I specialize in," Turner said. "I won the America's Cup, started the first 24-hour cable news network, and I'm sleeping with Jane Fonda. I'm a natural-born miracle!"

Brent dove into the Jeep, showed Turner his badge and asked him to head for Bonneau.

Turner pulled his blue Braves cap down tight on his head and slammed his vehicle into first gear. "Got a hunt club just up the road. Bubba can get you anywhere quicker than anybody. Hold on, son, next stop, Bonneau Beach International."

CHAPTER 61

S keeter Simms slept soundly until 4 a.m. on the couch in the Pinopolis Dam control room until Tony Ciuffo called in from a monitoring station down river.

"What the hell are you doing, trying to drown us?" Tony screamed into the phone. "We got three feet of river that wasn't here last night. Didn't you shut everything down because of that damn storm?"

"Le'me get back to you on that, Tony," Skeeter said. "Something ain't right. Better sound a flash-flood warning or something while I check it out."

"Hell, Skeeter, we done did that. This ain't good; ain't good at all!"

"Must be a pump stuck open somewhere," Skeeter responded. "I'm on it."

Skeeter looked down along the massive dam in front of him as the sun rose and a sea of orange illuminated Lake Moultrie behind him. The skin on the lake was smooth for as far as he could see. Then it hit him like a million tons of rocks and concrete:

"Holy Shit!" he yelled. "We got a breach!"

* * *

It was 8:35 when Junior Jones grabbed his beeper from the glove box of his company car and saw the URGENT! messages from Skeeter Simms.

"Damn!" Junior said to no one in particular, and walked unsteadily to a phone booth by the pier. As he dialed the office he tried to pull up enough saliva from his throat so he could say something audible.

"Hello, that you Junior?"

"Skeether, dith ith Junior."

"Where the hell you been, son," Skeeter said. "We got major shit going on at the dam, and you sound like you've been eating it."

Junior cleared his throat and lied.

"I'm home sick, Skeeter. Been drinking NyQuil like water all night."

"Well, get your ass in gear because I think we got a crack and my disaster-pre-paredness protocol sheet says I'm supposed to call Stoney, but he's out of country on Reserve duty, so I'm calling you. Round up all them big shots of yours; tell 'em the river's rising and ask 'em what the hell to do."

"On my way, Skeet," Junior said, trying to clear his head, which throbbed like a pimple about to burst. "Don't say nothing to nobody until I get there. Might not be as bad as you think."

Skeeter Simms considered that for a moment, then muttered half-heartedly, "Yeah, maybe. Hurry the hell up!"

CHAPTER 62

The brief message that Ascension Island operations chief Sam Tompkins received on his secure line was brief: "Detain Lieutenant Colonel Stonewall J. Sanders upon arrival. Instructions to follow."

Tompkins had been on the receiving end of government orders for 30 years and seldom got one that made much sense. While serving in the rice paddies of South Vietnam, some jackass from headquarters called in and said, "Take Sector 139 and report back when mission accomplished." Twenty-six dead Marines later, Tompkins reported the sector was secure, and the same jackass asked, "What sector?" Sam was oblivious to such crap now. He did what he was told, knowing it was probably wrong.

But he liked Sanders because he was a "Citadel Man." Sam graduated from Virginia Military Institute. Sam and Stoney were like brothers; they had been initiated into the brotherhood. You must go through the rigors of proper military colleges to completely understand, Sam told all who listened. But nobody did, except other members of the "brotherhood."

Citadel and VMI cadets have an honor code. They must not lie, cheat or steal, and must not tolerate those who do. So Sam gave Stoney the benefit of the doubt.

"Want some more coffee?" Sam asked as they sat quietly waiting in the Quonset hut for an explanation.

"No, thanks, just some sleep. Mind if I rack out here on the couch?"

Across the runway, the civilians were settling into their barracks.

"What a dump," sneered Billy Glover, the car dealer. "I had better accommodations in band camp. What are we supposed to do around here for the next 16 hours?"

The Methodist minister looked around the room and declared it was just fine. He stored his things in a footlocker and laced up his hiking shoes.

"I'm going with Sgt. Barnes, Miss Aiken and Mr. Gillespie on a hike up the volcano," the pastor said. "Want to go with us, Billy?"

"Naw," Billy growled. "I'm going to the bar. Anyone care to join me?"

Most of the group followed the pudgy car dealer out the screen the door to the Volcano Lounge, a shack with four tables that served only beer.

"So," Perry Barnes asked Berkeley Aiken, Bob Gillespie and the minister as the screen door slammed shut. "Want to rest or are you ready to climb?"

Berkeley finished tying her running shoes and declared she was ready. Gillespie, who popped another videotape into his camera, said he was too. The minister tucked his shirttail into his jeans and said, "Let's go!"

"Great. It's less than an hour to the top and well worth the trip," Perry said.

As they trekked across a narrow field of crushed volcanic rock, Berkeley gazed up at the green mountain with a condensation cloud that was perpetually gathered around the top and wondered what it was like when the volcano first erupted from the sea and claimed its lofty place in the middle of nowhere. Now, a million years later, what was once a catastrophic exception stood tall, transformed into a lush garden, 1,500 feet up, swept by ocean winds and watered by rolling clouds. She couldn't wait to reach the top.

Berkeley enjoyed being on top, even if getting there usually happened out of sequence. She never knew when or where or how she reached such heights, so it always surprised her. Like that night in 1982 at the Miss South Carolina pageant in Columbia. She remembered the flashbulbs exploding the moment Susan Patterson was named the new Miss South Carolina. Berkeley, who was standing next to Susan, was the first runner-up, an honor she never expected; one she got because of a silly dare.

Her college suitemates put her up to it. She'd never dreamed of being in a beauty contest until she sat editing a story for her college paper about the pageant coming to their campus and her roommate Louise said, "Bet you could win it, Berkeley. They've never seen anything like you."

The thought of sashaying like a cow at auction never appealed to Berkeley. Besides, she was too dark-skinned — an Angus among Guernseys. South Carolina queens were blonde and perky, perfect in every way. They walked, talked and oozed an insincerity that distinctly separated them from humanity.

But Louise was dogged in her desire to convince Berkeley to become a contestant. Louise pretended to be Master of Ceremonies Bert Parks. She grabbed a hairbrush and sang when Berkeley stepped out of the shower: "There she is, Miss South Carolina Moon Pie, Watermelon Seed, Tobacco Spit and Our Ideal..."

Berkeley threw her towel at Louise, and they giggled and laughed about beauty contests in general. A week later Berkeley received a letter in the mail from the Miss South Carolina Pageant director congratulating her on being chosen to audition.

Louise held her breath as Berkeley opened the envelope. Louise had sent in Berkeley's photo and filled out the registration form.

"Why'd you do this, Louise?" Berkeley asked. "You're just like my mother!"

The morning her mother died in Charleston's Roper Hospital, Berkeley, 13, walked with her father to the Battery and sat on a bench where they both cried. The tide was high and waves sloshed against the rock and concrete wall that protected the city.

Cancer is like the tide, Berkeley remembered thinking at the time. It comes in slowly, hangs around for a while then leaves, always taking something back out to sea with it. This time it was her mother.

Berkeley's rendition of "Somewhere Over the Rainbow" was passable as talent during the auditions. And she remembered how awkward she felt in the preliminaries, the only black-eyed Susan in a dressing room filled with Easter lilies, just as nice and refreshing as they could possibly be to Berkeley. It was a practiced form of pandering designed to disguise their hatred.

They learned deceit from their stage mothers, always hovering and teasing their Barbie Doll hair. Berkeley didn't have a mother, so short, chubby, red-headed Louise was her make-up and wardrobe consultant, advising her to wear the blue dress with the red shoes and to sing like Judy Garland in the "Wizard of Oz," because, because, because, because of the wonderful Wiz it was. It was Berkeley's and Louise's favorite song. It was one of only a few things they had in common.

Berkeley made it to the finals, much to the surprise of more than 500 people who jammed into Epworth Hall for the show, televised statewide on SC-ETV. And, one by one, the piano-playing, fire-baton-twirling, opera-singing Barbies were eliminated. The only three left standing were Susan Patterson, a busty, rising senior at Furman University; Lindsay Zurrender, a medical student from Myrtle Beach whose mom sprayed on her tan prior to the swimsuit competition; and Berkeley Aiken, who never planned to be up there on the stage to start with.

When Lindsay was named second runner-up, she managed a half-smile and just stood there, exposing her fake tan lines. Then, after a long pause, the announcer proclaimed Susan Patterson as the new Queen, handed her a bouquet of roses and helped pin the crown upon her freshly teased hair. That's when the camera flashes exploded.

Berkeley remembered looking through the glare and seeing her mother leaning against a gray stone wall, her head turned slightly upward and to the left toward the sun. Her image was the same as the one in Berkeley's favorite faded family photograph, taken on a sunny afternoon in Charleston along the Battery wall.

It's the picture Berkeley kept in her room, next to her bed and closest to her heart. It reminded her of the way her mother lived and of the day her mother died, when the tide took her out and didn't bring her back.

Seeing her mother through the blinding glare prompted the angelic look on Berkeley's face in the photo that ran the next morning in newspapers across the Palmetto State. It was the photo that made Berkeley shine. It captured the essence of a genuinely beautiful young woman's surprise, sadness and humility.

"Who is that lovely chocolate girl?" everybody wanted to know.

The Charleston Courier did a follow-up story on Berkeley, despite her father's professional disapproval. They re-ran the photo, only this time the other two contestants were cropped out. Berkeley Aiken soon became the pin-up girl in boys' dorms from Presbyterian College to S.C. State. She appeared as a special guest on several local TV shows, and rode on a float in the Charleston Christmas Parade.

Susan Patterson served her yearlong reign and soon afterward married a lawyer from Fort Mill. They moved to Charlotte and few people heard of her again. Lindsay Zurrender died in a car accident a year later when a drunk driver ran a stop sign on Pawley's Island. Berkeley Aiken got a job at WIS-TV in Columbia and her life was never the same.

CHAPTER 63

S id Rice was worried about special agent Brent Lee, but had bigger issues at the moment.

The information John Rhett gave the feds led them in several directions. Not only did it uncover Herman "Rolex" Bishop III as the kingpin of a huge smuggling operation, it exposed several other dealers in his network.

Among them were Ashmead Dawes, a downtown socialite who distributed mainly to the gay and party crowd South of Broad; and Stoney Sanders, a Citadel graduate, Santee Cooper executive and officer in the local Air Force Reserve wing. Dawes and Sanders were to be arrested in an early-morning sweep, which would be reported in the morning newspaper. But things did not go as planned.

A mammoth hurricane got in the way, which meant there might not even be a newspaper the next morning. Secondly, Herman Bishop III eluded what Rice thought would be a sure capture. Colonel Sanders, the drug-running pilot, was on a mission somewhere below the Equator and couldn't be arrested until he got back on U.S. soil, and the body of Ashmead Dawes was found on a Battery bench with a hole in his chest.

Meanwhile, Brent's wife and kids were missing and presumed kidnapped by Bishop's colleagues, none of which was the way Sid had drawn it up on the chalkboard in his office.

It also took four hours for the South Carolina Army National Guard helicopter to find the grass airstrip where Rice and his men, except for Brent, sat around and stewed, waiting for an airlift back to town. Federal agents don't like playing the fool.

"Tell the Air Force to hold Sanders until we can get another plane down there to bring him back into custody," Rice shouted to the radioman on the chopper as they lifted off the field at Sampit Plantation. "Also, I want to know where Brent

Lee's family is being held. That's a top priority. Somebody knows something."

As the helicopter cleared the pine tops and banked over the National Forest, Rice knew he had to horse collar this situation soon or the whole thing could come apart, including his career.

Meanwhile, Brent Lee was surveying an unusual 10-foot-long airboat at a broken down dock on Bonneau Beach.

"It's the fastest thing in the swamp," Bubba Hightower told him as he rolled a toothpick back and forth between his lips. "She'll scoot, Bo, and if the water's high enough, you'll sail right over the marsh, never touch the ground."

Brent figured his family was somewhere in a 50-mile radius between the lakes, a no-man's land of poachers and moon-shiners. He reached into his pants pocket and pulled out the mostly burned pack of matches he found on the ground near what was left of Herman Bishop's brief case. He examined the lettering again. "PEE LO" is all he could read. What could it mean? "PEE LO" was the only clue he had at the moment.

"Can I get to the lake in this thing?" Brent asked Bubba.

"No problem," Bubba said. "And it flies like a bird if you want it to. It's got a chute there on the back; opens up like one of them para-sailing things they got over at Myrtle Beach. Just give her some throttle and yank that handle there next to the seat and the chute will open. It'll lift the whole thing off the ground and you can fly it. It's amazing. So gimme a hundred-dollar deposit."

Brent grabbed his wallet and flipped out his badge.

"Federal agent," he said. "Take it off your taxes."

CHAPTER 64

Major Bonnie Bezner felt the airplane bump over uneven air currents as she held the nose of the WC-130 Hurricane Hunter steady in the wind. At 200 knots, the green-and-gray cargo plane was a mule in a stable of Air Force thoroughbreds.

It wasn't as big as the mighty C-5 Galaxy or as sleek as the C-141 Starlifter, but the Hercules was a war horse that could take troops closer to the battle, double as a gunship, and do it all in any kind of weather. Somewhere in California the Air Force was building a new plane, the C-17, which would replace all three. But Bezner knew her bird would not bow to anything when it came to hurricane missions.

She maintained a heading over the Caribbean Sea and directly toward the hurricane's swirling mass on the radar screen. She remembered the first time she flew a hurricane mission. She thought she was going to die. The sheer force and torque of storm winds ripping at the nuts and bolts of the wings and fuselage had her praying for her life. It wasn't until the plane broke through the eye wall that she opened her eyes.

The stillness of the eye amazed her. It was as calm as a cornfield back home. No clouds, no wind. Just a quiet, peacefulness that made her wonder if they had not entered heaven by a back door.

But the tranquility didn't last long. Within a minute the big bird sliced back into the storm's fury, bouncing wildly as Bonnie fought to gain control, tack against the hurricane's thrust and gather vital information as it passed through.

Hurricane Hunters work in an area about 800 miles off shore where the warm waters of late summer and early fall stoke the clouds and send them spinning like tops toward the eastern seaboard. Out there, with nothing but ocean as far as she could see, Bonnie felt at home, her landlocked childhood a geographical mistake. Since moving to the South, she had settled into another way of life.

It's not that Midwesterners aren't good people, she thought. They are the salt of the earth. But the South, with all its flaws, is a kinder, more genteel, place to live. People are friendlier. They actually care about neighbors having a nice day. All Bonnie's crew were Southern girls, raised on grits and oysters, with a touch of Tabasco in their hair and home-churned ice cream in their smiles. They teased Bonnie about being a Yankee, which she never thought about while growing up in Indiana. She even rooted for Notre Dame in football, something she kept to herself on weekends when everyone else was pulling for Ole Miss.

There were many things about the South she didn't know yet, but a hurricane wasn't one of them. She never took them for granted, approached them with extreme caution. And this one was a monster. Its outer bands stretched 200 miles across and it topped out above 50,000 feet. The previous Hurricane Hunter that flew into it registered sustained winds at 90 miles an hour with the millibars dropping fast. On this run, Bonnie estimated the winds at well over 100 miles per hour, perhaps a Category Three hurricane now.

"Touch up your lipstick, girls," she said over the intercom. "We've got a date with a stud named Hugo."

CHAPTER 65

After the tow truck hauled George Burr's patrol car out of the river, Maceo steered the Sister back into the channel and headed up stream, under the bridge and toward the dam. The Bull Street police officer spun slowly in the shrimp net, blood from his left foot dripping on the deck as stifling heat and humidity sapped what remained of his strength.

Maceo lay back against the bulkhead under his black Morton Salt umbrella. George had rubbed his face against the ropes enough to peel the duct tape from his mouth, which was dry as a salt mine.

"Water," he rasped. "I need water."

Maceo's head bobbed once, and he caught himself as the umbrella tilted forward allowing the sun to strike his face. So faded was the umbrella, it was difficult to see the image of the girl carrying a box of salt that spilled out behind her.

"W-w-w-what?" Maceo asked, raising the gun and pointing it at George.

"Water," Burr begged. "I'm dying."

"Who gives a sh-sh-it?" Maceo said.

Burr rolled his eyes and sobbed, "Oh, Mama!"

"M-m-momma?" Maceo asked with a toothy grin. "You w-want your m-m-omma?"

"Don't you have a mother?" George sighed.

Maceo thought about that and said, "I am your m-m-mother now, m-m-m-fo!"

"Maceo… Don't let me die this way."

Maceo thought about that for a moment, too.

"OK," he said.

Maceo grabbed the rusty levers that raise and lower the trawl net and shoved one forward with a screeching, scraping sound. The net and George winched up and over the gunnels and dangled above the river as a cool breeze enveloped him and the smell of his own parched puke dispersed in the wind.

Maceo wrapped his pink lips around the maw of his brown bottle, threw back a slug of whisky and yanked the control lever down. George and the net plunged into river and the Sister slowly dragged the trawl as if it had a giant, gasping grouper entangled in the webbing. Burr tried to crawl up the mesh spider-like and barely kept his nose above the swirling wake. He sucked the cool water through his cracked lips and sloshed it around in his mouth, but could not swallow. He gagged and coughed and couldn't breathe as the water filled his sinuses. He decided to give up and drown.

Maceo played him like a drum fish, jerking him up and dropping him down. Each time the net surfaced, George babbled and burbled, struggling to clear his nose and throat.

"St-sti-still t-thirsty, s-son?" Maceo cackled. "Want some m-m-more water, b-b-oy?"

Suddenly, out of nowhere it seemed, a ski boat filled with college kids roared up fast on the starboard side of the Sister. It pulled an inner tube with a girl holding on tight.

The boys in the boat hooted and hollered at Maceo, and one dropped his trunks and shot him a solid white moon. The other noticed a man in the net, dangling like a half-drowned tuna.

"Looks like fun," the driver screamed as the boat sped past. "Hey, Sally, wanna ride that ride?"

The girl couldn't hear a word, but leaned hard to her left and skidded across the boat's wake up close to the Sister. As she leaned back to the right, the tube sprayed water high and wide onto the shrimp boat deck. Maceo quickly opened his Disney World umbrella, blocked the spray and gave them the finger. On the side of the speedboat he saw a tiger paw.

As the ski boat and the laughter disappeared round the next bend in the river, Maceo cranked George back up and over the gunnels, released the gears and dumped him on the deck.

"You're j-j-just a s-sack of s-s-hit, a no good s-sack of s-shit," he yelled.

In the silence that followed, Maceo fell to his knees, grabbed his head, squeezed his temples between his hands and slowly rocked his body forward and backward.

"I c-c-can hear her, can't y-y-you?" he moaned. "It's S-s-Sister Santee! S-she's over there, on the shore! Sister, can you h-hear m-m-me?"

As Maceo felt the tarp tear loose and tug at the cleats of his sanity, Santee's pleas faded like her name painted on the bow. No one but Maceo remembered Sister Santee. Soon, he feared, no one would be left to tell her story to little wide-eyed Mazycks gathered up on the front porch and listening carefully. Then she would be gone forever.

"Ain' r-r-right," Maceo lifted his head and screamed unto the darkened heavens. "Ain' the way it s-s-s'pose to be…"

CHAPTER 66

Herman "Rolex" Bishop walked into the small Santee Cooper fishing lodge on Lake Moultrie, kicked open the door to the back room and looked down at the woman whose arms were wrapped tight around her two children. All three of the captives were blindfolded and trembling.

"Get word to Sid Rice that if his government goons get close to me again, these people are dead, got it?" Stacia heard him say. "Tell him we're flying out of here with Lee's wife and kids, and not to interfere. Do it! Now!"

Bishop's empire was collapsing. He trusted no one. This was his last chance to start over. He had transferred money to banks in Mexico and Venezuela. He could hold out forever.

First, he would slip into Venezuela, which had no extradition agreement with the United States. He had connections and would be safe there for a while. He'd live in a mansion by the sea and have the best security money could buy. When things cooled down, he'd slip up to Mexico and blend in with other gringos who had lots of cash and enjoyed colonizing Central America, where one dollar was worth seven times more in purchasing power.

The idea of getting caught was a joke until about a year ago when someone showed him an article in the Charleston newspaper about Operation Jackpot. While there had been other government attempts to shut down the smuggling along the coast, none came armed with a new federal law mandating that convicted drug kingpins get life without parole.

Until then, Bishop didn't think he was doing anything that bad. He was a businessman, an entrepreneur. Nobody got killed. All he was dealing was pot and hashish at first, then a little cocaine on the side. He knew his gig wouldn't last forever, so he took full advantage, made enough to be set for life. He came close to killing a few thugs but always made them disappear in different ways. "Geographical cures," he called them. "Get out of town or else."

But he loved to toy with cops, and laughed when they occasionally got a little grant money to upgrade their drug investigations. They'd buy new T-shirts embossed with a badge and lettering in a lame attempt to legitimize their latest boondoggle. Soon the funding would run out and everybody would go home.

But Operation Jackpot was a game-changer. Now Rolex was on the run and needed all his wits and resources to get out of the country. If it meant taking women and children hostage, even it if meant hurting them, then so be it. He vowed never to go to jail.

Rolex loved to gamble, and now he was playing the game of his life. He held three valuable bargaining chips — the woman and two children. They would guarantee him a one-way ticket to Venezuela, and federal drug agent Sid Rice would punch it.

CHAPTER 67

Stoney Sanders knew his time was running out, that when his buddy Sam received another radio message from the feds, it would be over. Sam assumed that the first one ordering him to detain Colonel Sanders was a practical joke by one of their pals in the Pentagon. Stoney knew no one would laugh when the truth came out that Sam's fishing buddy was an international drug smuggler.

Meanwhile, beyond the runway, Perry Barnes, Berkeley Aiken, Bob Gillespie and Pastor Ken Clamp began in earnest their trek to the top of Green Mountain. On the tarmac, a ground crew off-loaded supplies and refueled the *Spirit of Charleston* for the return trip.

Sam, who had stepped into the latrine, stood chuckling about how funny it will be when he and Stoney reminisce about what was happening some day. Sam hated to cuff his friend but orders were orders. At this point in his career, he'd hog tie his grandmother for an extra 50 bucks a month in retirement pay.

With Sam out of the room, Stoney stood up, walked over to the radio receiver and yanked a wire in the back of the unit. As he sat back down, Sam came out of the bathroom and said, "Those boys in Washington are taking their sweet time getting back to us, Stoney. They're getting a good laugh, I'll bet, knowing damn well that we'd have been catching fish by now."

Stoney grinned, rolled his eyes and nodded. "Those bastards probably got an office pool going on how long it will take you to figure out it's a joke, Sam."

Sam looked out the window, took a sip of his coffee and said, "This *is* a joke, right?"

Stoney raised his right hand on which he wore his Citadel ring. "On my honor as an officer and a gentleman."

Sam smiled, raised his right hand with his VMI ring. "Good enough for me, brother, good enough for me."

* * *

Berkeley Aiken was in great shape, as was Perry Barnes, who worked out in the air base gym three times a week. Not so for Pastor Clamp and cameraman Gillespie.

Ken Clamp was a sickly child growing up in Camden and cursed with asthma. When he headed off to Wofford College in Spartanburg, his mother packed his inhaler, which he always kept close. By the time he entered seminary in Nashville, his asthma attacks had worsened.

Gillespie was raised in Columbia and became a pothead at the University of South Carolina. He was an artist and enjoyed photography. He still took a few hits occasionally when he wasn't on assignment. He wished he had some now.

"Native peoples used to worship volcanoes," Clamp wheezed between huffs. "They thought God lived in the fire up there."

"This volcano is dead, pastor," Berkeley quipped. "God doesn't live up there anymore."

The minister looked up, smiled, wiped his brow and said, "Let's see if he left a forwarding address."

* * *

Colonel Sanders watched as the fuel truck driver pulled away from the aircraft. The other airmen now loaded pallets of trash and return mail into the back of his plane. All the while, Stoney tried to keep his buddy occupied by telling lies about how great it was to be a cadet and getting laid a lot by all the girls in Charleston.

"Speaking of which," Stoney added, "grab those binocs, Sam, and get a load of that thing hiking her sweet ass up the mountain trail."

Sam grabbed his field glasses and carefully focused on Berkeley Aiken's rear end.

"It's a beautiful thing, Stoney. "Who is she?"

"A TV gal from Columbia."

"What is she?"

"Iraqi or Pakistani or something; I don't know for sure."

"Mighty pretty, Stoney."

"Ain't they all…"

177

CHAPTER 68

The first 500 hundred feet of elevation along the Green Mountain trail brought a welcome respite from the stifling heat. Perry and Berkeley led the way. Bob was next and the minister lagged.

"A few Portuguese people still live on these slopes," Perry said. "Blown in on trade winds. Nobody knows how long they've been up here. They grow their own vegetables, raise goats for milk and meat."

As Berkeley and Perry passed the first hut, they saw an old woman tending her garden. The woman looked up at the hikers, waved and smiled. She had no teeth. She was dark-skinned — like Perry and Berkeley — homogenized and caramel. Perry and Berkeley shared her shade, toned by generations of crossed cultures. Yet they lived in a stark black and white world.

The atmosphere along the trail changed with each step closer to the top. They felt the high winds off the Atlantic whip across the cliffs. As they reached the three-quarters mark, Pastor Clamp was exhausted. He could climb no more. Perry pointed to a nearby flat rock custom-made by God for hikers with more ambition than ability. As the preacher huffed his inhaler, Gillespie set up the tripod for some panoramic shots.

Perry and Berkeley stepped over the stone railing and walked down a grassy slope on the southern face and sat down. Just below them was a wide expanse of flat, perfectly laid ballast stones that formed a trough that stretched all the way down the mountain to a large cistern at the edge of the runway. Rainwater and an almost continuous condensation from the clouds collected on this funnel-like series of stones and provided the islanders with their primary source of fresh water.

Berkeley stretched out in the grass,watched a huge cloud drift in, envelope the incline and embrace them like a friendly ghost.

"One of the best feelings in the world," Perry said. "When I can't fall asleep, I think of this place."

"It's wonderful," Berkeley intoned. "The most peaceful place on Earth, and you can come here again and again. Doesn't seem fair."

Perry leaned down on his left elbow and wrapped his right arm over her and looked her in the eyes. He could see the skies reflected in her deep brown irises.

"You're here now," he softly said.

"Nowhere else I'd rather be," she whispered.

Each kept their eyes open as their lips were about to meet.

At that moment Pastor Clamp poked his head from behind the rock and confessed, "I can't make it!"

The Methodist minister was exhausted, could hardly breathe. Berkeley and Perry looked at him and then at each other and smiled sheepishly.

"I've got plenty of footage," Gillespie said. "I'll take care of the preacher. Ya'll go on up to the top."

Perry and Berkeley stood, brushed off the grass and resumed their climb to the top. Both were flush but not from exercise. They held hands as they walked now, and together they looked out over the rocky coast of Ascension Island, at breaking waves and rolling seas as far as they could see. Soon they entered the mist surrounding the summit.

CHAPTER 69

Desperate to find his kidnapped wife and children, Brent Lee gunned the airboat through the marshes of the upper Cooper River toward Moncks Corner. He hydroplaned over mud flats and remnants of old rice fields, endless squares hewed out of the soggy bottomland handmade by slaves hundreds of years before as they toiled in the broiling sun.

Brent was hell bent on getting to the Berkeley County sheriff's office on the other side of Lake Moultrie where he could give more details about his family for an All Points Bulletin. The craft — half plane, half boat and propelled by a huge motorized fan — skipped across the surface with ease until he came face to face with dozens of alligators on a huge mud bank ahead; big gators mostly, their mouths wide open and waiting.

Brent jerked back on a lever next to the pilot's chair and a red-and-white striped parachute burst behind the boat, quickly inflated and lifted the flat-bottom contraption up and over the snapping gators. Brent was stunned as he floated over the mudflats like a snagged fish in an osprey's talons.

By trial and error he managed to guide the rig toward the western edge of the swamp. He leaned left and then right to control his direction and throttled up the fan to increase elevation. He spotted a paved road and followed it toward town.

Soon people in the streets of Moncks Corner heard something overhead, looked up and were astounded. Some had seen the unusual flying boats over the lakes, but never so far inland. Brent maneuvered above the power lines and over the K-Mart parking lot. He checked the chute, then cut the engine and glided in for a landing as a crowd of last-minute storm shoppers watched in amazement.

"Mind if I used your radio, sir?" Brent asked a man leaning on a pickup truck with a CB antenna on the back. Brent flashed his badge and said, "I need to call the sheriff."

The man held out his keys in front of him as if he was handing them to a robber. Brent thanked him, opened the truck door, switched on the radio, keyed the mike and said, "Breaker One Nine, calling anyone on this channel for assistance. I am a federal agent. This is an emergency request. Copy?"

The parking lot was silent except for static on the radio. A dozen people gathered around the boat, looking at the parachute and the special agent who fell from the sky. Suddenly, a voice came over the radio.

"This is the Dirt Dobber, can you read?"

"Loud and clear, Dirt Dobber, what's your 20?"

"Highway 52. What'cha need, good buddy?"

"I need the police."

"Well, this is your lucky day, brother. I am the poe-leese."

"I thought you were the Dirt Dobber?"

"Well, I'm also the poe-leese. Who are you and what's your problem?"

By the time Brent explained that he was a federal agent, a dirty brown Chevy pickup slid on two wheels with emergency lights flashing into the far end of the K-Mart parking lot. The truck roared up to the crowd and screeched to a stop. Down the window came and a man with a handlebar mustache in the driver's seat said to Brent, "Howdy. I'm the Dirt Dobber, aka Monroe Monteith."

Brent ran to the passenger side, pulled open the door and jumped in. He looked back into the truck bed and saw a collection of red, blue and yellow lights, black-and-white-striped road barricades, an assortment of rubber boots, rain gear and a stack of bright orange traffic cones.

"You a real cop?" Brent asked.

"As real as you gonna get right now, pal," Monroe said. "Where to?"

"Sheriff's Office," Brent yelled. "Now go!"

Monroe shrugged his shoulders, flipped on his siren, slipped the vehicle in first gear and slammed the accelerator to the floorboard. The Chevy's dual exhaust pipes roared like thunder and the back bumper dipped, almost hitting the pavement. The oversized rear tires squealed under the weight of the moment, and all that was left in the Kmart parking lot was a set of rubber burn marks, the power parachute and a gawking crowd.

CHAPTER 70

The higher Perry Barnes and Berkeley Aiken climbed Green Mountain, the muddier the trail became because it was watered almost constantly by condensation surrounding the peak. Berkeley leaned against a rocky ledge and breathed deeply.

"Only a few more yards up and we're there," Perry said. "It's just over that ridge."

Berkeley gathered her strength and resumed her climb up the slippery embankment covered in bamboo. She grabbed a thick cane shoot and pulled herself up the final two feet and peered over the rim. The sun shone brightly at the top and illuminated a perfectly round pool of crystal clear water at least an acre in diameter and as deep as her eyes could see. Perry reached the summit moments afterward, and they dropped down to a cinder path that encircled the lake.

"Amazing!" she gasped, and then she saw the fish— six huge golden carp swimming in circles at her feet as if they knew they were about to get a treat. "Just amazing!"

Perry smiled, dropped his backpack, reached in and pulled out a bag of specially prepared fish meal courtesy of the Charleston Air Force Base chow hall.

"Dinner time," he said and threw a handful of fish food into the water.

The carp swirled and splashed and gobbled it up as Berkeley and Perry showered them with more and more until the bag was empty.

"It's a tropical paradise up here, Perry. I never dreamed it would be like this."

"Mother Nature at her best," Perry said. "Leave her alone and she creates a masterpiece."

Berkeley turned and looked deep into Perry's dark eyes.

"Are you always so poetic?" she asked.

"Only with you."

There were no interruptions this time. When Berkeley opened her eyes again she was stretched out in the grass next to the path, and she knew her life had changed forever. She buttoned her blouse, stood and walked to the edge of the rim. The clouds broke and for a moment and she could see the tarmac and the Starlifter almost directly below. That's when she saw a man trotting toward the big jet as the fuel truck and ground crews were leaving the runway. Suddenly, her journalistic instincts kicked into gear.

"What is that all about," she asked Perry, who pulled out his binoculars from his backpack, joined her at the edge and focused his field glasses.

"Somebody who forgot his fishing gear, maybe?"

Berkeley grabbed the binoculars, pulled them to the bridge of her nose, squinted, adjusted the lens and said, "That's Colonel Sanders. Why is he running?"

Perry sighed, then took the binoculars for another look-see.

"Odd, but there must be a logical explanation. Other than you being here alone with me, this mission is about as routine as it gets. Not like going to Moscow, which is a field trip to the zoo."

Berkeley didn't laugh. She was worried. Something was not right.

* * *

Ascension Island station chief Sam Tompkins dozed on the couch and Stoney Sanders decided it was time to go.

After he slipped out the door of the shed, he trotted across the runway, trying not to draw attention as the members of the ground crew left the area surrounding the big jet. Most of the men just waved to him, paying no attention to his shiny new flight jacket, draped over his handcuffs like a leather tablecloth.

When he reached the first step of the ladder, he heard a voice, which stopped him cold.

"Forget something, Colonel?"

Sanders looked up and saw crew chief Sergeant Bill Hamilton at the top of the stairs. Nothing happens on a military aircraft on a runway without the chief's knowledge. Nothing.

"Uh, I forgot my flight cap, Chief," Sanders stammered and stepped to the ground. "Left it in the cockpit. Bad habit."

"I'll get it for you, Sir."

"Naw, that's okay, Chief. I, uh, left it up there along with some Hustler magazines that I brought for Sam … Um, wouldn't want you handling any contraband. Right?"

Hamilton grinned, nodded, skipped down the steps to the tarmac and cocked a perfect salute to the Colonel as his feet hit the ground.

Stoney, still handcuffed, was caught off guard by the salute. He knew he was supposed to return it, but said, "Hey, Bill, we're old friends. No need to be so formal way out here in the middle of the nowhere."

Hamilton slowly lowered his right hand to his side and eyed Stoney carefully as the Colonel doubled-stepped up the ladder, never touching the handrails.

"Sorry, sir," Hamilton said. "Bad habit."

CHAPTER 71

I t took Berkeley and Perry less than 15 minutes to get down the mountain. They took the most direct route available: Hand in hand they slid bottoms-first down the old stone aqueduct into the cistern with a huge slash. Soaked from head to toe, they crawled out of the enclosure, jumped to the ground then dashed across the runway toward the cargo plane.

Stoney cranked the mammoth jet engines, then ran back down the steps and kicked away the chocks. He yanked the auxiliary power unit loose from the plane and scampered back up to the pilot's seat.

Berkeley and Perry heard the high-pitched whine of the *Spirit of Charleston's* No. 1 engine as they sprinted the last hundred yards to the rear of the craft. Then engine No. 2 kicked in and the smell of jet fuel permeated the air.

"Just love smell of JP-4 in the morning," Stoney mumbled.

Sprinting now, side-by-side, Perry and Berkeley were hit by a blast from the engines. Suddenly the third and fourth jet engines sprung to life, and the ladder was raised into the body of the Starlifter. But the huge rear doors remained wide open.

From 20 yards back, they heard the plane's hydraulics kick into action. Running as hard as they could, Berkeley and Perry leaped onto the bottom ramp as it rose to meet the clamshell outer doors. The big craft was rolling now, and turned slightly to the starboard en route to the main runway. The outer doors slammed shut, sealing the cargo bay. Berkeley and Perry lay there on the rear deck for three or four minutes soaking wet and gasping for air as the big jet turned and positioned for take-off.

As they regained their strength, their eyes met again — but they were filled with fear instead of passion this time. Why was Stoney Sanders leaving Ascension Island like this? Was he coming back? What was he up to? Perry and Berkeley asked those questions of each other yet did not say a word. Then he grabbed her hand and pulled her between two pallets, where they stooped down among blocks of compressed, half-frozen garbage, broken antenna rods and other electronics.

"We need to strap you in," Perry said, "Quick, sit over there against the bulkhead while I go up and see what's going on."

Perry had never been on an Air Force plane in civilian attire and felt strangely out of place. What was even more uncomfortable was the fact that the plane was about to become airborne without a crew. As he maneuvered between the pallet straps, he looked up at the cockpit and saw that the door was shut. He felt the nose of the aircraft swing round 180 degrees, and he heard the brakes lock as the engines revved.

Stoney Sanders flipped toggle switches above his head as he held firm the brakes on the big bird, then pushed the throttles forward to increase the thrust.

"I'm taking this baby out of here," he screamed.

The authorities obviously knew he had been smuggling cocaine and he figured John Rhett was the rat. He knew better than to trust a politician, but it was too late now.

Stoney scanned the flight line and saw some of the ground crew running his way. But straight ahead was only concrete, and beyond that nothing but the wide Atlantic Ocean. Sanders knew everything about a C-141. He could fly it in his sleep, and if he could do that, he could go solo too. After checking his gauges one last time, Stoney pushed the throttles all the way forward with both hands because he remained cuffed. He held the wheel steady with his knee. That's when the cockpit door swung open with a bang.

"What the hell are you doing, sir?" Perry Barnes yelled. "Have you lost your mind?"

Stoney was stunned but turned around, attempting to smile as if everything were normal.

Perry stood there frozen for a second, not sure what would happen next.

Sanders slipped his hands down between the seats, jerked a flare gun from the emergency kit and stuck it in Perry's face.

Perry stumbled backward and suddenly was surrounded by a brilliant flash of light. His left foot got caught halfway down the crew ladder and his head slammed the corner of a pallet. He was knocked out cold.

Berkeley saw the flash as Perry fell and a blistering phosphorous flame ricocheted wildly from pallets to ceiling to walls in the cargo bay. She dropped to the deck and held her hands over her head. Suddenly all four of the engines sounded as if they had exploded and the jet rolled faster and faster along the runway.

She grabbed the webbing on the seats on the side of the bay and braced herself for the worst. The plane lifted off and jerked almost straight up. If she had not been holding on tight, her body would have slid all the way to the stern.

Slowly she pulled herself forward until she reached Perry. With her left arm she cradled his bleeding head to her breasts as she held on to the ladder with her right. She ripped off the front of his shirt and with one hand, wrapped it like a bandage around his forehead, and finished tying it with her teeth. The bleeding stopped almost immediately, but Perry remained unconscious. She laid his head on a life vest that had been stored beneath a nearby seat.

The plane banked to the right and she struggled to keep her balance. She reached for Perry's right foot, still wedged in the stairs. She tried to loosen his shoe and free him when she saw the duffle bag behind the steps. It was half opened and was chocked full of plastic bags of white powder.

"Wake up, Perry!" she said frantically into his ear. "Please, please wake up!"

CHAPTER 72

Junior Jones pulled into the parking lot at Santee Cooper's headquarters building in Moncks Corner and saw a TV satellite truck. His heart sank as he parked the car. He walked into the building and headed to his office.

"It has hit the fan," Skeeter Simms said as Junior walked through the door. "Looks like we've got a breach. The river's rising. The TV station called. They want to talk to somebody about it."

Junior was tired and frustrated. Earlier he tried tying his tie while driving up Highway 52, but it kept coming up short. He was in no mood to deal with Skeeter Simms.

"Where the hell is Stoney?" Junior yelled. "He's supposed to handle this shit, not me."

"Off flying with the Air Force again," Skeeter said. "You're next on the emergency contact list, Junior."

Junior looked out the window at the dam. The water that it was holding back was as smooth as glass. As he looked down on the Cooper River side, he noticed a bubbling turbulence, and indeed the water might be rising, he thought. Junior used the wide end of his still-untied tie to wipe a bead of sweat from his brow.

"What do the engineers say?" he asked.

"They're running some tests," Skeeter said. "Might be the clay foundation under the wall. Damn thing might be compromised."

Junior's head pounded now, echoing with remnants of cocaine, marijuana, Southern Comfort and Leona's scent trying to get out. He rubbed his eyes and looked toward the lobby door.

"Are they in there?"

"Waiting on you," Skeeter said.

Junior tried one more time to get his unruly tie in order, then took it off as he headed for the outer lobby door. That's where a television reporter and a cameraman cut him off.

"Your name, sir?" the reporter asked, shoving a microphone at Junior.

"I, um, am Grover Jones Jr., assistant vice president for Santee Cooper Authority. Who are you?"

"Harve Jacobs, Live 5 News. What's wrong with the dam? The river is rising and lots of folks down stream are worried, Mr. Jones. They say the Pinopolis Dam has a breach. Can you confirm that?"

Junior tried to remain calm, like Stoney Sanders advised him to do when cornered by the media. He cleared his throat, blinked his bloodshot eyes, looked directly into the camera and said, "We want to thank the public for keeping a watchful eye on the river. It takes the cooperation of everyone in Santee Cooper Country to maintain the high level of services from recreation to the generation of power that we use to service our community.

"I want to assure everyone that we're doing everything possible to ensure the public's safety while getting to the bottom of this situation. As always, our customers and our employees are our number one concern."

Nice, but the reporter was relentless.

"Answer my question, Mr. Jones. Is the dam going to break or not? Will there be an evacuation? The public needs to know."

Junior wet his lips, as Stoney taught him, then blinked his eyes slowly, a sure sign that a lie was forthcoming.

"We don't anticipate that kind of action being necessary at this point," Junior said. "As you know, everybody's main concern right now is the hurricane that threatens our coastline. In the event of an emergency, Santee Cooper will take all precautions to make sure the public is informed and protected. Now, if you'll excuse me, I have to check on a few things. We're very busy. Thank you."

Junior backed out the door as the reporter and cameraman followed in hot pursuit.

"What do we know, Skeeter?" Junior asked as they squeezed through the doors of the inner office, cutting off their questioners.

"The river is rising six inches every six hours and our engineers don't know why," Simms said. "That's what we know."

Junior thought for a few seconds and said, "Call Timsdale. Get his ass down here."

CHAPTER 73

Two miles down river, a flight of mallards tapped the water with their wing tips as they took off fast, low, headed north. Maceo was going the same way but had trouble steering the Sister into the strong current. Earlier a whirlpool created by the rapidly rising water spun the shrimp boat around, slamming it against an old dock, damaging the rudder.

With the bilge pump straining to keep up with the water pouring in through the hole in the bulkhead, Maceo struggled to maintain his course toward Pinopolis Dam. But it wasn't easy with the boat's busted rudder and his own fractured brain. An hour earlier, he saw Indians — their bodies smeared with war paint — running along the bank. They launched canoes and came toward him, so he took aim and fired at them.

"F-f-fourteen."

Suddenly, to his left on the opposite shore, he saw British dragoons, driven hard by an officer in full dress uniform, slogging through the swamp. Maceo fired two more shots at them.

"T-t-thirteen. T-t-twelve."

Then, to his right, he saw Klansmen riding hard on horseback swinging a noose.

"Eleven."

In the distance through the thick stand of cypress trees, he saw a large hairy creature being led on a leash by a bundled up Scandinavian boy. But instead of trudging through snow, the monster and its young handler slogged through South Carolina swamp mud, out of place, out of time, like most of Maceo's hallucinations. He didn't shoot this time because of the boy.

It was during moments like these that the tarp flapped fiercely in Maceo's head and he no longer had even the slightest ability to make decisions. His manic behavior did not go unnoticed by his captive. From inside the net, dangling a few feet above the deck, George Burr had already made peace with his maker, asked for forgiveness for his sins and was prepared to die. As the blood from his wounds dripped onto the deck, he figured death would come slowly but surely, like nightfall on the river.

Burr no longer felt pain, having numbed his mind to it. And as the sun slowly rose that morning from behind the pines, he thought he may have already reached Paradise, that God and Jesus and Moses and Saint Peter were there waiting to say he had lived a good life, didn't hurt anybody if he could help it, was charitable, nice to animals and that he was welcome to join them.

What he got at precisely that moment was a kick in the ass from Maceo, who ripped the duct tape from his lips and shoved another Vienna Sausage in his mouth.

"B-b-breakfast in b-b-bed," Maceo smirked, spit drooling down his cheek, as he wobbled weak-kneed in the mid-morning heat. "Th-the only th-th-thing w-w-worse th-a-than a hospital c-c-cop is a white hospital c-c-op. Those b-b-black bastard orderlies were bad, but you white m-m-mother f-f-fuckers with g-guns and badges, you were b-b-brutal."

George said nothing as he dangled in the net and watched the madman pop open another umbrella, which featured the family dog pulling down the bathing suit of the Coppertone girl.

George thought about attempting to yell at a passing sport-fishing boat headed for safety upstream, but it was useless. It was running wide open and the captain was too busy dodging floating logs in the high water. But the captain did give Maceo the finger as he whizzed by. The "Pink Nigger" was infamous from one end of the river to the other.

Maceo started to slap the duct tape back across his captive's mouth when George begged for water again. Maceo smiled a crooked smile, unzipped his pants and happily obliged.

CHAPTER 74

S antee Cooper electric cooperative CEO Rod Timsdale was moving the deck chairs away from his swimming pool in Pinopolis when a maid walked across the patio and handed him a portable phone.

"Call for you, Mr. Timsdale. It's the power plant."

He took the phone and sat down in one of the deck chairs.

"Timsdale," he answered curtly.

"Mr. Timsdale, this is Skeeter down at the power plant."

"Yes, Skeeter. Everything okay?"

"Not exactly, Mr. Timsdale, sir."

"What's wrong?"

"Well, sir, it looks like we have a problem."

"Look, Skeeter, we're trying to leave town because of the storm, and I don't have time for chit-chat. Can it wait?

Skeeter looked out at the rising water on the riverside of the dam and said, "No sir, sir."

Rod Timsdale had been executive director of Santee Cooper for exactly six months and knew nothing about hydroelectric power, coal power or any of the nuts and bolts of the state's largest utility company. He was a banker by trade and was appointed to the job by his best friend, S.C. Gov. Robert Hodgkiss. Timsdale planned to be there for five years while he finished up work on a huge real estate deal. His state retirement benefits would dovetail nicely with his new investment portfolio and leave him set for life.

Timsdale knew all he needed to know about Santee Cooper. It was one of the biggest boondoggles ever foisted on the citizens of South Carolina. Despite all the promises of delivering low-cost hydroelectric power to every dirt farmer from Lake

City to Low Bottom, all it actually did was relocate thousands of people, stores, shacks and graves from a huge swath of land between Columbia and Charleston and create two giant man-made lakes and hundreds of miles of waterfront property.

Now, almost 50 years later, a mere one percent of all the power Santee Cooper generated in an area that covered almost half the state came from water that flowed through the turbines of the dam. The rest was produced by coal, which rolled into South Carolina by a network of trains that snaked their way to four black-smoke-belching generating stations which pumped tons of carbon daily out of the incinerator stacks.

Timsdale's job was to keep the State Legislature happy with Santee Cooper so the utility's private stakeholders could broker the coal and continue to develop all those thousands of acres of prime lakefront property. And he did that quite well, especially since he had a stake in it himself.

As a banker, Timsdale spent years brokering land deals in conjunction with the international paper companies in the area. Few people knew it, but a 30-square-mile swath of Santee Cooper Country was on its way to becoming the largest retirement community east of the Mississippi. It would be filled with "half-backers," older folks mostly from New York and New Jersey who retired to Florida, found it too hot, too sandy and too crowded down there, and moved halfway back to South Carolina.

That Rod Timsdale was a silent partner in the development company was one of the state's best-kept secrets, and that's the way he wanted to keep it until he got all he thought he deserved for his service to the citizens of South Carolina. To him, the State Motto — *dum spiro spero* — meant what it sounded like. That's what he'd say to his associates every time he had too much to drink, which was more often the closer he got to retirement.

But for now, the huge tracts of pine woodlands — especially the Francis Marion National Forest — were ripe for exploitation. "National Parks are protected; National Forests are tree farms," Timsdale liked to say, "and we're the ones who have the keys to the gates."

Until recently, logging trucks fed the paper mills an endless supply of pulp. But Timsdale knew the economy was changing, thanks to the dawning of the computer age. It would not take long before the land would be worth more as "planned communities" instead of tree farms.

Timsdale's strategic plan, dubbed the "Swamp Fox Project," would turn the ecologically rich Santee Delta into the economically rich "Santee City," largest retirement community on the east coast.

Unless the dam broke.

Timsdale's face flushed as he listened to what Skeeter Simms was trying to explain.

"Are you shittin' me, Skeeter?" he suddenly screamed.

"Uh, like I said, sir, the damn thing's sprung a leak and we ain't sure we can plug it," Skeeter said.

"You can actually see the water rising?"

"Yes sir, pretty steady, sir."

"Okay, okay. I'm on my way."

CHAPTER 75

It didn't take long for word of a hijacked C-141 to reach the White House. Within an hour, fighter jets from Florida scrambled in search of the stolen cargo plane. Extrapolating available information on who did it, why and where he was going was extremely difficult.

Getting one government agency to communicate with another is always a problem. The federal drug task force trying to arrest Lieutenant Colonel Stoney Sanders was reluctant to disclose information to military officials, who were hamstrung by various intelligence agencies that were vulnerable to various bureaucratic and political interests.

The only person who knew for sure what was going on was Staff Sergeant Rick Nelson, who had the *Spirit of Charleston* on his radar screen inside central command headquarters at Homestead Air Force Base outside Miami, Fla.

"Think he'll go to Cuba?" Sergeant Nelson asked his commander, Major Bob Burdette. "Does that make any sense to you, sir?"

Burdette, a maintenance officer, was holding down a shift for his bowling buddy who was rolling strikes in the Ft. Lauderdale Open. Chasing down a stolen C-141 was not Burdette's field of expertise. In fact, it was nobody's specialty.

"Nobody goes to Cuba anymore," Burdette said.

"That's his heading, sir," Nelson responded.

"Do we have any fighters aloft?"

"Yes sir, a group of F-16s on a training mission in that sector right now."

"Well, have them check it out," Burdette said.

"Yes, sir."

F-16 pilot Captain Henry "Hot Rod" Hanks was cruising toward the Florida coast with his squadron of Fighting Falcons when he got the call. They had just finished an exercise in military air space off the Atlantic coastline.

"Gotta be a mistake," he squawked to his wingman. "Who steals a 141? And why? The Russians don't need it. They've already stolen those plans. And the thief is going to have a hell of a time hiding the damn thing."

Hanks radioed for a KC-135 Stratotanker to meet his six-plane formation near Key West for a refueling. With their tanks topped off, they could intercept the errant aircraft and shoot it down if necessary.

Stoney Sanders was psyched. He dropped the big Starlifter to a thousand feet above the seas to keep himself under the radar even though flying low burned more fuel. For the first time since flight school, he felt like a fighter jock, the job he always wanted. He waggled the big wings of the C-141 to give him a better feel for the aircraft at such a low altitude. It felt good knowing he was in complete control. Mostly computers flew big planes now. Pilots were just along in case the hard drive crashed.

All he could see was ocean in every direction but up. He was headed to Cuba in hopes of getting political asylum, but how could he be sure Castro wouldn't shoot him down first? He also had a more immediate concern. Somehow his loadmaster had joined him on the mission. Was there anyone else back there with Sergeant Perry Barnes?

So he flipped on the autopilot, got out of his seat and shoved several stacks of flight logs against the cockpit door. There were no locks on the door — Air Force regulations — but it was better than nothing.

Meanwhile, Berkeley Aiken was terrified as she peered forward from between two large pallets and wondered what to do next. She tried to make Perry as comfortable as possible as she held his bloodied head.

"Perry? Perry? Can you hear me," she asked, but all he could manage was a deep moan.

Berkeley knew that this was the biggest story of her life. Problem was, she didn't know what it was about. So she just sat there holding Perry's head. Then she pulled a silk scarf out of her side pocket and wrapped it around her neck and asked herself, "What would Christiane do?"

CHAPTER 76

Two hours after getting airborne, Stoney Sanders heard chatter on the radio. He had flipped off his transponder to maintain a silent run but could monitor what was going on around him. Captain Henry "Hot Rod" Hanks and his F-16 squadron were reaching the outer limits of their reserves and calling for fuel.

"Looking for that pit stop from McDill," Hanks squawked. "Are you out there, tanker?"

Stoney listened closely as the pilot of the KC-135 called in her puppies to line up for juice from the tanker's hind tit. Stoney also heard the fighter pilots receiving orders to split off into pairs, high and low, and commence radar pinging so they could spot the C-141 on their screens. That's when Stoney decided to scrap his unscheduled appointment with Fidel.

He dipped the right wing, set a new course north-northeast toward Bermuda and hoped for a miracle. What he did not realize was he was about to enter through the backdoor of the biggest hurricane on record.

Back in the cargo area, Berkeley sat tired and scared but determined to get her story and save the lives of herself and Perry, who moaned occasionally, his head still in her lap.

Berkeley was not sure how serious his injuries were. The worst of it appeared to be the phosphorous burns on the side of his head. She had cleaned those wounds with towels from the latrine and applied antiseptic she found in the first-aid kit. That's what Christiane would have done for sure.

As the C-141 streaked low across the open ocean, Sanders saw a Panamanian-flagged freighter dead ahead and steaming his way. A jumbo jet flying below a thousand feet at 500 miles an hour must have been a sight to see for the freighter crew, most of whom scrambled for cover as Stoney roared directly over their heads.

But in the broad scope of things, the C-141 was only a speck on radar. And if Stoney did have to put her down out there, no one would ever find him. There would be no memorial service for sure, he thought.

He had once attended such a service when his Air Force Reserve wing lost a C-141 in Sicily. The Starlifter was taking off when one of the right engines blew up, sending red-hot rotors slicing into the fuselage. The cargo included an undocumented container of unauthorized flammables, which exploded on contact.

The six crewmembers were remembered a year later after the official reports were submitted. The sky was clear, but there wasn't a dry eye on the ground when three Starlifters flew over in the "Missing Man Formation."

It wouldn't be that way for Lieutenant Colonel Stoney Sanders, he thought. Everybody knew military aircrews smuggled contraband from one country into the next. Things like elephant tusks from Kenya and Cuban cigars. Stoney even slipped in a belly dancer from Istanbul once for a birthday party. This time, however, the brass would prefer that Stoney ditched his 30-year-old bird and simply disappeared.

CHAPTER 77

R od Timsdale swung his Lincoln Continental into his reserved parking space outside the Santee Cooper headquarters and rubbed his beady eyes. He could not believe what he was seeing.

Two TV satellite trucks had set up in his parking lot and the driver of a third one was looking for a place to do the same. That's when somebody began banging on his side window glass.

"Mr. Timsdale! Mr. Timsdale! Harve Jacobs with Live Five News. Is the dam going to break? Do you have a contingency plan? Mr. Timsdale …"

Timsdale found a parking space and tried to remember all the things he learned in "Executive Crisis Class" at Bankers Trust. Actually, it was a four-day junket to Cancun where CEOs and their companions spent a few hours trying to answer tough questions by make-believe reporters during mock interviews at poolside. Timsdale was so drunk that he grabbed his secretary by her bikini bottom, pulled her on camera and buried his face in her ample cleavage when asked what he would do if there were a nuclear accident at one of his power plants.

The only advice Timsdale could remember as a result of his crisis training was to tell the truth because it's too hard to remember all the lies. But the truth did not come easily for Rod Timsdale.

"I'd love to give you a statement, Harve," Timsdale said, emerging from his car into the glow of the klieg lights. "As you know, we at Santee Cooper always level with the public. We have nothing to hide. Apparently, some warning signals have been activated and we're in the process of determining why."

At that moment, a gust of wind blew down a light stanchion and swept it across the parking lot where it slammed into the side of a satellite truck. The reporter turned to Timsdale and asked, "Which is more dangerous, sir, a leak in your dam or a hurricane on the doorstep?"

Timsdale pushed his graying hair to one side, leaned into the wind and said, "We've handled hurricanes before, Harve. If the storm knocks out power, we'll have crews on the scene and restore power as soon as possible."

"And a dam breach, sir?"

"It's a big dam, Harve, and a tiny leak as best we can determine. No big deal, Okay?"

A few miles away and 180 feet below the surface of Lake Moultrie, a tempest swirled around a 40-foot long crack in the base of the mile-long, 60-year-old Pinopolis Dam. Not since the lakes were created in 1940 had anyone laid eyes on this portion of the concrete barrier. Sensors along the structure were designed to alert security personnel if anything unusual occurred below the water. But the only movement ever detected was that of a 130-pound catfish snagged by local fisherman three years ago.

Meanwhile, Skeeter sat in his office watching the sensor panel. Three lights flashed in the section directly above the Cooper River's main run. Timsdale walked in shaking off rainwater like wet a dog. The severity of the situation was obvious on Skeeter's face.

"There really is a leak?" Timsdale asked, grabbing Skeeter by the sleeve and moving to a corner of the room where no one could hear them.

"Seems so," Skeeter said. "Started small but getting bigger fast. Probably should send somebody down with a camera."

Santee Cooper had a dive team that trained in the company pool occasionally. But only once did they venture more than a hundred feet below the surface of the lake. That was five years ago when Lex Johnson, the team leader, called it off about two minutes after they started, saying the bottom was so littered with logs it was too dangerous.

By June 1940 the utility had obliterated more than 170,000 acres of trees to create lakes Moultrie and Marion. More than nine hundred families, most of them African American, were relocated along with 6,000 graves. Each family got their shack moved to higher ground, a brand-new screened porch, a low-interest loan to purchase farm seeds and 100 chickens.

Approximately 30 plantation houses, many of them in disrepair, were either dismantled and moved or left to drown along with church buildings, country stores, the Ferguson lumber mill, worker's housing and a Revolutionary War battlefield.

More than 9,000 men were hired to cut by hand — there were no chainsaws then — two hundred million feet of timber. But when Japan bombed Pearl Harbor everything changed. Hundreds of thousands of fallen trees where tied down to stumps to keep them from floating as the lakes were filled and most of the men went off to war.

CHAPTER 78

It didn't take an investigative reporter to figure out that Berkeley Aiken was in a tight spot. As she cowered in the cargo bay of the Starlifter, she knew Stoney Sanders was connected to the duffel bag full of cocaine she had found and that he was running scared.

She lifted Perry from her lap then slipped on a flight jacket that one of the loadmasters left nearby. She raised herself up from behind the pallets and looked out a port hole to get her bearings. She saw nothing but ocean, but judging from the position of the sun she determined they where flying low and headed north. She had no idea what Colonel Sanders had in mind.

Would he ditch the plane? Would she and Perry have to swim for their lives? Or would the Colonel simply bail out and let the aircraft crash into the sea? Maybe some fighter jets would shoot them down, putting a quick end to the drama, she thought. She peered forward at the cockpit door, trying to think of a way to get inside, disable the pilot and attempt to fly the plane herself. That's what Christiane would do.

Soon after Berkeley Aiken landed her television job in Columbia, she imagined that she would have an interesting career. She'd start out infiltrating a Soviet spy ring or uncovering a murderous KKK plot in the Ozarks or find and disclose top secret documents about a Joint Chiefs of Staff plan to take over the United States government.

Now, she re-wrapped her silk scarf around her neck, sat back and waited for Christiane to somehow tell her what to do next.

Meanwhile, Stoney Sanders slipped his handcuffed hands into a pocket of his flight suit and pulled out the fat marijuana joint he had been given, flicked a Bic, lit up and inhaled. He'd wondered what it would be like to fly an airplane while stoned. The pot was powerful and he was ripped, which reminded him, he hadn't eaten anything since Antigua.

Back at Homestead, Sergeant Rick Nelson was frustrated as he tried in vain to find the hijacked plane on a large radar screen inside the control center. Just outside the door, the dayroom was filled with officers anxiously waiting for him to get a reading. He could see them milling around through the glass double-doors.

Then, two men wearing plain clothes arrived. This was not a good sign within the confines of an airbase headquarters building. One of them wore a blue seersucker suit.

The station boss, Colonel John "Soupy" Campbell, poked his head into the radar room and asked if Sanders had changed course, speed or altitude. Nelson shook his head again as he had been doing all along. How was he supposed to know if Sanders changed course, speed or altitude? He had no idea where Sanders was other than somewhere over the Atlantic Ocean.

Colonel Campbell walked back into the day room to confer with the suits.

Sergeant Nelson, an eight-year veteran of the Air Force, had been involved in enough special operations not to ask questions. The military's "need to know" doctrine applied to practically everything regarding his job. Soupy stuck his head inside the radar room again and asked, "Where are the Falcons, Sergeant?"

"Our F-16s are two hundred clicks offshore and calling for another fuel tanker, sir," he responded.

Soupy returned to the dayroom where the man in the seersucker suit spoke for the first time. He was older than the others. His hair was longer and graying.

"The word from Ascension is there are two other people on board," he said to Colonel Campbell softly. "One is a loadmaster, Sgt. Perry Barnes. The other is a TV anchorwoman, Miss Berkeley Aiken ... my daughter."

Soupy Campbell stared at Bernard Aiken and asked, "What do you want us to do about that, sir?"

"Call in your Falcons, Colonel. The tankers are grounded due to the weather. There is no way to refuel those F-16s in flight. Call them back now or you will lose them too."

Sergeant Nelson flipped two switches and did as he was told. Within minutes the squadron of F-16s banked back toward the Atlantic coastline, the crews happy to dodge the storm. "Roger that," Colonel Henry "Hot Rod" Hanks said as his team of fighters broke off and headed for home.

As the huge hurricane roared across the Atlantic, all Air Force, Navy, Marine and Coast Guard aircraft on the East Coast were evacuated inland.

Except one.

CHAPTER 79

"Keesler, this is Momma Bear, do you read me?"

The response from the Air Force Base was loud and clear.

"Yes Ma'am, Momma Bear, go ahead."

"We're within a hundred clicks of the target and request permission to fly the triangle," Capt. Bonnie Bezner said, looking out the window of her WC-130 Hurricane Hunter as it approached the outer bands of Hurricane Hugo from the west.

"Proceed, but maintain radio contact."

"Roger, Keesler, we'll pick our point, fly the usual entry from northwest, cut the eye, exit the southeastern wall, then back up the eastern side and cut it again, northeast to southwest," Bezner said calmly as if she were about to wax the kitchen floor. "We're dropping two dropsondes and will relay wind speeds and pressures in real time."

As Bezner said those words, the plane slammed into a wall of turbulence that jerked the nose of the aircraft sideways, jolting everyone on board. But the crew was experienced. Each simply tightened her seatbelt. So far, so good, thought Bezner, a veteran of 28 intercept missions with tropical storms and hurricanes.

But she wasn't always so calm. She was often reminded by her maintenance crew chief that her aircraft was nothing more than a lot of spare parts flying in formation, and that winds gusting up to 200 knots could rip the wings off if the pilot didn't know what she was doing.

She thought about this each time she took a Hercules through the outer walls and into the eye of a storm, and she always was amazed at the stability of the craft after she flew back out. People often asked if her plane had extra support built into the wings, and they were stunned when she said no; they were built strong from the start.

At least she hoped so.

The sky grew dark as the Hercules entered the outer bands of a storm and heavy rain assaulted the aircraft. Then, out of nowhere, an invisible hand grabbed the plane and shook it like a gallon of paint. Bezner threw up at this point during her first mission, and there was no shame in it. Almost every crewmember grabbed the barf bag at least once in their careers. But no one did this time.

"OK girls," she said over the intercom. "We're going in. It's all about penetration, right?"

CHAPTER 80

Monroe Monteith lived with his mother and spent most of his monthly disability check on police equipment from mail-order magazines. It didn't matter much to him. The half-million-dollar trust fund left to him by his grandmother paid for the rest of his toys.

His favorite uniform was gray, like those worn by highway patrol troopers, but he also liked his camouflage outfit for going into the swamp. Most folks in Berkeley County knew Monroe was strange. The sheriff warned him about impersonating police officers, but never did anything about it. Monroe was harmless and everybody knew it.

Monroe even worked traffic duty on Friday nights during high school football games. It made him and his mother proud. The locals called him Barney Fife, and often asked if he remembered in which pocket he kept his bullet. Actually, Monroe had lots of bullets and lots of guns. Monroe also had an uncanny ability to show up at crime scenes and accidents before the police did.

Like the time a man got his arm chewed off by an alligator at the Navy's recreation area on the lower lake. Turned out the only person within 10 miles was Monroe Monteith, who clamped a tourniquet on the victim and got him to the Emergency Room before EMS left the station. Monroe also shot the gator and retrieved the man's arm from the belly of the beast in case the surgeons wanted to sew it back on. They tried, but failed.

Last year a little girl fell down a well in St. Stephen. Monroe showed up within 20 minutes, lowered himself down and brought the child back up, much to the delight of the neighbors who had gathered round. The local Red Cross gave him a plaque for his heroic action and the St. Stephen's Chamber of Commerce provided him a year's supply of doughnuts.

Now, with his truck's emergency lights flashing and siren blaring, Monroe Monteith was in the thick of it again as his passenger Brent Lee flipped switches on the police radio under the dash.

"Which channel you looking for?" Monroe asked as he ran a red light. "I got 'em all? You want city police, county police, state troopers, fire departments, Coast Guard? I got 'em all."

Brent was frantic to figure out where his family was.

"Have you heard anything about a woman and two kids being kidnapped?"

"No," Monroe said. "You got any clues?"

"Only this," Brent said as he reached into his pocket and retrieved the singed matchbook cover that he found near the landing strip. "What do you make of it?"

* * *

Huddled in a backroom of the cabin, Stacia Lee and her children were given Snickers bars, bottled water, and orders to keep quiet or else. She entertained Graycen and Grant with whispered stories about how their father was planning their rescue. She convinced them it was all a game and everything would turn out fine.

"I don't know when he'll get here," she said softly. "But you know Daddy won't let anything bad happen to us. He just wants us to play along until he arrives."

Graycen was old enough to know this was not a game, but her little brother Grant was not.

"Shut up in there," one of the men hollered from the other side of the door.

Stacia lifted her index finger to her lips and looked at Graycen, who was on the verge of tears.

"Daddy's coming," she whispered. "I promise."

CHAPTER 81

Rolex Bishop thumbed a microphone as he sat in the backseat of a black van and spoke to the Berkeley County Sheriff's Office dispatcher.

"Patch this through to Sid Rice or you're going to have some dead kids on your hands," he said. After a brief pause, he added, "How in the hell would I know where he is? Just find him. Fast."

Sid Rice was not far away. In fact, he was standing directly behind the dispatcher, who was trying to keep Rolex on the air long enough for agents to pinpoint his position. Unfortunately, Rolex had instructed his driver to move the van every three minutes, roaring 10 miles down dirt roads and firebreak lanes, then stopping, just to keep the feds guessing.

Sid Rice grabbed the phone and said, "Talk to me, Herman."

Rolex's face reddened. He hated his first name.

"Don't call me that!" he responded. "Sidney!"

Sid Rice knew better than to get into a war of words with a desperate man.

"What do you want, Mr. Bishop?"

"You know the drill, Sidney. I've got the woman and the kids. I want a flight out immediately. No kidding around. I'll kill 'em."

There was a long pause as Rolex listened to the static on the radio.

"Where do you want to go?" Rice asked.

More static.

"Santee Cooper's got a corporate jet at the Summerville Airport. Fuel it up and have it ready to go in an hour. I'm taking the woman and kids with me, so no tricks. You hear me?"

The airways crackled some more.

"I hear you, Mr. Bishop. Jet at Summerville, one hour. Anything else?"

Silence.

"Yeah, Sidney, stock the galley with dinner for six from that rib joint you like over in Kingstree!"

"Brown's Barbecue?"

"Yeah, I've seen you and your family in there on Friday nights. Nice family you got. A lot like Mrs. Lee and the kids," Rolex chuckled.

Sid Rice adjusted his headset and sighed. The thought of this drug dealer watching his family gave him the creeps.

"See you in an hour," he said. "Don't be late."

Rolex threw the microphone into the front seat.

"Haul ass," he yelled to the driver, who wheeled the van from a dirt road onto Highway 52 and sped past Monroe's truck, which was sitting in a church parking lot.

"That's it," Monroe said to Brent as he pulled his night-vision goggles down over his eyes. "The rats are headed to their hole."

CHAPTER 82

"You have got to be shitting me!" Billy Glover yelled, then slugged down his eighth Rolling Rock beer while sitting in the Volcano Lounge on Ascension Island. "That crazy-ass pilot of ours took off in our plane and just left us here in the middle of nowhere? That sorry son of a bitch stole a C-141 and hauled ass, and there ain't another airplane in the entire U.S. Air Force that can come get us?"

The folks sitting around the table were as astonished as Billy Glover about the situation, but not as outspoken. Some saw the cargo plane take off a few hours earlier. Others heard it. All thought it was routine until the word spread that it wasn't.

"The station chief told us we might be here for a while," the mayor of Gaston said. "They can't come get us until they know exactly where that hurricane's going."

Glover slammed his beer bottle down and screamed, "That hurricane is headed straight for South Carolina, and I've got 600 brand new shiny Chevrolets sitting outside under a whole lot of tall light poles. Even worse, my dumb-ass son-in-law's in charge of things while I'm off on this snipe hunt on an island halfway between Brazil and Booga Booga land!"

"Well, maybe the storm will turn and everything will be all right," Pastor Clamp said, hopefully.

"Hell's Bells, Padre!" Glover snorted. "There's a big-ass hurricane headed toward our homes and we can't even make a friggin' phone call."

Glover stared at the group, his eyes wide open and his nostrils flared. "Not only that, we're about to run out of beer!"

CHAPTER 83

J unior Jones stared into space as he listened to three civil engineers discuss the ramifications of a dam break.

"Basically," one said, "a rupture of this nature could cause a chain reaction all along the spine of the structure resulting in a major collapse."

The idea of a 50-foot wall of water barreling down the Cooper River, drowning everything in a 50-mile-wide swath to the Atlantic Ocean was more than most at the table cared to think about.

Junior's head pounded from a combination of ingredients he had flushed through his system the night before, all of which, taken individually, would kill a bull. But he knew he didn't have nearly the headache that Rod Timsdale suffered.

And of all the people who could have been sitting at the head of this table on this day, Timsdale would have been everybody's last choice. Mainly because he wasn't a Santee Cooper man. He didn't come up through the ranks. He was a political appointee, primed to spearhead a mega-million-dollar joint land development project between Santee Cooper and the timber companies.

Timsdale's expertise was in organizing fundraisers, not fixing broken dams. He preferred discussing fiscal matters over cocktails at the Summit Club instead of a heavy dose of physical reality.

"We should do something," said Timsdale, who showed up for the meeting in a light blue University of North Carolina jogging suit. "What's the consensus of the group?"

The engineer clones huddled quickly at their end of the table, rolled out maps and scratched their heads. They quickly concluded that it would be best to slowly open the floodgates, lessen the pressure in the area where the dam was leaking and allow the water to permeate the entire flood plain before filtering out to sea.

"But there's a hurricane coming," Junior reminded them, noting that if Charleston gets a direct hit, the high winds combined with the massive storm surge would double or triple the amount of water in the basin, and when it all finally did rush toward the Atlantic, the flooding would be immeasurable.

Skeeter sat next to Junior. On each side of them sat a bevy of assistant vice presidents who didn't have a clue about what to do. Junior, thick-tongued and dead-eyed, cleared his throat and asked sheepishly, "Why don't we just plug the hole?"

Everybody turned and looked at him with astonishment.

"How?" Timsdale asked.

Skeeter could tell that Junior was at a loss for words, so he did what any good utility pole cat would do: came to his rescue.

"I think what Junior means is that maybe there's a way we could assess the size of the leak, jury-rig some sort of plug and, you know, stop it up until the storm passes, giving us time to implement a permanent solution."

One of the engineers raised his hand, asking for permission to speak. Timsdale gave him a nod.

"We've got a large steel slab down at the shop that I asked them to save for something like this. If we can locate the leak, we could slide the slab into the lake and down the concrete wall and the suction might keep it in place for a while."

The row of vice presidents nodded in unison.

"But our dive team has evacuated," Timsdale said.

Skeeter lowered his head, rubbed his bald spot and said, "I know somebody who could do it."

CHAPTER 84

J osh Jenkins was packing up his minivan when the call came in from Santee
Cooper headquarters. His daughter was strapped into the car seat and his wife,
Dora Ann, was inside cleaning out the refrigerator of their mobile home.

Josh, who was on the Sheriff's Department recovery team, had planned to take
his family to spend a week at Dora Ann's sister's house in Camden. But Hurricane
Hugo changed all that. Weather forecasters made it clear that the storm was headed
straight for the Lowcountry and it would be best for everyone in its wide path to
head for higher ground. Josh would use the back roads to avoid the traffic on the
interstates. Then he would be in a position to come back immediately after the
storm and relieve the other officers.

"Yo," he answered the phone.

"Hey, Josh, this is Skeeter. Glad I caught you. Where are Dora Ann and the baby?"

Josh thought for a moment before answering his father-in-law. They never did
get along, Josh being of mixed blood and all.

"What's up, Skeeter?" he finally answered.

"Josh, we've got a real serious situation here at the dam. I need your help."

"Situation?" Josh asked.

"We need a diver, Josh. All hell is about to break loose. We got a leak and we
gotta plug it!"

The coffee-colored baby was crying in the car and Dora Ann was ready to go.

"Santee Cooper has lots of divers, Skeet. I got Dora Ann and the baby in the
car ready to go."

"Look, Josh," Skeeter said. "This is urgent. We need somebody to go deep. Thousands of lives are at stake."

Josh felt his stomach flip. He never planned to go deep again. Too dangerous.

Too many things go wrong down there. He'd lost friends to snagged lines, pricked pressure suits. He had nightmares he never told anybody about.

"How deep?"

"Pretty deep," Skeeter answered.

"Where?"

"Pinopolis Dam."

Josh looked out the window and watched his daughter throw her pacifier from the back seat to the front seat.

"I'll be there in 30 minutes."

CHAPTER 85

Maceo's madness was almost complete. He could not distinguish halluci-nation from reality and George Burr represented everything evil, every-thing insulting, and everything unfair in the world. Burr's agonizing death would be the ultimate payback. Burr would be held accountable for horrors the security guards inflicted on him and all the others who were imprisoned on Bull Street.

Although Burr himself did none of the awful things that seared Maceo's terror-ized mind, he wore the uniform — that was enough. Burr symbolized the torment and he must suffer the consequences. That was the only thing that mattered now to the half-baked captain of the *Sister Santee*. Maceo was the victim, the judge, the jury and the executioner. And he would make his prisoner pay dearly.

As Burr hung half-conscious in the damp night air — injured, infected, ex-hausted — Maceo considered his options for carrying out the sentence. Now that the sun had set, Maceo was free to roam about the boat without his umbrellas; free to taunt Burr with streams of slurs and spittle, both of which dripped off the condemned man's face like drool off a mad dog's jowls.

Burr wished he were unconscious. Unable to free himself of the netting, he was Maceo's slave, doomed to suffer whatever punishments the albino's demons demanded.

"No more," Burr pleaded in a futile appeal to Maceo's fractured humanity. "Please, no more. Shoot me now. Just shoot me, Maceo!"

Maceo's rage blazed. In the recesses of his mind he could hear the cries in the bowels of the wards on Bull Street as the men in uniform beat their prisoners unmercifully. Their screams were malignant. They multiplied Maceo's madness. Although nurse Eleanor's medications tamped it down temporarily, the madness always won out.

His madness was so much stronger than drugs. Its mission was to show the world the pain and anguish and injustice inflicted on those who have no control of their lives; those whose wires are frayed, trapped behind doors that have no keys; those pitiful souls imprisoned in hell, without hope of escape.

As the winds whipped the Cooper River into a sea of whitecaps, the shrimp boat pitched and rolled. Maceo removed his camouflaged hat and allowed the slashing rain to wash over his pink-and-brown splotched face. So much of his life was in the darkness, hidden in the shadows, where sweat drips into a convergence of stench, and only he suffered the consequences, felt the hopelessness, and experienced the rage. That's why he shot the Gullah girl and left her body floating in Schitt Creek. Abandoned and afraid, she ran toward the Sister, slopped through pluff mud, knee deep until she reached the stream.

"Takes me wi'cha," she screamed as her left breast fell from the top of her white cotton dress. She waded deeper and deeper until she reached the side of the boat and tried to scratch her way onboard.

Maceo pretended not to hear her cries, poling the boat steadily off the muddy bank and into the shallow channel. She had scorned him. She was a slut, a nasty Gullah whore, he thought as he looked down into her eyes.

"Da storm he come," she said, as she slipped and fell. "Takes me wi'cha, Maceo. Takes me wi'cha."

Maceo looked down at her, leveled the gun barrel and shot her between the eyes.

Then he turned the bow toward the river while remembering his brothers joking about the difference between a whore and a bitch. "A whore," they said with a laugh, "is a woman who fucked everybody; a bitch is one who fucked everybody but you."

"B-b-bitch," Maceo said softly as he pulled away.

CHAPTER 86

Perry Barnes moaned as he regained consciousness and looked around, trying to figure out where he was. He saw Berkeley and thought it must be heaven.

"What happened, Angel?" he asked.

Berkeley was rummaging through the emergency kit.

"Perry," she said, leaning down to his face. "You okay?"

"What happened?" he asked.

Berkeley checked his eyes and mopped his brow with her scarf.

"Do you remember anything?"

Perry thought for a few seconds and said, "Stoney was stealing the plane."

She leaned close to his left ear and whispered, "He hijacked it, Perry, and he shot you with a flare gun. You fell down the stairs, and I think you broke your ankle. We're airborne, just you and me and Stoney."

Perry winced as he tried to move his right leg. He attempted to lift himself up, but fell back in agony.

"Don't," Berkeley said, holding him down. "We'll figure a way out of this. I don't know where he's going or what he plans to do with us. And I have a feeling he doesn't either."

In the cockpit, Stoney Sanders, still high as a kite, ate a bagel from a bag he found under the co-pilot's seat. It satiated his hunger, but did nothing to satisfy his anxiety. He knew from listening to the radio that the Air Force was tracking him, and he was pretty sure from the sound of foreign chatter on low frequencies that the word was spreading. He had nowhere to go except home.

He looked at a huge green blob on the screen of his radar. Hurricane Hugo, now a Category Four storm, was dead ahead and headed north, northeast. Riding it in was his only chance. What better place to hide than in the middle of a hurricane?

CHAPTER 87

Brent Lee knew Monroe Monteith was a crazy cop impersonator. Every town has one, or two. While most are harmless, some use the badge and flashing lights as a license to perform unspeakable acts in the name of the law. Their disguises can be purchased at any Army-Navy surplus store.

But Monroe was relatively tame. He just liked to dress up. One day he would be a sheriff's deputy, the next a park ranger. Tonight he was a genius. He had pulled his Chevy into a church parking lot not far from Pinopolis after Brent retrieved his only clue — a partially burned match book he found on the ground near Rolex's shattered brief case.

Monroe took one look at the mysterious letters "PEE LO" and said, "Fasten your seatbelt, Bubba, we're headed to Wampee Lodge!"

That's when the black van carrying Herman "Rolex" Bishop pulled out of a dirt road and onto Highway 52 across from the church parking lot.

"You see that?" Monroe asked as he fell in behind them. "Ain't nobody who lives round here got a black van, and it's headed to Wampee!"

As they got closer and closer to the gate to the lodge, Brent became more and more convinced that Monroe was not as dumb as he looked.

"Let's pull them over and see what happens," Monroe suggested.

"You think they're gonna just pull over if you hit the blue light?" Brent asked, sarcastically.

"Well, it worked on 'Cops' the other night," Monroe said.

"You mean that new TV show?"

"Yeah," Monroe said. "Last night they had a deputy from Tampa, I think it was Tampa, it might have been Orlando, chasing bad guys all by himself, and he hit the light and they pulled over. Just like that. He said it was a natural-response thing."

Brent didn't think it would work but was willing to try anything at this point. "You got an extra gun?" he asked.

Monroe looked at him with a smile, reached behind him and lifted up the back seat. Under the cushion were five semi-automatic pistols, a deer rifle and a sawed-off shotgun.

"These will do," Brent said slipping a .45-caliber Beretta into his belt while grabbing the rifle.

With a nod, Monroe picked up a Smokey-the-Bear style hat from a hook behind him, pulled it down on his head and tightened the chinstrap.

"Stay back 20 yards or so," Brent said. "I'll slide out and come around on their blind side. You do the cop thing. But don't get too close."

Monroe pulled up behind the van and flipped on his blue lights. The van driver slowed then pulled off onto the side of the road. Monroe stopped about 20 yards behind. Brent used the barrel of the Beretta to smash the inside dome light, opened the passenger door and slid into a drainage ditch.

Monroe turned on his side-mount 20-million-candle-power spotlight and shined it on the van. There was no traffic, only two vehicles on a two-lane road in the middle of the forest.

"Step out of the vehicle, now!" Monroe announced over his loudspeaker. "Step out of the vehicle with your hands visible and get on the ground."

Nobody moved. The van sat idling.

Monroe used his CB radio to send out an SOS to anyone listening.

"Breaker, breaker, this is Monroe. I'm with a federal agent and we got some bad guys stopped out Highway 52 near the fish hatchery. We need backup. Over."

There was no answer, just static on the radio, which didn't surprise Monroe. Every available law officer was working traffic and security by this point, trying to get people evacuated ahead of the storm.

Monroe slowly opened his door, stepped out onto the highway and walked toward the van. As he approached, he did what every law enforcement officer does. He touched the back of the van with his hand, to leave his fingerprints. At least that way, if everything went wrong, the forensic folks would be able to prove this was the vehicle involved in his murder. He learned that from watching "Cops," too.

Monroe would have made a good police officer if he were halfway normal. In his mind he was Wyatt Earp and Melvin Purvis incarnate. He drew his revolver without a hint of nervousness and kept his eyes on the driver-side door. He tapped the side of the van with the barrel of his gun.

"This would be a good time to exit the vehicle," he shouted. "I'd like to see your driver's license, registration and proof of insurance."

That's when the back tire of the van dug in to the roadside gravel and began to spin. Monroe pumped two bullets into both tires on the left side of the vehicle, two more shots into the driver's window, rolled into the ditch and came up firing.

The van careened off the road and into a stand of pine trees. Two men burst out of the back doors with automatic machine guns blazing. The headlights, side-mounted spotlight and four of the six blue-and-white flashing lights across the top of Monroe's Chevy were blown to smithereens.

Brent, who had climbed into a deer stand, took aim with the Beretta and snuffed two of the gunmen in their tracks. He didn't know how many more were still inside. Monroe's shots into the driver's window blinded the man behind the wheel. The driver fell across the front seat screaming. Rolex wriggled out through the front passenger door and headed on his hands and knees toward the woods.

At that moment, Brent especially appreciated Monroe's attention to detail. He pulled his night-vision goggles down over his eyes, brought the 30.06 caliber deer rifle to his shoulder and zeroed in on Rolex's fat ass. Brent took a deep breath, caressed the trigger and pulled gently as he exhaled.

The round slammed into Rolex's backside and exploded out of his chest like a cannonball. In an instant, it was over. When Brent rolled the big man over, Rolex had a look of complete surprise on his face, as if frozen in time.

Monroe yanked open the driver's door and smiled. One more shot echoed through the endless woods.

CHAPTER 88

The Cooper River parade of boats fleeing the hurricane had stopped and the skies were grim as Hugo zeroed in on Charleston. On his transistor radio, Maceo heard the voice of WTMA's Dan Moon advising listeners in the area that it was too late to run.

"This storm is a killer, folks," he said in his deep baritone voice. "Don't fool with it. I'm telling you straight up. Hunker down as best you can. We've never seen one like this."

Maceo's head was about to explode. The drop in air pressure was a vice on his temples, squeezing his brain, bulging his eyes, causing him to see things that were not there. He saw a church choir, dressed in purple robes, standing in water up to their knees, singing…

"Some say Peter, some say Paul.
Ain't but one God for we all.
You know the storm is passing over,
Hallelu."

Then he saw Eleanor running naked through the forest. She was scratched and bleeding profusely, and being chased by a man. Maceo took aim and fired at him. The echo was quickly swallowed by the howling wind.

"N-n-nine."

Then he saw hospital cops behind every tree. They smirked and began rolling up their sleeves.

Blam! Blam!

"Eight. S-s-seven."

He saw doctors in white coats sitting at tables stacked with folders and speaking in foreign tongues.

Blam!

"S-s-six."

He heard a familiar scream. It was Santee splashing in the water, crying out for help, dying for the millionth time as a group of white men held her down.

"F-five. F-four."

He saw his brothers, stripped to the waist, hands tied behind their backs, holes in their heads. Before Maceo left Schitt Creek, he walked into the containers where they slept and heard them snoring. He shot them in quick succession.

"Three. T-t-two."

He dragged their bodies out back, leaned them against a tree, then loosed the starved and angry dogs, which tore into their flesh and spread their entrails across the dirt yard.

Maceo felt the slash of rain sweep across his face and reached for another umbrella. As he opened his favorite Donald Duck, a powerful gust tore it from his hands.

He fell back inside the old bus and sat down.

"They're telling us to shut down our broadcast, folks," Dan Moon explained. "They're cutting the power at the station, so be safe, be smart and I'll see you on the other side."

Maceo leveled the barrel of his pistol at the radio and fired again.

"One," he mumbled.

What followed was the silence before the storm. Maceo didn't mind. He liked silence.

Living in the forest spared him the complications of a bustling world. Some days he could hear deer walking in the woods, the swish of an owl's wings low beneath the canopy, a squirrel scrambling up the bark to its nest. The forest spoke only in whispers and with no concern about man.

Maceo liked that about his home. The trees protected him from the blistering sun. Yet, unlike him, the forest could not run when fire comes. The forest stands bravely when the blaze races through, scorching the underbrush, torching the lower limbs. Yet, in the aftermath, when the smoke dies to smoldering swirls and men in heavy boots tramp through with saws and rakes and heavy machinery, the forest is stoic, saying nothing to nobody.

It was the same with hurricanes, Maceo decided. So he would stand his ground.

As darkness enveloped his boat, a single deck light illuminated the net that ensnared George Burr, swinging slowly, soaked with rain, clinging to the last thread of his sanity, praying for a miracle.

And his prayers were answered. It felt like a slight sag at first, almost imperceptible, but his shackles of heavy, waxed hemp suddenly loosened some. As the winds whipped George's battered body back and forth above the deck, the net then shredded at his knee and his left leg jutted through. Then his right foot was freed along with his right arm. His smelly, rotten prison was unraveling.

CHAPTER 89

For two days, Interstate Highways 26 and 95 were bumper-to-bumper with cars and trucks as a half-million people fled the South Carolina and Georgia coasts. But the eastbound lanes of I-26 from Charleston to Columbia were empty except for a few emergency vehicles. Nobody in state government ever considered the enormity of such a massive evacuation, so only the westbound lanes were available for retreat.

Shortly before midnight, the eye of the 200-mile-wide hurricane turned inland It was too late for anyone between Charleston and the North Carolina line to run. They had no choice but to ride it out.

That was the decision Brent Lee made soon after he and Monroe Monteith broke through the front door of Wampee Lodge and found Stacia and the children unharmed in a back bedroom. The guards were long gone, having heard the shooting and screaming over Rolex's two-way radio shortly before he and it went dead.

Brent, Stacia, Graycen and Grant huddled in a bathtub as Monroe sat next to them and led them in prayer. Only Grant, who held his hands together reverently, got a few of the words mixed up:

"Our Father, who art in heaven," the boy prayed, "Howard be thy name …"

Just outside the door of the lodge, Lake Moultrie roiled and churned with white-caps for miles. At the Pinopolis Dam, Josh Jenkins snapped down his diving helmet, turned to his father-in-law Skeeter Simms and said through the glass, "I hope those engineers of yours know what they're talking about."

Skeeter had explained to him that the mammoth steel sheet would be lowered down the inside wall and over the crack in the dam with the hope that the pressure from the leak would hold it in place until the storm passed. The engineers stood in the wind and rain and watched as a crane lifted the 10,000-pound slab of steel from the bed of an 18-wheeler truck parked on the road across the top of the dam.

CHAPTER 90

Stoney Sanders glanced at his wristwatch, trying to figure how long it would be before he hit the outer bands of Hurricane Hugo. When he did, he noticed the date, September 21, his birthday.

At age 40, his life had come to this: flying across the Atlantic in a stolen Air Force jet, smoking pot and looking for a place to hide his cocaine. Not exactly what his father had in mind when he sent his son off to The Citadel, stood proudly in the crowd at Altus Air Force Base in Oklahoma when they pinned on his wings, and served as his best man when he married Helen Hart, the former Miss Lone Star.

Stoney remembered giving his father's eulogy inside the First Baptist Church of Elloree. The place was packed. Everybody loved his old man; only said good things about Jerry Sanders.

Stoney drummed his fingers on the yoke and wondered what people would say about him after he's gone. That's when the aircraft hit the first band on the backside of the storm. The plane dipped and rolled, and it was all Stoney could do just to hang on. His seatbelt was loose so he could defend himself from the stowaway.

The plane plunged violently and Stoney's head slammed into the ceiling. Blood gushed from a gash above his right eyebrow.

"Great!" he screamed, as he used both hands to mop the blood out of his eyes. "It's my birthday; I'm a fugitive; I'm injured; I'm handcuffed; I'm starving and there is no cake or ice cream. Happy fucking birthday to me!"

Another squall slapped the aircraft from the port side as Stoney struggled to pull the plane back onto its northwesterly course.

"Pay attention, dumb ass," he hollered to himself, and decided he needed a hit of cocaine to better focus himself. He wondered what had happened to Sergeant Barnes, the stowaway. Was he still alive after taking a live flare in the face?

Stoney never liked Barnes anyway; never trusted him. He was too coy for an enlisted man. Probably because he was an Indian, Stoney decided. It was like Barnes knew something nobody else did. Hell, you could just look at him and tell he wasn't a real American, Stoney thought.

Stoney once saw Barnes in his dress blues; saw all the ribbons for combat in countries that the United States never fought against, officially. Stoney was envious, sort of, like the Vietnam thing.

He didn't consider himself a killer. No. He was a lover, a lady's man, who looked good in his uniform and never got it dirty.

Some of his Citadel classmates called him "Jody" at their 10-year reunion. Jody is the fellow who stays behind while the others go off to war. Jody is the guy who snakes your girlfriend when you're gone. Stoney laughed it off like he always did. But laughing didn't ease the pain. It was like his best friend stuck a knife in his back. It wasn't his fault that he was a no-show. He volunteered. He wanted to go. But he became a flight-training officer in Oklahoma and shuttled diplomats back and forth to NATO meetings in Germany. They don't give out ribbons for that. But his retirement check would look the same.

It had been a while since he thought about his retirement. He had this vague notion that when he turned 60 he could walk away from Santee Cooper and the Air Force Reserve, get a couple of fat monthly checks and spend his days on his pontoon boat cruising Lake Moultrie, snorting coke with a few friends.

Now he had no friends. If he survived he would have to start over somewhere. Maybe he'd look up Rolex down in Mexico, where liquor is cheap and the senoritas live. Maybe he'd run cargo back and forth across the border, hugging the ground, avoiding radar, stuff he learned in flight school.

Again he was jolted back to reality. The air currents lifted the aircraft up for several seconds before slamming it back down. After blotting the blood on his forehead with the back of his hands, he tightened his seatbelt straps and held on tight to the yoke. For the first time, he felt a massive tailwind, ramping up his airspeed by 50 knots. It was as if he didn't need the engines — which was a good thing, because soon he wouldn't have any.

Back in the cargo bay between some pallets, Berkeley Aiken munched on a granola bar she found stashed in the rigging along the walls of the Starlifter. She secured Perry to the deck with a cargo strap after a powerful wind shear shoved the aircraft sideways, knocking her flat. Now she looked forward at the cockpit door. There was movement. The door handle turned and she saw Colonel Sanders peering out. Berkeley lay down beside Perry and did not move.

Stoney Sanders had loosed his seatbelt, set the autopilot, climbed out of his seat, opened the door and surveyed the plane, which was gliding smoothly now with a steady drone. In a flash Berkeley thought of Christiane and knew what she had to do.

CHAPTER 91

Rain pelted Josh Jenkins' deep-sea diving helmet as he told himself, "This is about the dumbest thing I've ever gotten myself into." And that was saying something.

In the Navy, he had completed 25 deep dives, repairing equipment and retrieving lost parts, including an admiral's 60-foot sailboat that sank off Rhode Island. He was a member of an elite squad, each man possessing exceptional nerve and stamina.

Most of his dives were around 100 feet or less. The maximum was 250 feet while breathing compressed air. That's when your hands become antennae in the darkness, tactile extensions of the brain. The pressure is enormous. Josh swore he was through with diving after three years service on the dive team. It was a young man's game, and upon completion of his 25th dive, he swore he would never go down again.

Skeeter tapped on his son-in-law's helmet and Josh gave the thumbs up, then grabbed hold of a thick steel handle welded securely to a massive metal plate.

"Think it'll work, Skeet?" one of the engineering clones asked as a tall yellow crane lowered the huge slab down the inside wall of the dam. The metal screeched and pounded against the concrete barrier, which vibrated under everyone's feet as it sank into the deep.

The plan was simple. They had already determined the general vicinity of the leak. Josh would ride the big steel plate almost to the bottom of the dam, then feel his way along the wall and pinpoint the crack. When he found it, he would guide the slab over the leak and let the suction of the escaping water seal it in place. The trick would be to keep himself, his air hose and his lifeline from getting trapped between the wall and the plate.

Once the plate was lowered to the proper depth, the crane operator locked the cable and waited. Skeeter Simms removed his cap, lowered his head and crossed himself.

"It'll work," Skeeter said. "It's got to."

CHAPTER 92

A hundred miles off the South Carolina coast, Bonnie Bezner and her crew churned through the thick outer bands of Hurricane Hugo. The WC-130 Hercules bucked like a bull in the turbulence as the veteran crew looked forward to entering the eye of the storm.

"Prepare to launch dropsonde," Bezner said loudly to be heard over the roar of the winds.

"Ready to drop," Sergeant Nina Logan responded.

"Launch dropsonde," Bezner ordered.

"Dropsonde away, Ma'am."

With that a small plastic tube, about two feet long, was ejected from the bottom of the aircraft into the savage winds, delivering real-time data on wind speed and barometric pressure as it fell 5,000 feet into the sea.

"Prepare for the eye," Bezner said. "We're punching through in 5-4-3-2-1."

Silence.

The outer wall was behind them now, the breakthrough heralded by the steady drone of the Hercules' engines. The crew looked out the windows and saw the gray spinning storm wall swirl behind them. From the cockpit, Bezner could look straight up and see stars, as clear as a September night back home in Indiana. But it was only a brief respite.

Maintaining a steady grip on the yoke of the Hercules, she prepared her crew for the next jolt.

"Re-entering eye wall," she said, "in 5-4-3-2-1."

Despite a thousand successful missions and the assurance of those who build and maintain the Hercules aircraft, every crewmember experiences a moment of terror when the plane hits the wall.

"That's leg one and leg two," Bezner reminded her crew. "Hang on ladies, we're going to break out, give it a good turn and plow through one more..."

The pilot was quiet for only a second or two, and then added, "Damn! Shit! Unbelievable!"

"Crew to flight deck, crew to flight deck," Sergeant Peterson shrieked through the intercom. "What's going on, Bonnie? What happened?"

The crew waited nervously for the response, but all they heard for a few seconds more was the creaking of the aircraft. Then came a click on the intercom, followed by the pilot's response:

"Flight deck to crew. Ladies, we're not alone up here. We've got a strong ping on the radar; there's another plane up here. The transponder says it's a C-141!"

Once clear of the outer bands, Bezner checked and rechecked her radar but could not find the blip on the screen. There had been one for sure, off her starboard side about 20 miles out, but now it was gone.

"Keesler, this is Momma Bear," she said, collecting her thoughts. "Are any other planes authorized for this sector?"

Her call also came through loud and clear to Sergeant Rick Nelson in Homestead, Florida. He looked up at his superiors and shrugged.

"What do I tell her?"

"Tell her it was her imagination, Sergeant."

"Think she'll buy it?"

"I don't care if she does or not, Sergeant. She's a United States Air Force pilot and she'll do what she's told."

Nelson leaned into his microphone, keyed the switch to override the Keesler command and said calmly:

"This is Homestead, Momma Bear, trying to confirm your report. Must have been that pizza you had for lunch, Major. You're the only one authorized or crazy enough to be flying in this weather."

Major Bezner stared at her radio receiver, gave a skeptical look over to her co-pilot and responded:

"Never needed a traffic cop out here before, Homestead. We've got enough to worry about without having to dodge joy riders."

There were a few clicks and a rush of static on the radio before Bezner heard the familiar voice from her home base back at Keesler.

"Break off that last leg, Momma Bear," the dispatcher in Mississippi said. "We've got enough. Looks like he's going to be a bad one. See you back at the ranch. Out."

Bezner knew better than to argue with dispatch, but something was not right. She'd never been called back like this before. Still she did as she was told. She banked the big plane away from the outstretched arms of Hurricane Hugo and headed for home.

CHAPTER 93

Junior Jones went to his office and tried to clear his head. This had been a day from hell, the kind he was not prepared for. Nothing in his South Carolina State undergraduate education or three years in the University of South Carolina Law School taught him how to face death.

His perspective had changed dramatically in the last 12 hours. Ever since he staggered away from the beach, he'd come face to face with a reality he never dreamed possible. For decades, the massive lakes held tight behind the utility's dams. The lakes were only recreational playgrounds for Junior.

He'd spent years certifying and renewing leases for people from Elloree and Orangeburg and Summerton and other surrounding communities who had lakefront parcels where they parked mobile homes and spent most of the time fishing in calm waters.

He'd spent countless hours bobbing aimlessly on the surface of Lake Moultrie himself, hundreds of feet above the sites where his ancestors lived as slaves. All of it seemed like fodder for tourism brochures now.

Santee Cooper was an engineering marvel that tamed the flow of three great rivers, harnessed the power of water and created places for people to play. The idea that all these people and all this money and all this effort could wash away like a sand castle on the beach blew Junior's mind.

He sat at his desk with his head in his hands and wept. But his tears were not for the pending disaster. He cried when he noticed an envelope that arrived earlier on his desk, addressed to him in a familiar handwriting and postmarked Columbia.

Inside was a colorful card that said, "Happy Birthday, Son" on the outside, next to a drawing of a rising sun. Inside the message read, "You make every day a great day in our lives."

It was signed, "Love, Mom and Dad."

Junior had turned 40 and wondered if this birthday would be his last.

* * *

Not far away near the headwaters of the Cooper River, a flock of gulls winged quickly across the darkening sky as George Burr's foot touched the deck of the *Sister Santee*. It was the first time in two days he'd put weight on his right leg and the pain was unbearable. He saw streaks of infection running up his calf in search of fresh blood. He knew his left foot, still folded underneath him, was worse, although he had not felt it in the past 12 hours.

But slowly, the rotted sling gave way, thread by thread. He used his hands to ease himself onto the deck while his captor slept inside the wheelhouse. Maceo retreated inside an hour earlier while cursing the rain and the wind, screaming at figments in the fog.

As George worked himself loose, he came to rest on the boat's deck, slimy with urine and feces, littered with Vienna Sausage cans and broken umbrellas. His immediate impulse was to slip over the gunnels and into the water and try to swim to shore. He'd rather drown than continue to be tortured by a maniac.

But George took a look over the side and changed his mind. The river was a tempest. It would be impossible for him to make it. He decided to lie quietly for a while, regain his strength, crawl up next to the wheelhouse door and strangle Maceo with his bare hands.

CHAPTER 94

The fuel gauge on the Starlifter indicated Stoney Sanders was almost out of fuel. His only chance was to put her down in the lakes of his youth. He was born and raised in the Lowcountry swamps, and all he could think of at the moment were the good times. Such was his delusion.

Stoney was a golden boy, capable of achieving anything, always laughing, sure to grow up and become a good ol' boy like his father. But few people knew the Sanders family secret; that his father had worked for Santee Cooper when the utility began clearing the land; that he'd been accused of stealing wedges and saws and was fired.

Old man Sanders begged to get back on with Santee Cooper, tried to explain he'd been framed. Stoney wanted to believe him, but couldn't justify the gaps in the story or the guilt in his father's eyes.

These memories rushed through his mind as he guided the aircraft into the wind field and prepared to land. That's when he heard something just outside the cockpit, turned and saw a chocolate chip cookie slide half way under the door.

After getting a whiff of marijuana smoke in the cargo bay, Berkeley decided that food was the only weapon at her disposal. She had searched the inside of one of the plane's life rafts and found a first aid kit, bottled water and a flare gun. She had looked a little more and found that some of the crew had added a stash of their own: a box of chocolate chip cookies. Christiane would know what to do with them. Berkeley did too.

Stoney wasn't sure who was outside. But he did know one thing. He should not have smoked the entire joint. His mind was muddled and he was starving. He released his seatbelt again, slipped over toward the door and took the bait.

"Got any more?" he yelled after returning to his seat. "You are the Keebler Elf, aren't you?" he added with a giggle.

Silence for a few seconds, then another cookie appeared on the floor from beneath the door.

Stoney stared at the second offering, then quietly lifted himself out of the seat, reached back with his handcuffed hands and the trap was sprung.

Berkeley saw Stoney's shadow under the door, grabbed the bar above the entrance of the flight deck, swung her body backward and slammed both feet forward against the door, which, despite the pile of flight books stacked against it, smacked Stoney square in the face.

By the time Berkeley's feet hit the floor, Stoney was sprawled on his back halfway across the pilot's seat. The blow knocked him out cold. She quickly rolled him over onto the floor and used her scarf to tie his handcuffed hands to the co-pilot's seat. Exactly the way Christiane would have done it. Then she turned, sat down in the pilot's seat and stared blankly at the C-141's wide instrument panel.

CHAPTER 95

B ernard Ishmael Achem, aka Bernie Aiken, walked out of Homestead Air
  Force Base headquarters and climbed into the back seat of a black CIA staff
limo. It was a balmy evening in South Florida. A flight of pelicans glided low and
in perfect formation overhead as the sun sank and the shadows faded. But all was
not in good order. Bernie Aiken was worried.

The Company had recruited Perry Barnes soon after he graduated from Marine Corps boot camp. Perry was strong, smart and Cherokee. During the Korean
Conflict the agency relied on Native Americans just as the Allies used Navajos as
code breakers during World War II. Their language skills and the color of their
skin qualified them to be trained as Special Operations chameleons for undercover
assignments in Asia, Central and South America, Indonesia and elsewhere.

Sergeant Perry Barnes was more than an enlisted Air Force loadmaster. The
unassuming Native American boy graduated from high school, spoke to a recruiter
and gave his life to the U.S. Marine Corps in 1966. His initial pay was $101.31 a
month, and it was more money than he had ever seen before. But he proved to be
a priceless commodity.

His subsequent assignments left him well-traveled and well-versed in espionage
operations. Recently he'd been assigned to Bernie Aiken, a Southern gentleman,
newspaper editor, covert CIA officer.

"Sergeant Barnes happened to be down there on another assignment," Bernie
said to the general who sat beside him in the limo. "He was gathering information
on a Columbia-area car dealer who sells imported Yugos. It's a front for a heroin-
smuggling ring — a Russian Mafia operation. Perry uncovered that scheme while
working on a nuclear matter."

Bernie Aiken explained that Communism in Soviet bloc countries was collapsing and the Berlin Wall would soon fall. He had arranged for Billy Glover to get invited on this junket to Ascension Island so Perry could spend time with him to learn more about the smuggling ring.

"So what happened?" the general asked.

"Everything happened," Bernie snapped back. "How my daughter Berkeley got asked to join them is beyond me. Go figure! Then, some whacked-out light-bird colonel steals a Starlifter. A Starlifter, mind you! And on top of all that, we've got a Category 4 hurricane bearing down on the southeastern seaboard like a freight train off the tracks, a missing jumbo jet carrying one of our best Special Ops guys as well as my only daughter and … and …"

"And what?" the general asked.

"And I forgot to renew the flood insurance policy on my house," Bernie said with a sardonic smile. Bernie Aiken, after all, was still a journalist who had not lost his appreciation for gallows humor.

Then came two sharp knocks on the car window next to the general, who lowered the glass slightly and stared.

"Excuse me, sirs," a young airman said, stiffening to attention and popping a salute at the sight of two stars.

The general feigned a return salute and said, "What is it, son?"

"Yes, sir," the airman said. "Major Burdette says we've made contact with the stolen aircraft and you should return quickly to headquarters. The pilot is a girl, sir, and she's not one of ours."

CHAPTER 96

Josh Jenkins' teeth chattered as he rode the steel plate down the side of the inner-wall of the Pinopolis Dam. The engineers assured him it would be a relatively safe dive; that he could avoid being sucked into the crack in the massive dike as long as he stayed above it. Once he was in position atop the plate, he could position the slab with his weighted boots and physics would take care of the rest.

What Josh already knew was that at 200 feet down, his entire body would feel as if it were caught in a giant vice, and each foot deeper he went, the pressure would feel as if it had increased tenfold.

Josh had experienced numerous close calls underwater, most of which he tried to forget. Once, when he was dropped onto a sunken research vessel in the Mediterranean, he was supposed to retrieve a computer chip that was vital in gathering evidence about nuclear dumping by Middle Eastern countries.

It was top-secret stuff. There would be no record of the dive. And if he failed to come back alive, the only thing his family would be told was that he had drowned in a freak accident in a training pool back at the base. Josh asked for no details because he knew he would get none. Later he learned that the sunken vessel was full of radioactive nuclear waste. His commander topside was under orders to sever his lifeline and his air supply and leave him down there to feed the fish if anything went wrong.

Thanks to dumb luck, Josh managed to find the chip and avoid exposure to the radioactive trash heap, much of which was spilled when the ship slammed onto the ocean floor. In fact, it was his buddies topside who saved Josh by quickly yanking him up, computer chip in hand, while the brass bickered about how safe it would for them if he got back onboard.

He never told anybody about the assignment, not even his wife. Now, he wished he had not told Skeeter he would ride this massive steel plate down and try to plug this leak. The only reason he agreed was because his father-in-law was desperate and he wanted to please the old man.

That's what he was thinking as something big knocked his legs out from under him. He fell several feet between the plate and the dam wall. As he glanced down, the light on his helmet illuminated the tail of a giant catfish bumping its nose and whiskers on the inside of the plate as if it were trying to figure out what was going on in the neighborhood.

Josh had heard stories about local fishermen hooking giant catfish near the dam. The few who managed to bring one of the bottom-feeding beasts to the surface swore the fish were at least 10 feet long and weighed 400 pounds.

Josh had always considered them fish tales, until now.

Meanwhile, atop the dam, Skeeter paced back and forth despite the wind and rain saying, "I wish there was another way. I don't like to the looks of this."

As a former pole cat, Skeeter understood the danger. He'd been up a hundred feet working on 10,000-volt transmission lines during a lightning storm because he didn't want to let his buddies down. He lost an arm doing his job. Bravery is a personal thing. It's why soldiers charge into withering machine gun fire knowing they will be cut down; why firefighters rush into burning buildings; why Josh Jenkins went down into the dark, cold lake during a hurricane to plug a leak in the failing 49-year-old dam.

"We ain't got time to figure out another way, Skeeter," the man lowering Josh's air hose said as rain raked their bodies. "If this doesn't work, we're all gonna wind up 50 miles downstream, our bodies tangled in the bells of St. Michael's."

CHAPTER 97

B erkeley Aiken settled into the pilot's seat and searched the giant control panel for anything that looked like a radio. She assumed the plane was on autopilot because it was holding its course and altitude. She just didn't know it was about to become a big glider.

Colonel Sanders was unconscious, so she leaned down under her seat to make sure his handcuffs and her scarf were solidly secured to the stand, which, of course, was bolted to the deck. She thought about using a large wrench she found in a side panel to bash the pilot in the head, just to make sure he would not regain consciousness any time soon, but decided she may need his advice on how to fly the thing.

As she fumbled with the headset and pressed buttons on the panel, she nervously repeated, "*Spirit of Charleston* to base, *Spirit of Charleston* to base, this is Berkeley Aiken. Can you read me? This is an emergency. My name is Berkeley Aiken. Can anybody hear me?"

All she heard was static that rattled her headset at various pitches and volumes.

"This is the *Spirit of Charleston*. My name is Berkeley Aiken and this is an emergency. Can anybody hear me?" she said again and again.

Finally, through the high-pitched screams of radio beams and beacons across the spectrum, Berkeley got an answer.

"*Spirit of Charleston*, this is Homestead. We can hear you loud and clear. Repeat. We can hear you loud and clear. Come back …"

Berkeley almost fell out of her pilot's seat. She grabbed what appeared to be a tuning knob and slowly dialed the voice in. "Homestead, I can hear you. Homestead, this is *Spirit* and thank God I can hear you! Somebody needs to tell me how to fly this thing. Please?"

By the time Bernie Aiken got to the communications console, Sergeant Rick

Nelson was fully engaged in conversation with the new pilot of the C-141.

"This is Homestead, we read you loud and clear, Miss Aiken. What is your situation?"

"We're over the ocean, in the eye of the storm. The pilot, Lieutenant Colonel Stoney Sanders, is knocked out cold. He's wearing handcuffs and I've managed to secure him to the flight deck. I've never flown a plane before, but I have sailed a few boats. I'm scared!"

Bernie grabbed the microphone, keyed the pad and said, "Berkeley, this is your father, do you read?"

Berkeley stared at the control panel and shook her head, wondering if perhaps she had passed out and was dreaming.

"Uh, excuse me? Could you please repeat that? Uh, over," she said.

"Berkeley Aiken, this is Bernie Aiken. It's me, Baby. Can you hear me?"

"Daddy?" Berkeley asked.

"No time to explain, dear, we'll have a nice long talk when you get home. For now, listen carefully to what Sergeant Nelson here in the control room tells you. We can get you down safely. Don't panic. He knows what he's doing. He will talk you through it. Okay?"

"Okay, Daddy. Over."

"Where is Sergeant Barnes?" her father asked.

"Perry?" she asked.

"That's correct. Where is Sergeant Perry Barnes? I understand he's in that plane with you and Colonel Sanders."

"Perry is injured. He has a broken ankle, I think, and is semi-conscious. He's in the cargo bay. Colonel Sanders is unconscious, too, and lying here at my feet in the cockpit. He's crazy, Daddy. I don't know what he's liable to do when he comes to. Uh, over..."

Before she could finish the sentence, the aircraft had drifted to the port and had a scrape with the hurricane wall. The plane twisted left then right and plummeted 500 feet like a kite in a dive.

Berkeley, dazed and confused, struggled to secure her seatbelt and grabbed the yoke, wondering what to do next to keep the aircraft from coming apart.

"Um, Daddy, I've got a problem here," she said calmly.

Realizing the autopilot had switched off, Sergeant Nelson leaned into the microphone and spoke slowly:

"Berkeley, this is Sergeant Nelson. Listen carefully now. I can help you. Grab the yoke — grab the steering wheel in front of you, and pull it up steadily. Pull up steadily, do you read me?"

Berkeley squeezed the two pistol grips on the wheel and pulled back steadily at first, and then as hard as she could. But she was not strong enough to even slow the dive.

"I can't do it!" she screamed. "We're going down! We're going down, and I can't stop it!"

"Just keep pulling back, Berkeley. Secure your feet to the deck as best you can, grab hold and pull. Pull, Berkeley, Pull! You can do it," Nelson said.

That's when Sergeant Perry Barnes slipped in behind her, stepped over Colonel Sanders and slid into the co-pilot's seat beside her. His leg was severely injured but he was there sitting next to Berkeley. She managed a sigh of relief as she continued to pull back as best she could on the yoke.

"I've got it Berkeley," Perry said calmly. "I've got it now."

Barnes pulled the nose of the aircraft up and maneuvered back into the eye of the hurricane.

"Homestead, this is Sergeant Perry Barnes, United States Air Force. I'm here in the cockpit with Miss Aiken and await further instructions, over."

"What happened to Stoney?" Perry asked her.

"I fed him, then put him to bed," she said.

"Great, so where are we?" Perry asked.

"I have no idea, Perry. Ask the guy on the radio."

"Still awaiting instructions, Homestead," Perry said. "Do you read me?"

"Loud and clear, Sergeant, glad you could join us," Nelson said, adding, "Standby, Perry, someone here wants to say Hi."

"Perry, this is Bernie Aiken, what the hell are you doing up there with my daughter?"

"Uh, nothing, Sir … Uh …," Perry stuttered. "All is above board, Sir. It's way past curfew and we're trying to get her home safely."

"See that you do, young man. See that you do, over."

Bernie Aiken handed the microphone back to Nelson, mopped sweat off his brow and asked for a cup of coffee.

"OK boys and girls, this is Sergeant Nelson. From the looks of things, you appear to be close to the northeast quadrant of the storm. What does it look like outside? Over."

The aircraft jerked and rocked as Perry located the altimeter and tried to determine their position.

"Which way should we turn to exit this joy ride?" Perry asked. "It all looks bad out there to me."

By now three pilots from another squadron had joined the group in the headquarters radio shack and were eager to lend a hand.

"Any of you guys ever flown in a hurricane?" Major Burdette asked them.

All three shook their heads negatively. "We're jet jockeys, Sir," one of them, a captain, replied.

Within minutes Nelson had patched through his communications dispatchers trying to locate the W-130 Hercules, commanded by Major Bonnie Bezner. It didn't take long to find her.

"Homestead, this is Major Bezner," the radio squawked. "How can we help you?"

Bezner and her team of Hurricane Hunters were well out of harm's way by now, cruising toward their home station in Mississippi.

"Major, we've got a C-141 hung up smack dab in the middle of Hugo, do you read?" Nelson asked.

"Loud and clear," Bezner said. "I thought I saw that plane while cruising the neighborhood."

"Here's the deal, Major," Nelson responded. "The pilot is out of commission and we've got a loadmaster and a TV reporter at the controls. Can you help us?"

"What is the Starlifter's position?" Bezner asked.

"In the eye, Ma'am, near the northeast quadrant," Nelson said.

"Roger that," Bezner said. "Tell them to climb to 20,000 feet on a heading of north-northeast and hold on tight. If they're lucky they'll slingshot out the right side like a rock from a lawn mower."

CHAPTER 98

Inch by inch, George Burr dragged himself along the slippery deck of the *Sister Santee*, worried as much about the boat sinking as he was about Maceo awakening to his current state of madness. The vessel had taken on a lot of water and listed badly. The bullet that tore off George's left toe also blew a gaping hole in the bottom of the boat, and the bilge pump couldn't keep up with the leak.

George — one leg numb and infected, the other barely functional — managed to strip the duct tape from his hands, legs and face, but he was extremely weak. Inside the wheelhouse, he could see the pink man slumped in the driver's seat with the pistol in one hand and cradling six sticks of dynamite in the other.

Dynamite? George wondered. What was Maceo doing with dynamite? He had enough to blow the boat and everyone on it to Kingdom Come. That's if the hurricane didn't do it first.

The Sister chugged slowly upstream and around a final bend and straight toward the locks of the Pinopolis Dam. On the other side of the massive concrete structure, nearly 200 feet below the surface of the Lake Moultrie, Josh Jenkins struggled to maneuver a huge steel plate attached to a chain from a crane into place, just above where the safety engineers pinpointed the leak. Visibility at that depth was minimal, but sound was magnified.

As the steel plate swayed and banged against the concrete base of the structure, the clanging reverberated in Josh's metal helmet and rattled every bone in his body. He could also hear a swooshing sound of water swirling around him in a rush to escape through the crack to the other side of the wall.

In theory, covering it would be a relatively simple procedure. Just lower the plate to the crack, waddle it over the leak, let the vacuum suck it into place and pull the diver back up to the surface. Once the hurricane passed, permanent repairs could be completed.

But as Josh inched the plate closer to the target, something slammed him from behind, spun him around and sent him reeling against the wall. As he flailed in the darkness and grabbed for his lifeline, something hit him again. Trying to regain his balance, he felt his body being sucked into the vortex between the plate and the wall. Josh tried frantically to climb the wall, his gloves slipping on the slime and his legs unable to find a foothold.

Again he was hit, this time on the side of his helmet. Josh quickly turned his head, peered through the window of his helmet and was eye-to-eye with a giant catfish!

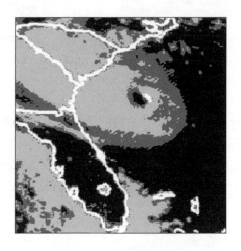

CHAPTER 99

As the eye of Hurricane Hugo crossed Charleston Harbor around midnight, observers at the National Weather Service in Bethesda, Maryland, could not believe what they were seeing.

"Hey, Sam," one said. "What the hell is that thing?"

As both men leaned closer, the massive green swirl filled the radar screen as it swallowed coastal South Carolina. And there, moving fast in the northeast quadrant, was a dark, missile-shaped object headed straight toward the shore.

"Should we tell anybody about this?" Sam asked. "Make a note or something?"

"Nah," the other said. "It'll be gone before you can write it down."

Meanwhile, in the cockpit of the C-141, Berkeley Aiken and Perry Barnes were on the ride of their lives. Perry held the yoke in a death grip and scanned the instrument panel: Altitude 10,000 feet; groundspeed 200 miles per hour; fuel gauge empty. Moments later, the engines shut down, and all they could hear outside was the horrendous howl of Hugo's winds.

The huge transport plane was now the world's largest glider. It was as if a giant hand grabbed the *Spirit of Charleston* and hurled it like David's proverbial stone toward shore.

"Can you see anything, Berkeley?" Perry screamed. "Look for a place to land!"

Berkeley wiped the windshield and searched through the angry skies for land. Then she saw a flash, and seconds later another.

"It's the light house!" she yelled. "I see the lighthouse!"

"Which one?" Perry asked.

"Sullivan's Island, I think!"

"Okay, that means the Santee Cooper lakes are dead ahead," Perry said. "I'll try to put her down in the lakes. It's our only chance!"

About 30 miles inland, hurricane-force winds and heavy bands of rain raked the top of the Pinopolis Dam as Skeeter Simms and the others struggled to keep their balance while diver Josh Jenkins positioned the steel plate over the leak far below the surface. The tall Santee Cooper crane that held the plate pitched violently from side to side, its cable swinging wildly. Something happened down below. Something was terribly wrong, and Skeeter knew it.

"Pull him up!" Skeeter screamed. "We've got to Josh out of there now!"

That's when he saw it. He looked down at the roiling surface of Lake Moultrie and saw his son-in-law's air hose snaking loosely and slapping against the concrete wall. For a full minute, he watched and waited, hoping Josh would surface. Then someone behind him hollered: "It stopped! The leak stopped! Josh did it, Skeeter! He did it!"

But Skeeter could not move. The plate was in place and the leak was sealed, but his son-in-law was gone and there was no one there who could save him.

"Skeeter, we've got to get off the top of the dam. The crane could go at any minute. The winds are increasing. We have to go inside," one of the workers screamed. The others grabbed Skeeter, pulled him back from the edge of the wall and into the guard's shack atop the wall. They scurried down the stairs deep into the bowels of the concrete dam, hunkered down and waited for the storm to pass.

Skeeter was in shock. What would he tell his daughter and his grandchild? Josh Jenkins was dead. He gave his life to save the dam.

CHAPTER 100

Bits of concrete, nails, sheets of tin, tree limbs and other flying debris hammered Santee Cooper's headquarters, located on high ground just east of the Pinopolis Dam. Down the hall from the control room, Junior sought refuge in the executive washroom. As he pulled back a shower curtain, he found Rod Timsdale, cowering in the tub, saying his prayers.

Junior closed the curtain and selected a toilet stall where he did some praying of his own.

If God would let him survive this, Junior vowed, he would change his ways; he'd go home to Columbia and marry Della with the big tits and ample ass; he'd join the church, make babies and his momma and daddy would be proud.

Just south of the bunker-like Santee Cooper headquarters, the *Spirit of Charleston* screamed down from the sky headed straight for the Pinopolis Dam. Inside the cockpit, Perry and Berkeley pulled back on both yokes as hard as they could, trying to keep the plane's nose up. As a powerful flash of lightning illuminated the sky, each saw the dam ahead. It would be only moments before they reached the wall at the northern most point of the Tail Race Canal.

"We've gotta clear the wall!" Perry yelled. "We've gotta clear the wall! Pull up! Pull up!"

As the silent Starlifter sailed directly over *Sister Santee*, George Burr was on the deck, fighting desperately to keep the savage winds of a thousand small tornadoes from sweeping him over the side.

George again pulled himself up to look through a window of the wheelhouse to see what Maceo was up to. But the madman was gone.

As he wiped the rain from his face and looked around, George recoiled as another lightning flash lit up the sky and a clap of thunder rattled the wooden deck. That's when George saw the maniac only a few feet away, balancing himself at the bow.

Falling to his knees and facing the dam, Maceo held the pistol in his right hand and clutched the explosives in his left. He cursed the storm and God who created it, but again his protest was ignored, his anguish expressed in vain; his words empty, swept away by the wind as soon as they left his lips; his tattered and tangled life just another piece of debris hopelessly lost in the storm.

Maceo turned toward George and glared at the Bull Street cop through eyes as red as blood. He slowly raised the pistol and aimed at George's head. He struggled to steady his arm as the rain pummeled his pink face. Gone were Maceo's jungle hat and aviator sunglasses — stolen away along with his words by the angry storm.

George could not move now. The last ounce of his strength expended. He knew his life was about to end. He held his breath and waited. Would he hear the sound as the firing pin hit the 38-caliber round? Would he feel any pain?

Maceo's finger tightened on the trigger and …

Click.

Click, click, click.

The madman had miscounted.

Again, Maceo looked up and cursed heaven, only this time the wind stopped blowing momentarily, followed by a deafening clap of thunder and a flash of lightning that hit the bow with the force of a thousand jagged swords.

George remembered being thrown backwards into the rotten nets, and as he fell into the slimy deck again he saw Maceo's face, which seemed only for an instant to be relieved of all his agony.

Through the twisted limbs of his mangled mind, Maceo saw the early morning sun breaking over the tops of hundreds of thousands of pine trees. It was as if he was in the fire tower again, waiting for the blue hues and pink ribbons of light to flood across the expanse of the forest. Maceo, it seemed, was happy.

A million volts of electricity struck Maceo's gun that night, ran up the barrel and through his veins, broiling his skin, frying his innards and leaving his body smoldering and sizzling in the rain. The gun, its handle melted into a puddle of plastic, lay on the deck nearby along with the bundle of dynamite, unexploded and exposed for what it really was — a dud, long lost in some sort of military simulation.

George looked at the charred and worthless heap of what used to be Maceo Mazyck and thought: The long-suffering Pink Nigger finally, undeniably was completely black.

CHAPTER 101

The bright lightning strike that took Maceo's life also allowed Perry Barnes and Berkeley Aiken to see the crane atop the Pinopolis Dam. They did manage to keep the cargo plane's nose up just enough to miss the crane and clear the wall.

As Skeeter Simms lay flat on the floor inside the dam, he heard the loud, grating sound of the aircraft as it scraped across the concrete. Perry managed to land the plane in Lake Moultrie as it skipped like a smooth stone and came to rest near what was left of somebody's dock.

"Hurry," Perry said to Berkeley as they unhooked their seat belts. "It's about to sink."

From the pilot's seat, Perry flipped the windshield clamps and used his right foot to kick out the side window of the cockpit. Berkeley helped Perry as they clambered out and onto the wing just as the last of Hugo's fury passed.

Later as the sun rose, the lake resumed an eerie serenity, except for the sounds of pontoon boats working their way through flotsam strewn across the waters.

Berkeley and Perry got a good look at what the storm left behind – rooftops, baby carriages, lawn furniture, lampshades, mattresses and an orange Volkswagen, bobbing around, as if it were looking for a place to park.

"You know, if Ted Kennedy had been driving a Volkswagen that night at Chappaquiddick, he would have been president," Perry quipped.

Berkeley smiled half-heartedly, but was too numb to respond.

As they were helped off the wing and into a boat, Perry noticed a large billboard floating by that read, "Welcome To Santee Cooper Country!"

The grandfather's face was completely gone but the boy's image, holding up the glistening striped bass, remained.

Then, to his left and right, Perry heard an unusual, bubbling sound. Hundreds of coffins popped to the surface of the lake — same pine boxes that contractors claimed to have dug up and re-interred on higher ground a half-century before.

"You all right?" a man yelled at Perry.

"We're okay," he said. "But there's another one inside. Bring plenty of rope. You'll need to tie him up so he won't steal your pontoon boat."

CHAPTER 102

Eight hours later, Berkeley Aiken stood atop the Pinopolis Dam as she wrapped a paisley scarf around her neck.

"We're going to satellite, Berkeley, stand by," the CNN cameraman said.

In her earpiece she could hear the producer briefing the network anchor in Atlanta.

"Her name is Berkeley Aiken, a reporter for WIS-TV in Columbia. She was on the plane. She's the heroine. She kept the plane from hitting the dam. Okay, 30 seconds…"

Berkeley scanned the crowd for Perry's face. He was the real hero. He saved her life. But he slipped away shortly after the rescuers arrived. Knowing it was only moments before she went live, she asked her cameraman if her hair was okay, still looking to maintain her "maximum minimum," even in a disaster zone.

"You look great, baby," the cameraman said, using the same line he always did when talking to female reporters getting ready to go on the air.

"This is a national feed, right?" she asked.

"No, baby," he said. "This is global. And remember, the anchor will go first and introduce you in 5,4,3…"

Berkeley took a deep breath and waited for the red light on the camera to come on. Her hand shook as she held the microphone, so she thought of Ascension Island, and the clouds sweeping in off the Atlantic, filling the gaps and ridges as it rolled in. She visualized Perry's face, illuminated in the cargo bay by St. Elmo's fire, and his deep brown eyes looking up at her.

"…2,1…" the cameraman said then pointed at her.

"Good evening, ladies and gentlemen. This is Christiane Amanpour at CNN headquarters in Atlanta. We have an incredible breaking story in what's left of

Charleston, South Carolina — ground zero for the storm of the century, Hurricane Hugo. We're switching live now to the scene where we're talking to Berkeley Aiken, a local news reporter and one of many heroes of this harrowing story."

Berkeley was suddenly taken aback. She blinked once, then said, "That's right, Christiane, it was a harrowing night here in the South Carolina Lowcountry, one that people here will never forget. The devastation is widespread; the death toll is more than a dozen and continues to climb as survivors claw their way out from the rubble.

"But there's more. Caught up in the middle of the destruction and carnage is another developing story. It's about an international drug smuggling ring, espionage, the hijacking of a U.S. Air Force jet, and the heroic efforts of a man who lost his life trying to prevent this hydro-electric dam on which I am standing from collapsing and drowning a half million people downstream."

On cue, the CNN cameraman pulled back from the close-up of Berkeley to a wide shot of the dam, then panned the cluttered landscape to show the Cooper River as it wound its way toward the Charleston.

"We'll be back at the top of the hour with more details," Berkeley said. "Now, back to you in Atlanta, Christiane."

As the monitors faded to black, Berkeley took another deep breath and dropped her head in sheer exhaustion. In the background, caught up in a mass of broken tree limbs, *Sister Santee*, her name barely visible on the bow, sank slowly into the swirling waters of the river, and disappeared.

EPILOGUE

Eight weeks later, Berkeley Aiken walked into the garden behind the Governor's Mansion in Columbia for a cocktail party. She knew her new job as anchor of the "Six O'clock News" was a result of her new star-reporter status. That was fine with her. She deserved it. She hit the trifecta. She was in the right place, at the right time, with the right stuff.

Now she and other heroes of the storm were escorted to the stage and seated. They were about to be awarded the Order of the Palmetto, the state's highest honor.

Seated to her left was Monroe Monteith. Nobody knew exactly why he was wearing a bright red Royal Canadian Mounted Police uniform. And nobody asked.

Dora Ann Simms Jenkins, holding her young daughter, was up there too. She would accept the award for her late husband, Josh, who lost his life plugging the leak in the Pinopolis Dam.

On her right was her father, Bernie Aiken, who was getting used to introducing himself as Berkeley Aiken's father, yet another identity he comfortably assumed.

Absent but accounted for was Perry Barnes, who sent Berkeley a note that she had pinned inside her suit jacket next to her heart: "Dear Berkeley, sorry I am not there for this special occasion. But our suspicions were correct. The Berlin Wall will fall soon, and I must be here to make sure all the players behave. Please wait for me. P."

As the crowd quieted and took their seats in the garden, a jazz trio played "Lullaby of Birdland." Not far away, a slow-moving coal train clanked past and a flock of starlings flushed from a leafless tree. They darted left, then right, then directly over the crowd in silent formation.

George Burr took his seat in the second row from the front. He cradled his crutches in his arms. He was flanked on one side by Special Agent Brent Lee and on the other by former Congressman John Rhett, an unlikely pair.

Arriving late was James Brown, the "Godfather of Soul," resplendent in a bright green jumpsuit. Brown, a South Carolinian, never missed an opportunity to be photographed with the governor. As he walked past he looked up at Berkeley and said, "Hello, Cleopatra. When are you coming to see me?"

She ignored him, feigning conversation with Monroe.

Behind Berkeley sat the Jones family, invited because Grover "Don't Let Nobody Down" Jones, was receiving a special citation for his many years of service to local government. Seated with him were his wife and son, Junior, who held hands with Della, an African queen, who wore a low-cut black dress and flashed a sparkling new one-carat diamond engagement ring.

They were all there together on this crisp, November morning, sitting in folding chairs, just six inches apart, unaware they were so much like the birds who flew through Maceo's mind, each on a different course, assigned different altitudes, following various flight plans, within the same small airspace in a very small state. Parallel lives. Different colors. Different shades. So very close, yet so very far part.

Berkeley was thinking about this when she felt a hand touch her shoulder. She turned and saw Grover "Don't Let Nobody Down" Jones, who had been admiring her poise, personality and caramel color.

Grover leaned forward, cupped his hand to Berkeley's ear, and said, "Excuse me, Ma'am. But have you ever thought of running for guv'nor?"

THE END

Dum Spiro Spero
(While I Breathe, I Hope)